AN
HONORABLE
MURDERER

Other titles by the same author

Sleep of Death

Death of Kings

The Pale Companion

Alms for Oblivion

Mask of Night

AN
HONORABLE
MURDERER

PHILIP GOODEN

CARROLL & GRAF PUBLISHERS
New York

Carroll & Graf Publishers
An imprint of Avalon Publishing Group, Inc.
245 W. 17th Street
New York
NY 10011-5300
www.carrollandgraf.com

AVALON
publishing group incorporated

First published in the UK by Constable,
an imprint of Constable & Robinson Ltd 2005

First Carroll & Graf edition 2005

Copyright © Philip Gooden 2005

ISBN 0-7867-1528-6

Printed and bound in the EU

An honourable murderer, if you will

Othello, 5, ii

The insolent foe

The August sun glittered on the water. The boats jostled each other in the swell as though, like the spectators, they were trying to position themselves for a better view. The river smelled as bad as it usually did in the late summer but I don't suppose any of us were more than occasionally aware of the stench. We were too busy watching out for the enemy.

Both sides of the river were solid with craft, bobbing in expectation. Ferries and wherries overshadowed little sculls and skiffs. There were herring buses and eel boats, temporarily diverted from the fish trade. There were primitive vessels which looked to have been made out of logs and kept afloat by bladders, and which I personally wouldn't have boarded even to see the arrival of the Queen of Sheba. All of these craft were stuffed with goggling Londoners.

We were moored on the south bank of the river between the Globe playhouse and Molestrand Dock. And we – the King's Men – were in something of a privileged position because we were standing on the deck of our very own barge. Dick Burbage and the other senior shareholders in the Globe had splashed out a hundred shillings a year on hiring a big boat. This vessel was moored near to the playhouse and was used to ferry us to important places on the other side of the water such as Whitehall Palace and Somerset House, so that we should arrive in style.

Our boat was painted with the image of the Company symbol which stands on top of the thatched roof of the theatre – it's a figure depicting Hercules the strong man holding up the globe – so that everyone could see who we were and where we came from. Sometimes we advertised our forthcoming productions with banners draped over the sides.

But on this glaring August afternoon no one was looking at us. All eyes were directed towards the middle of the river where a fleet of bedecked barges was making its way up-stream to the beating of drums and the tootling of trumpets. The painted oars caught the sun as they cleared the water in unison and threw out a curtain of sparkling spray with each stroke. Church bells rang out from both shores.

"Oh, look at the Dons!" said Mrs Burbage. "Look how many of them there are."

For this special occasion some of the women had been invited on board the *Hercules*, as the Globe barge was called. Dick Burbage's wife tried to sound careless enough but there was an undertone of something else in her voice, a note between fear and admiration perhaps.

"It's a proper armada," said her husband, and there was a bit of laughter from the older members of the Company, the ones whose memories stretched back that far.

I'd barely been into my teens when the Spanish had last attempted to make a landing in England. It was during the summer of '88 in the previous century. Of course the news did not reach our little Somerset village for many days, not until it was all finished with and (had we but known it) we were safe and sound. But by God's grace – and with a little help from the stormy weather and the fighting prowess of our sailors – that great fleet of foreigners had been scattered in all directions. We'd tweaked the King of Spain's beard, we'd given him a bloody nose, I remember my father saying. That was immediately before he sank to his knees in thankful prayer.

I was more surprised at my dad's jubilation and his language than I was at the defeat of the Spanish since I'd been too young or simply too ignorant to understand the danger we were in. Maybe I only began to appreciate the threat properly after the church bells were ringing out and our neighbours were dancing and drinking on the village green by the pond. My father used the Spanish defeat as material for the first of several fiery sermons.

But whatever my youthful ignorance, if it hadn't been for the grace of God, if it hadn't been for the weather et cetera, we English might have been very used to this vision by now. That is, the vision of a grand procession of boats floating on *our* river Thames and containing the flower of the Spanish nobility. Might have been so used to it that we'd scarcely have looked at it twice. Instead, we would all have been trying to wrap our tongues around Spanish vowels at this moment, in submission to an all-conquering power.

As it was, we were viewing the people whom Mrs Burbage had called the 'Dons' as guests, as honoured visitors to London. They came in peace. There was no reason to feel fear. Even so, I shivered slightly. Perhaps it was the breeze which had suddenly sprung up and which broke the light on the water into ten thousand fragments of silver.

"A long time ago I fought those people," said Abel Glaze.

"And now they are to be welcomed," said Jack Wilson.

"Welcomed with open arms rather than with unsheathed weapons," said Laurence Savage.

My friends were standing next to me by the railing and gazing across the water. Even before the Armada and its defeat, Abel Glaze had taken part in the Netherlands campaign against the Spanish. He too had scarcely been into his teens. But during the period when I was ignorant of pretty well everything outside the boundaries of my father's Somerset parish, Abel was fighting for his life and watching others lose theirs over the sea. Jack Wilson was a bit older and had been a member of the King's Men for longer. In fact I'd obtained my first foothold in the Company by filling in for him during a temporary absence. Laurence Savage, an amiable fellow with a cowlick of dark hair topping his round face, had run away from his unhappy home and joined the Company years earlier.

"The enemy," I said, for the sake of saying something.

"Yes," said Abel. "But the cold was the real enemy in the Low Countries, the cold and the shortages. General Frost and Sergeant Hunger killed many more of us than *they* ever did."

We had a fair view of *them* now. The *Hercules* was a large boat, suitable for the King's Men, and it raised us a couple of feet higher than the nearest craft on the river. We were able to see Spanish gentlemen – and some Spanish ladies too – sitting or standing on the grand barges. From this distance they looked little different from an equivalent helping of our royal court. Finely dressed, naturally, and with an arrogant tilt to their postures. You might even have called them insolent.

I wondered whether the Spaniards were as curious to see us as we were to see them. Probably not. If you're high-up you are used to being gawped at rather than doing the gawping. A few Londoners were waving their hands in a tentative way but there were no answering waves from the foreigners.

"Nine – ten – eleven boats . . . I can see so far . . . and there are more of them coming," said Jack, squinting into the sun-dazzle downstream. "How long will this line stretch out?"

"Till the crack of doom," said a voice behind us.

It was William Shakespeare. We turned to see our shareholder, playwright and occasional actor standing at our shoulders. There was an intent expression in his face. Even WS – the friend of the high and mighty, a man at home with kings and queens (on and off the stage) – was impressed by this floating procession, it seemed to me.

"We shall look dowdy by comparison, Will," said Laurence Savage. "Are we getting new livery? Have you asked Secretary Cecil for new livery?"

"He's probably got more important matters in hand at the moment, but you could ask him yourself," said WS, jerking his thumb at a barge which was moored fifty yards or so upstream. It was the largest boat on this side of the river and, strangely, it carried no identifying marks. From our position we were unable to see the interior, which was lavishly curtained off.

"Cecil is over there?" said Jack.

"Not only him but the Lord High Admiral, I believe – oh, and the Queen."

WS enjoyed the little ripple which this information caused among those standing nearest.

"Do you think we're the only people to feel anything as vulgar as curiosity about our new friends?" he went on. "Or that no one else has wondered whether the Spaniard will arrive with horns on his head and belching hell-fire? The King may have to stay in Whitehall and wait for the grandees to come to him, but that doesn't mean his wife must do the same. If she wants to watch the Spaniards arrive from the privacy of her own river-boat then she will."

"Queen Anne goes her own way," said Jack Wilson, throwing in his own bit of insider knowledge.

This was true as far as I was aware (which wasn't very far at all). After countless years of being governed by a single woman who had no consort, it was odd to find ourselves being ruled over by a King *and* a Queen. Odd also that the English were now governed by a couple neither of whom was English by origin. James of Scotland kept his state in Whitehall Palace while Anne of Denmark kept hers a full mile to the east in Somerset House. They were separate in many things – for example, we Globe players were the King's Men, while the Queen bestowed her theatre patronage on the Earl of Worcester's Men. But the royal pair had come together on at least three occasions during their marriage and produced two princes and a princess.

"Maybe Anne's got nowhere to stay except on that boat," I said.

The Queen had voluntarily given up her residence on the banks of the Thames when the Spanish ambassador had chosen it as the only place in town splendid enough to accommodate his country's envoys while they were staying in London. It really was a voluntary move. In some quarters, Anne was whispered as being of the Spanish party.

"She is back in Whitehall Palace for the time being," said Shakespeare.

"And back in the King's bed?" said Abel.

"She'll have to kick Pembroke out first, it is rumoured," said Jack.

"A handsome youth, that Pembroke," said Laurence.

"But I have heard that the King thinks Pembroke's brother is a handsomer one," I said.

Listen to us talk! As though we were fully fledged courtiers. We waited for Shakespeare to confirm or deny these latest scurrilous stories about our King. But if he knew anything he wasn't saying. In fact WS turned away, with a look of slight disapproval on his face as if we were gossiping out of turn. Another strange feature of the new reign was that, whereas under Elizabeth most of the gossip had been to do with state affairs and the succession, the current tattle mostly concerned James's favourites. It was all about who was in and who was out and who was elbowing his way to the front of the court queue. It felt to me that things weren't quite as *serious* as they used to be – or maybe I was just getting older.

I noticed that WS had moved away without answering Abel's question about whether we would be issued with new livery for the forthcoming peace celebrations. To mark James's coronation in the summer of the previous year we'd each received precisely four and a half yards of red cloth to make doublet and breeches for the procession. By that stage we were no longer the Chamberlain's but the King's Men. (Our ailing patron, Lord Hunsdon, had died though not of the general pestilence but of the pox.)

"Eighteen – nineteen – twenty boats I have seen," said Jack Wilson, "but these ones now are nothing like so grand as the leaders."

All of us could see the way this Spanish 'armada' was dwindling to its conclusion. I glanced upstream at the large, anonymous barge with its lavish curtains. Behind them apparently sheltered Queen Anne as well as Robert Cecil, the crookback Secretary of State, and Charles Howard, the Lord High Admiral. Everyone knew Howard, even relatively new Londoners like myself. He had commanded the English fleet against the '88 armada and was no doubt curious to see an old enemy whose less ceremonial arrival he had fought to prevent all those years ago. I had a more particular reason for recognizing his name since, when I'd first come to London, I had been temporarily taken on by the Admiral's Men, who played under his protection – not that I'd ever seen the great man at any of our performances. He kept away. In this he was like many patrons.

There were only a handful of barges passing now. They were workaday ones rather than brightly decked out, while their oars were coated with plain varnish. Even the spray coming off them seemed not to glitter quite so much. They were full of dark-suited attendants with a scattering of soldiers. The boats in the very rear were low in the water on account of the canvas-covered cases and trunks which they carried.

The attention of the Londoners bobbing on the Thames waters had also dwindled and a buzz of talk was breaking out. The main action was over. The principal actors of the invading party – all those foreign Constables, Counts and Dukes – were on the leading craft which had already travelled upriver and were preparing to dock at Somerset House, or Denmark House as it was officially called. What was travelling in front of our eyes now was like the baggage train of an army, no doubt important for general sustenance but not very interesting.

The *Hercules* rocked slightly as the senior members and shareholders of the King's Men began to disembark. Our own little group by the railing – Jack Wilson, Abel Glaze, Laurence Savage and I – also turned our backs on the water. The show on the river was finished. And there would be no show for us in the Globe theatre this afternoon or for several afternoons to come. We were enjoying a break from playing. There was a festive, holiday spirit. The sun was out.

We jostled our way to the gangplank, the others in the lead. I felt my shoulder being grasped by a firm paw. I recognized that grasp. Only one man connected to the King's Men had that power in his fingers. I turned about to look full into the gaze of Master Benjamin Jonson.

"Well, Nicholas Revill, have you given thought to my suggestion?"

"Yes."

"And?"

"I would be honoured to join you and your friends."

"They're your friends too. Good man. You will come tonight then?"

"Where to?"

"There is a fish tavern in Bread Street – "

"The Mermaid. I know it."

"Good man," repeated Jonson with real approval. "We will be enjoying ourselves from seven onwards. *'Pine kai eufrainou'* is what Palladas of Alexandria tells us."

"I expect he does," I said.

"Drink and be merry, Nicholas. Drink and be merry. We never know whether the next day will be our last."

The grasp on my shoulder tightened even further before Jonson allowed his hand to fall away. He had a pock-marked face and a manner of getting up close when he spoke to you, even if he was only talking about the day's weather. Mind you, with Jonson, any comment about the day's weather was usually accompanied by a classical garnish – just a sliver of Latin or a sprig of Greek, as above. He prided himself on his learning

8

and lost no opportunity of showing it off. He thought William Shakespeare was quite an ignorant, unrefined man.

Like WS, Benjamin Jonson was a player and writer, though a much more touchy one. He was always on the lookout for snubs. You'd never have thought that he was the son of a bricklayer and had served an apprenticeship in the trade or that, like Abel Glaze, he had fought in the Netherlands or that he'd killed a man in a duel and only just escaped the noose – at least you wouldn't have thought any of these things until you experienced the strength in his hands.

At this moment, from our vantage point at the head of the gangplank which linked the *Hercules* to dry land, we could see over the heads of the people milling about on the river bank. There was a stir of activity in the region of the anonymous barge moored further upriver. There was nothing really anonymous about it, of course. How could there be when the Queen of England and Scotland was involved? A knot of uniformed yeomen blocked our view but between their shoulders I could glimpse a figure being ushered into a closed carriage. The figure's face was concealed by an elaborate mask. From a practical point of view this was silly. (If you want to draw attention to yourself, wear a mask. If you're looking not to be recognized, go about bare-faced and with some tiny difference from the usual.) But it was said that Queen Anne liked dressing up and taking part in dances and masques.

Ben Jonson was still at my elbow as we paused on the gangplank, caught up in the line of our departing fellows. Beneath us was a ten-foot drop into the greasy water between the barge and the bank. I was almost fearful that a careless movement might pitch me into the river. Jonson gestured towards one of the individuals who had disembarked from the royal barge and was pacing in the Queen's wake. This was a quite elderly man with a fine, fair moustache and a forked beard.

"Look at Howard, look at the Lord High Admiral," he said. "Observe the spring in his step. That's what a young wife will do for you. Young wives are a great preservative."

Like Shakespeare, Ben Jonson was fond of showing his familiarity with the court high-ups. He did it more nakedly than WS, however. But it was true that Charles Howard – or the Earl of Nottingham – or the Lord High Admiral – walked with a bounce that denied his age as well as the weight of titles which he carried. He'd recently married a much younger woman.

"Get a move on, Ben," said someone to our rear. "You're holding everyone up."

"I'll move when I'm ready, thank you," said Ben, deliberately not budging even though there was now space in front. I would have moved forward but he had me firmly by the elbow.

"And Cecil. You know Cecil, Nick? There he is."

It was easy enough to spot Sir Robert Cecil, Secretary to the Privy Council. Cecil was a short man with a large head topped by a great brow. But his main emblem was the crooked back that accompanied him everywhere. Today he was on his feet although usually he would not walk any distance in public and must be transported in a chair. Seeing Cecil I felt a queasiness in my guts.

"I have met Secretary Cecil, yes."

"*You* have met him. When?"

I recalled being taken blindfold through the midnight streets of London for my meeting with Robert Cecil in the closing days of Queen Elizabeth's reign when the Earl of Essex was plotting his treason. I recalled the task with which Cecil had entrusted me. The secrecy of it.*

"It's of no account," I said. "I've no wish to meet him again. He is dedicated to his plots."

I pulled out of Jonson's grasp and started to move down the gangplank before the people behind grew impatient enough to shove us into the Thames.

"Dedicated to plots? You must tell me about it some time," said Jonson. "I can smell a story."

---

* see *Death of Kings*

"Who's that man and the woman too?" I said to distract him.

A slight individual with prominent ears was leaning down so that Cecil might whisper something to him. He looked grave, as you would do if the second most powerful (some would say *the* most powerful) man in the kingdom was addressing you. Nearby stood a largish woman.

"That is Sir Philip Blake. I know him, know him well. The lady next to him is his wife, Lady Jane. They are both involved in this business with us. You might call them patrons."

By this time we were on the shore. There was a certain interest from the passers-by in the presence of such important visitors to the south bank but, being sophisticated Londoners, none of us wanted to show it very much. A glimpse of Queen Anne was hardly comparable to a sight of Queen Elizabeth in the old days. And it may be that everyone's appetite for spectacle had been sated by the river-borne Spaniards. I looked about for Abel and the others but they'd made themselves scarce.

The black carriage containing the Queen stood a few dozen yards off, sealed up like a sepulchre, the horses waiting patiently in the shafts. Sir Robert Cecil was evidently going to depart with Anne but was allowing himself to finish his conversation with Sir Philip Blake first. It was a mark of Cecil's standing – some people might have said, his arrogance – that he could afford to keep the Queen waiting like this.

The Lord High Admiral strode away from the royal party. He was by himself, a fine old gentleman in an elegant ruff. Closer to, his beard was more white than fair.

"What do you bet that he's going to take a little walk on this side of the river," said Ben Jonson. Hs eyes tracked the admiral's back. "See, I told you."

Charles Howard had turned off in the direction of Paris Garden.

"*He* has no fear of wandering by himself in these lawless realms. Every waterman, wrinkled or otherwise, in South-

11

wark is familiar with the victor of the Armada, and would be honoured to see him board his boat. And if we were to follow him now, Nicholas, we would no doubt see him entering the hallowed precincts of Holland's Leaguer – or some other knocking-shop."

"Where every woman, wrinkled or otherwise, would be honoured to have him board *her*," I said.

"Good, good, Nicholas."

"You're very curious about the Lord High Admiral, Ben," I said.

For myself, I was surprised rather than curious. Not so much that a man of Howard's rank might be visiting one of the local brothels – assuming that's what he was doing – but that he should be so careless about it. As Ben said, the Lord High Admiral would be easily recognized by most of the older watermen, many of whom were ex-sailors.

"There is encouragement here for all of us who are merely in our middle years, Nicholas Revill," said Ben Jonson, almost gleefully. "Look at Nottingham. He marries when he's touching seventy, he gets his young wife with child almost straightaway, and while she is in that state which the French term *hors de combat* he takes himself off to the Southwark stews because he must have it. He must have *it*."

"I'm not in my middle years," was my feeble reply. But Jonson wasn't even listening.

"I will follow my admirable admiral, I think. He has given me my cue for this hot afternoon," he said, moving off in the direction taken by Nottingham and pausing only to shout out a reminder that I should present myself at the Mermaid tavern that evening, if I chose. And so Jonson left, presumably for one of the stews which are studded across Southwark like so many buttons on a whore's outfit.

I might have done the same, I suppose. I used to frequent Holland's Leaguer sometimes when my friend Nell worked there (although I enjoyed free what others paid for). But I have lost my taste for that particular place ever since her sad departure. And because the heat which was stirring up Ben Jonson had left me feeling spiritless I made my way back to my lodgings.

Where lodges he?

The story of my lodgings is part of the story of my time in London. Sometimes I thought my changing accommodation was a reflection of my fortunes in more than a monetary sense and, if this was so, then even the most favourable observer couldn't have said that my fortunes amounted to much. Recently, though, there'd been a welcome and overdue change, or at least a hint of it . . .

Among my earliest accommodation in the capital had been a sty on the third floor of an establishment in Ship Street. It belonged to a stuck-up woman called Ransom, who kept a slovenly house and gave herself airs and graces. The only merit of this room was a view of the river which was obtainable if you risked your neck by craning out of the little window. There were various reasons why I'd had to leave this place, reasons connected to a carelessly emptied chamber pot and a rampant daughter of the establishment.

Then I'd sunk even lower by putting up with a peculiar quartet of women in Broadwall who charged four pennies a week for a 'chamber' that was more holes and gaps than it was floor, walls or ceiling. My landladies called themselves after the sunnier months of the year – April, May, June and July – and had a local reputation as witches. One of them was murdered at the time of the Essex uprising.

And after *that* I had spent more than two years in a room in a household belonging to Master Samuel Benwell in the

14

street known as Dead Man's Place. This room of his, which was an improvement on my previous lodging (in the same way that purgatory may be said to be an improvement on hell), had the advantage of being close to the Globe playhouse. Master Benwell and I had our troubles – at one time I found myself lodging in prison rather than under his roof – but he remained faithful to his single tenant. Not so much on account of the shilling a week rental which I paid, as for the playhouse gossip which I fed him from time to time. Some of the gossip was actually true.

And now Master Benwell was no more. He was dead. No, not murdered, if that's what you're thinking, but died naturally. Or as naturally as anyone could who perished in the great plague which had started even while our great Queen was on her deathbed and which continued for many long months into the reign of her successor from Scotland. Indeed, the rising bills of mortality had caused James to delay his coronation procession – the very one in which we'd marched with our four and a half yards of cheap red livery – until the summer.

By a miracle, none of the Chamberlain's Men was directly touched by the pestilence. True, we'd spent large parts of the year of 1603 away from the city and out on the road. When Queen Elizabeth died we were playing at the Golden Cross Inn in Oxford, although that brainy town did not escape the plague either. Subsequently we returned to London, but it was plain that there would be no theatre business for many months to come. So we took ourselves off to places like Coventry and Bath, and at each stage we seemed to be stalked by a disease which, like a chess player, made unexpected moves to check and frustrate us. When we got to Bath, for example, we found that the plague had made a knight's jump into Bristol, killing many in that city.

Eventually the winter months arrived and we decided to lie low in Mortlake for no better reason than that Augustine Phillips, one of the Globe shareholders, had recently bought a house there by the river. Mortlake seemed as good a place as any. It was a safe distance from town and so the family men summoned their wives and children to join them while the rest of us made do with whatever temporary accommodation we could find.

Anyway it wasn't until early in the new year of 1604 that the playhouses were allowed to open once again and the King's Men could resume their London living in both senses. But the city was a changed place. Weeds flourished in many streets and the doors of infected houses hung aimlessly in their frames. Holes were left unrepaired in roofs and walls. The price of property went down, at least away from the fashionable spots like the Strand or Westminster. Although parts of the town seemed less busy or bustling, I was never sure whether this was because some of the people who would normally have thronged there were dead or on account of trade and activity being generally slack.

As far as we players were concerned, our audiences had held up but they didn't seem to have the old appetite for comedy, or at least not such innocent comedy. Maybe we didn't have the appetite for it either, and so we turned to rather darker stuff. Shakespeare produced a play about jealousy and a Moor from Africa who turned suspicious of his wife before killing her. This piece drew them in. The other principal diversions of the Southwark shore – the bear-and-bull-baiting, and the brothel business – held up too. But it would require the end of the world to draw the curtains on those trades.

I may have taken a bit of a ramble away from the subject of my present accommodation but, trust me, it *is* connected to the plague and its aftermath. I was now, in August 1604, lodging with a family called Buckle in Thames Street. This thoroughfare runs parallel to the river on its upper side and, though nowhere near as grand as some streets a little further to the north or west, it still enjoys its own smell, as the expression goes.

Not so long before I'd had a friend and comforter called Lucy Milford who lived in Thames Street until she quit the town at the first outbreak of plague, and so I was quite familiar with it. By lodging here I'd gone up in the world, I suppose.

My landlady Mrs Buckle had been widowed by the plague and her house left without a man. She did have a daughter, though, who was not yet paired off and so remained at home, though I hardly ever saw her. Two other daughters were married and had establishments in Finsbury and Kingston.

I'd met Mrs Buckle and her daughter Elizabeth in an unusual way. You could almost say I'd come to their rescue. It was soon after we'd returned to London from Mortlake and the spring season at the Globe playhouse had begun. We hadn't performed at home for almost a year and it was odd to be striding about on the familiar boards once more. Our audience welcomed us back with a warmth which touched our hearts.

Late one day in the spring – after we'd played a piece called *The Melancholy Man*, a drama of blood and disguise by a satirical writer called Martin Barton – I stepped out of the players' entrance to the theatre and straight into a real-life drama. Our costume man, Bartholomew Ridd, had detained me over some piffling piece of damage to my outfit for which he held me responsible. We'd argued about it, although I knew I wouldn't get anywhere, and so I was just about the last person to leave the playhouse. In contrast to my mood, which had been aggravated by Ridd, it was a mild evening. The promise of better things to come was in the air. Two women were standing in earnest conversation with a well-dressed couple. The couple had their backs to me but I saw on both the women's faces signs of distress and confusion.

As I got nearer I overheard the man say, "I did my best – but he was too quick – he was too quick for me."

He was out of breath, and panting in a way that was very obvious.

"You had better check – that you are all complete – ladies – make certain – you haven't lost anything."

"My husband is right," said the lady standing next to him. "Best make sure."

She put out her hand to touch the younger of the two women on the arm before turning and patting her husband on the shoulder. "So brave you are, Anthony," she said. Then to the others, "So brave he is. I have heard that there are many villains round these parts and now I see it is true."

I might have walked on and left them to it but something made me slow down and draw closer to this little group. Perhaps it was a sense of obligation to the patrons who had stuck by us after our year's absence. Perhaps it was a desire to prove myself after being put down by the costume man – Ridd had threatened to report me to Burbage for a forfeit because of a tiny tear in the cloak I'd been wearing in my part as a murderer (I can't help it if cloaks will catch on nails that shouldn't be sticking out in the first place). Or perhaps it was that the two women were, despite their distress and confusion, quite attractive.

So I stood at a little distance and watched the proceedings. The couple, apparently husband and wife, were well past the first flush of youth. They were properly turned out. From their outfits you would have said that this particular gentleman and his lady were unlikely to be from our southern side of the water, while their *refined* accents told a similar sort of story. He was clean-shaven in the latest style while her cheeks were fashionably whitened. The two women facing them, the quite attractive ones, looked as though they might be mother and daughter. They had the same turn to their mouths, from the little which I could glimpse under their wide-brimmed hats, and there was something similar in the way they were standing.

"The rascal took nothing, I do hope," said the gentleman called Anthony. "Best see to all your things. Do not delay now."

He'd recovered his breath by this point. He glanced side-ways at me and looked away again. The lady smiled at the mother and daughter, giving all her attention to them and pretending not to notice my presence.

Taking the repeated hint, the women made a kind of inventory with their fingers of what they were wearing or carrying, touching various objects or bringing them out into the light of the spring evening. Item: one locket on a silver chain worn around the neck. Item: one silk purse briefly glimpsed under a mantle. Item: a nicely worked pomander filled with sweet-smelling stuff and attached to a girdle. And so on.

Seeing that everything was still in its place, they visibly relaxed. Smiles all round. The chalky-faced woman again touched the younger one's arm in reassurance.

For the first time, the woman I thought of as being the mother spoke.

"We haven't lost anything, I think. Have you, Lizzie?"

The younger one shook her head.

"I am Mrs Buckle and this is my daughter Elizabeth. Whom have we to thank for this good service?"

"I can answer that," I said, moving forward.

"What business is this of yours?" said the gentleman.

"An honest citizen's business," I said, stepping between the couple and the two women.

"Allow me to introduce Mister Anthony Thoroughgood, madam," I said. "How do, Tony. And this lady here is his wife, Mistress Charity Thoroughgood."

"This has nothing to do with you," said the woman called Charity. "*Nothing.*"

All smiles gone now. I could almost feel the hostility coming off the couple like the heat from an oven.

"These good souls have been helping us," said the daughter, speaking for the first time. She had a soft voice but sounded wary, if not hostile – not towards the couple but towards me.

"I don't know about you, sir," said the older woman called Buckle, "but it is not every day a gentleman will risk his life in

19

pursuit of a wrongdoer. A bad man tried to rob us as we came out of the playhouse and Mister, er, Thoroughgood gave chase."

"I don't think Tony was ever at risk of losing anything more than a few lungfuls of air," I said. "As for the bad man who tried to rob you . . . Who was it this time, Tony? Phil the Foist? Or Nip Drinkell? Or have you got some new lifter on your books?"

"Oh, begone . . . whoever you are," said Charity Thoroughgood, a tinge of red peeping through her chalky cheeks.

"I am Nicholas Revill, player and member of the King's Men."

"Oh, now I recognize you," she said, with quite a convincing shudder. "You have just played a murderer on stage, in disguise."

"The difference is that I don't wear my disguise in the street. But you two I recognize as well. Think back to the Goat & Monkey ale-house last Thursday night. I was sitting in a corner while you were boasting about your latest haul and drinking away most of the proceeds."

"Oh, piss off, will yew."

Her words and her delivery, in which vehemence struggled with the attempt to hang on to her accent, almost gave the game away. I saw the simple gratitude and relief which had appeared on the faces of the two women being replaced by puzzlement, even suspicion. But it was still me they were more suspicious of. After all, I'd just enacted a murderer's part. A few evening strollers had halted to watch the outcome of this little scene.

Tony Thoroughgood decided to go on the attack.

"Oh, this is good," he said, to no one in particular. "Very good. I suppose this is one of those Southwark tricks I've heard about. It's the device of some cheapjack player to cause mischief and deprive these good folk of their property by impugning honesty. *My* honesty."

"It's a device all right," I said. "Let me tell you how it works. A playgoer is accidentally banged into by a passer-by on the way out of the theatre. A moment later a gentleman shoots off in pursuit of the passer-by, yelling out 'Stop thief!' or similar words. Meantime the gent's companion – usually a lady because it's more persuasive that way – stays behind to reassure the victim and to prevent them moving off. And a few moments after *that* the pursuer returns, all puffed out. 'Oh dear, the thief has managed to get away this time. I do hope nothing's been taken.' And nothing *has* been taken up to that point. Best make sure, though. Best produce your goods, and so provide a display of everything valuable which you're carrying. That's when the real thieving starts."

I saw that my account carried a bit of weight with the Buckle mother and daughter. That's exactly what happened, they were thinking. In a distracted manner both of them started to feel about for their valuables once more.

"This is the reward of virtue, to be slandered by a player. A common player!" said Charity Thoroughgood.

"I will forswear honesty in future since this is all the thanks we get," said Anthony Thoroughgood.

"Honesty and you haven't been on nodding terms for years, Tony," I said.

"That's God's truth," said another voice. "Mister Thoroughgood wouldn't recognize honesty even if he found it in another's purse. And as for *her* virtue . . . well, her virtue's been well handled, believe me."

"Not handled by you, Bartholomew Ridd," said Charity. "Never been handled by you. You wouldn't know where to put it."

I turned to see the aforesaid Bartholomew Ridd. The tireman had been on his way out of the Globe, having finished brushing down his costumes and hanging them up and working out who should pay their forfeits for the little harms done. Although I could have clouted him earlier I was glad enough to see him now. It was the playhouse pair versus the husband-and-wife coney-catchers.

The Buckles, the mother and daughter coneys or dupes, looked from the Thoroughgoods to Bartholomew Ridd and me and back again, still not knowing whom to believe but with the balance swinging in our favour, especially after Charity's last outburst. But the lady with the painted cheeks wasn't quite finished.

"Come along, my dear," said Mistress Thoroughgood. "We will never prevail against such impudence."

With a shoulder-shrugging show of indignation, the couple made to move away. We were only a few yards from the corner of the alley known as Brend's Rents. They'd be round it in a second and then they'd take to their middle-aged heels. But I was quicker. I yanked at Charity Thoroughgood's cloak. It was a long garment, longer and fuller than necessary considering the mild spring weather. Underneath the cloak, tucked into an elaborate belt which was hung with straps and hooks, was an engraved pomander. The object looked familiar. It looked familiar because it was familiar. It had been dangling a few moments earlier from the waist of young Elizabeth Buckle. I grabbed for it as Charity twisted away. Luckily she hadn't had time to secure it properly and the pomander pulled free in my hand.

In the confusion the Thoroughgoods managed to make their getaway down Brend's Rents. In a more respectable area of town the bystanders might have raised a hue-and-cry after the couple, but thieving was commonplace in our district and the pursuer was as likely to be tripped up, or worse, as the pursued. It was quite possible that among the little group of watchers starting to disperse was the very accomplice whom Tony Thoroughgood had been 'chasing', come back to observe the successful conclusion to their scheme.

The Buckle women stood open-mouthed at this latest turn of events. Meantime I kept a firm hold on the engraved pomander. Sold on through one of the Southwark brokers, who never ask any questions, this item alone would have kept the Thoroughgoods in liquor for a week. As far as I'd been able to tell from my glimpse of Charity's bare belt, the pomander was all she'd been able to lift in this foist. Her fingers were more nimble than her husband's – his task was simply to pursue the 'wrongdoer' and to distract the victim on his empty-handed return, while it was left to his good lady to pick and choose among the articles so recently on display. People are less guarded around a woman, especially when she is all smiles and reassurance. And if you believe you've just been robbed, and are then relieved to find that you *haven't* been robbed after all, your guard is already down.

"Well done, Nicholas," said Bartholomew Ridd. "And farewell, ladies."

The tire-man moved away down the street. I was inordinately pleased at this casual compliment from a man who'd recently been telling me off. If I had expected gratitude from the women, though, I was mistaken. Mother and daughter both looked wary underneath their great hats. I suppose they thought that this was merely another scene in an elaborate exercise to trick them out of their property. Thought that, soon enough, a third or fourth trickster would crawl out to expose me . . . and another one afterwards to expose *him* . . . and so on.

I hurriedly surrendered the pomander to its owner. From the scent left on my hands, it contained cloves. The young woman took hold of the engraved sphere without comment. It was a sensible thing to carry about in the aftermath of the plague and, for some of our more delicate playhouse patrons, it would provide a counter-smell to the odours of the common crowd. She examined it carefully as though, in handing it over, I might have performed some sleight of hand. Then she glanced up at me from under the brim of her hat. I had the impression of a small animal, a timid one perhaps, gazing out of its burrow.

I did not suggest that they check through their possessions for a second time. I bowed, or rather I inclined my head a fraction, and moved off. Good deed done for the day. So why should I expect any thanks for it?

My route lay away from the theatre to the south and east of the town. Since the Company's return from Mortlake I'd been staying with my friend Abel Glaze at his lodging house in Kentish Street. Dusk was closing in.

I didn't hear her coming up behind me, just felt a feather-tap on my shoulder. It was the mother, Mrs Buckle.

"I should thank you, Master . . . *Devil*, was it?" She laughed – a young laugh – and clapped her hand to her mouth. "No, I must have misheard. It can't be Devil?"

Her face was pale in the half-light but her eyes were bright under the rim of her hat. In the distance stood her daughter.

"It's *Revill*. And it was nothing, madam. Only, when you next come to see us at the Globe playhouse, could I suggest that you keep your, ah, wits about you. That Thoroughgood woman was right enough in one thing she said."

"What was that?"

"When she claimed that there were plenty of villains round here – even if she is one of them."

"This is the first time we have been to the playhouse, Elizabeth and I."

I wasn't surprised at this but asked instead whether they'd enjoyed Martin Barton's *Melancholy Man*.

"Yes, for all the blood and gore. We did not expect that. My husband would not have approved," she said.

"Many people do not approve. He wouldn't be alone."

"Perhaps we are justly rewarded for coming here by . . . by what has just happened."

"Your husband wouldn't think you deserve to be robbed, surely," I said, though not as certain as I sounded. People are odd.

"My husband is dead," she said. Her eyes seemed to glitter more brightly in the gloom.

"I am sorry to hear it, Mrs Buckle."

"In the late outbreak."

"I lost my parents to the plague some years ago. But that was in another place, a long way away."

There was a pause.

"We thought we would be going back in the daylight," she said. "If it hadn't been for this business we would have been."

"Going back?"

"To the other side of the river."

"You live there?"

"In Thames Street by Skinners' Hall."

"Then I shall keep you company on your return."

"This is too much trouble, Master . . . Revill. This is a second kindness."

"It's nothing," I said.

"You're wrong," she said.

"Then it is such a little something that you should not mention it again."

"Do you treat all your playhouse customers like this?"

"Every one. That way we can be sure they will be happy to come back and see us again."

Together we walked towards where Elizabeth Buckle was standing. I had no strong motive for doing what I was doing, and certainly not a disreputable one. It was not going to put me to much inconvenience to cross from here to Thames Street. I probably wanted to show these innocents from the north of the river that there was honesty on the south bank too. Besides, Elizabeth Buckle and her mother were quite attractive.

Now the mother was confiding to me in a low voice that, for herself, she could happily have threaded her way through the alleys between the Globe and the river but it was her daughter for whom she was concerned. Elizabeth smiled to see her mother, who quickly explained that I had offered to escort them home. The usual half-protestations followed but I sensed that both women were relieved. The encounter with the Thoroughgoods had shaken them up more than they realized. Perhaps they believed that our borough crawled with glib tricksters (and they wouldn't have been altogether wrong in this belief). I wondered whether Mrs Buckle had deliberately set out to pluck at my chivalrous string with her talk of the late hour and the return across the river.

By the time we reached the stairs by St Mary Overy it was almost dark. The watermen had lit their lamps and their craft were so many fireflies. On the right-hand side, lights flickered in the grey-blue bulk of London Bridge. Filling our ears was the roar of the water, forced between the great piers. I hailed a ferryman, and one of the fireflies changed course and started to hover towards us through the air. We were picked up by a brawny waterman (the fellows who regularly work this part of the river need to be stronger than usual because of the pull of the water through the bridge piers) and snugged ourselves down in the stern. I sat between the two women. It was a little time since I had sat between two women, so tightly. We rapidly became familiar.

It happened like this.

Within a few yards of quitting the shore, with the ferryman gruntingly pulling on his oars as he struggled against the tug of the tide, I was told that the late master of the Buckle household had been a minister of religion. That he had selflessly served his parish of St Thomas's during the plague, unlike many clergy who either walked away from their posts or refused to step outside their houses at all. The Reverend Buckle had fallen sick as he was giving the sacrament in church. He had gone home and died without fuss the next day (which was a Thursday). The older woman, whose name was Ursula, poured her story into my ears, with the younger one making very occasional comments. It was as if a dam had been unblocked.

By the time we were nearing the northern shore, with the lights of the Bridge glimmering above us, I'd told the women of how their situation echoed my own. My father too had been a parson, down in the wilds of Somerset. He had been absent from our village when the plague struck but had come back, at certain risk to his life, to tend his flock. He and my mother perished together with many of his parishioners.

From the way that Ursula Buckle grasped my knee and from the heartfelt sighs of Elizabeth, I knew that I had found ready listeners. But while my wounds were old and nearly healed over, theirs were still raw. They knew that they were lucky to have survived. I think they felt some odd sense of guilt because they were still living while so many around them had perished. They said nothing of this, naturally, but I had been through the same mixture of self-blame and relief.

By the time we disembarked at Old Swan Stairs we were fast friends. It took a short time to walk to their house and then not much longer before I was sitting at their table, being refreshed with wine and gingerbread, and only a little while longer than that before it was settled that I should move into their house as a lodger.

Maybe I had been angling for this. Maybe, in turn, they had been angling for a male presence in their household. It was a comparatively large dwelling – most probably a one-time merchant's property, like so many of the houses near the Bridge – which was rented to Mrs Buckle by a distant cousin of her husband, the Reverend Hugh. In a way mother and daughter were lucky still to have a roof over their heads. Had they been living in the parsonage belonging to St Thomas's, they might have been dispossessed by now in favour of the new incumbent. Anyway, Ursula and Elizabeth rattled around in their rented place in Thames Street like a couple of loose peas in a pod. They'd brought their own furniture with them but these few objects were not up to the task of filling the place. They'd also employed a housemaid, a young girl with a very runny nose. The other servants, including a male cook, had died during the plague outbreak or quit the area for somewhere safer.

When I told Abel Glaze that I was moving out of his lodging in Kentish Street, which had never been meant as anything more than a stop-gap, my friend said, "A mother and daughter, eh, Nick, and all alone in the world."

"These are respectable people."

"I thought you liked it down here among the less respectable people."

Abel was a little hurt that I was abandoning him. Besides, he said, hadn't I always claimed to prefer the air of Southwark to the more refined stuff that blew about in the confines of the city?

"Others live on the north side," I said, referring to a small handful of the King's Men, mostly the seniors.

"And don't you get ensnared by the mother and daughter," he said.

"What could be better than being ensnared by the pair?" I said. "I intend to be ensnared."

As usual in such disputes, there was a measure of truth in the insults we threw at each other. Perhaps I did have a hankering towards a touch more respectability – I was approaching thirty, for God's sake, and I owned none of the items that many men of my age possessed (such as wife, children, property). As for Abel: in my view, he would have liked nothing better than to be 'ensnared' by a mother and daughter. He didn't have much luck in love, did my friend.

Anyway I soon moved into the Buckle house in Thames Street. It was highly convenient being so close to the Bridge and therefore within easy reach of the playhouse on the other side.

It was highly convenient too being cared for by women again. I was something between a friend, a lodger and a cousin. They charged me a low rent but more than repaid me with meals. With a bit of encouragement, Mrs Buckle visited the Globe playhouse and admired some of the performances, provided I promised to escort her home afterwards. We discussed poetry and the drama together. The Reverend Buckle had been a good man but, like many other good men and including my father, he had not approved of plays, players or playhouses. He'd never ranted against them in the pulpit, or not much, but he had shown his disdain clearly enough by forbidding his wife and daughters to attend the place. I didn't realize until later how much Ursula and Elizabeth Buckle had had to steel themselves to venture into Southwark to see *The Melancholy Man* at the Globe. Ursula told me they'd gone to see it only because the title promised something gentle and reflective. They did not bargain on the feast of revenge, blood and rough humour which Martin Barton the playwright served up.

My few months in the Thames Street house had been pleasant ones. For the first time in London I was quite content to stay where I was. As I said, I'd gone up in the world.

But it wasn't just to do with a change of place. Of course I had fallen in love, slightly in love. Not with young Elizabeth Buckle, of whom I saw little, but with Ursula. She was considerably older than me, although not old enough to be my mother. My love was unrequited, needless to say. And unrecognized, I hoped. My small secret.

I would have said that Mrs Buckle was settling into widowhood, perhaps before she started looking round for a fresh husband. But she had a small secret too, which she confided to me one evening. She had started to glimpse the ghost of her late husband, the Reverend Hugh Buckle, in various places round the house.

Give me your hand

The Mermaid tavern, where Ben Jonson had fixed to meet me on the evening after we'd watched the advance of the Spanish party upriver, is situated in Bread Street. This thoroughfare runs up at right angles to Thames Street in the area to the east of St Paul's and not too far from where I was lodging with the Buckles. The Mermaid tavern is a well-run house, and so offers a different world from the usual players' dens like the Goat & Monkey. Its fish and wine are recommended by those who know their food and drink.

When I got there on this fine summer's evening Ben Jonson was already installed at the end of a table, his invariable position.

"Ah, Nicholas, sit yourself there – and help yourself to this and afterwards to these."

Jonson was a casually commanding person and a generous one too, with himself as much as with others. William Shakespeare rarely put himself at the helm in this manner. But then perhaps WS didn't need to.

Jonson gestured once more. In front of him was 'this' and 'these': a large flask of wine and a heap of opened oysters. I wondered whether the playwright needed to fortify himself after an energetic afternoon in the stews of Southwark. But the truth is that he was a man of large appetites, on any occasion. Now he reached for one of the oysters and tilted his head. I watched his Adam's apple bobbing about as the oyster slithered down his gullet.

Already sitting to one side of the table was a red-headed man called Martin Barton, whom I knew glancingly. He was a poet and playwright, an up-and-coming satirical writer. He had recently written that play called *The Melancholy Man*, after a performance of which I'd first met Ursula and Elizabeth. And then there were Jack Wilson and Laurence Savage. I expected them to be present. I hadn't expected to see Abel Glaze on the opposite side of the table. I was surprised that my friend had said nothing to me earlier about coming to this tavern meeting, but then we were no longer living in each other's pockets.

"We were talking of the whelp," said Ben Jonson.

"The whelp?"

"The whelp that was born to Elizabeth in the Tower of London," said Abel.

"Oh, the lioness," I said. I was with them now. There was a lioness among the animals in the Tower. She was named for our old queen.

"It was a rare thing, her whelping," said Abel.

"But the whelp has died," said Ben Jonson.

"Died unbaptized," said Martin Barton. "Do you think it will go to purgatory now?"

"Do not be flippant, Martin," said Ben. He took his religion seriously and, according to some, had turned Catholic during one of his spells in gaol.

I saw Barton's eyes flare for a moment at Jonson's rebuke. Barton had a mercurial temper, which was in keeping with his red hair and which he was said to have inherited from his Italian mother. He and Jonson had fallen out in the past, and although there was a truce at the moment, it might be broken at any time and then they'd be back to slanging each other again.

"There is still a *lion* in the Tower though, as well as a lioness," said Barton, perhaps determined to show that he was willing to steer the conversation in a risky direction. "Walter and his Elizabeth are together even in their captivity."

No one had to ask the identity of the 'lion' for it was Sir Walter Raleigh, currently languishing at the King's pleasure after being found guilty of treason. He had been a favourite of Queen Elizabeth's but, unlike many others, he had not succeeded in making the smooth – some might say, the greasy – transfer from favour under one monarch to favour under her successor.

At this moment a newcomer joined our party. He was a dapper fellow who smiled round at the four of us before sitting down at the tavern table. Jonson introduced him as Giles Cass. He repeatedly dabbed at his lips as if wiping away some fragment of food stuck there. I learned later that he had some sort of ill-defined function in Robert Cecil's office, being used by the Secretary to flit between King James at Whitehall and Queen Anne at Somerset House.

Whatever part he played, he was indiscreet. Perhaps because he'd heard Martin Barton's remarks about Raleigh, he pushed the talk further in the same direction. Had we seen them, he asked, the Spanish party that afternoon? What did we think of their impudence in floating up the river in full fig? It would never have happened in the days of Queen Elizabeth, he claimed. You could have cut out her heart before she would have welcomed them.

I thought Giles Cass was overdoing it a bit, protesting too much. Perhaps he was doing it to elicit a response from us but, if so, I couldn't think why.

"I have heard," said Laurence during a pause while Cass poured himself a glass of wine, "that some members of the Spanish party were so seasick that they had to recover at Dover before they could travel on to Gravesend."

"That's true," said Cass, dabbing at his mouth.

"A fine armada they'd make now!"

"While I have been informed that they brought two loads of ice with them in the barges," said Jack Wilson.

"The ice is for their wine," said Giles Cass. "Or for the Constable of Castile's wine, to be precise. The Spaniard puts it in his drink in his own country."

And we all gawped at those foreigners who'd put ice in their drink.

"Gentlemen," said Ben Jonson, "this is quite enough about the Spaniard's drinking habits. To work."

Ben did not like attention being diverted from himself, or rather he was always eager to keep control of any conversation. This was his Mermaid meeting anyway. We were to discuss the presentation of a masque in a few days' time at Somerset House.

Masques were one of Ben's things. They are mixtures of song and dance and verse, as well as of fine costumes and effects which cost a great deal of money.

"I bring good news and better news, Benjamin," said Giles Cass. "Sir Philip and Lady Blake are eager to participate in your *Masque of Peace*. They have offered their house for practices."

I remembered the thin man and the large woman we'd seen that afternoon standing next to Robert Cecil by the river.

"That's good. And the better news?"

"Oh, nothing much. Only that the Queen herself is willing to take part."

There were little sounds of surprise, even amazement, from the six of us.

"That is good, very good," said Jonson with real gladness. "Thank you, Giles. What role should we assign to her now?"

"The part of Jealousy," said Martin Barton. "She could come on and drive away a host of those new knights from her Scottish husband. Those well-known parasites Sir Duncan McLeech and Sir Lennox Bloodsucker."

I glanced at Cass to see how he responded to this suggestion, which was risky enough. But he laughed with the rest of us.

"Anne could be the Queen of the Arctic, they say she is so cold," said Abel Glaze.

"Then perhaps the Spaniards ought to be borrowing their ice from her," I said.

"And perhaps *we* ought to be more careful of our tongues," said Jonson, glancing round the tavern, although no one seemed to be paying much attention.

"Of course, Ben. I forgot you had reason to fear for your bodily parts. For your tongue and your thumb," said Martin Barton.

"I am thinking of the law of slander, which applies even to queens. Anyway there is a difference between fear and a proper respect," said Jonson.

"All the same, show us your thumb, Ben Jonson," said Barton.

"Not for you," said Jonson.

"I have not seen it," said Giles Cass. "Give me your hand, do, good Benjamin."

With a resigned expression – though I thought I detected a touch of pride in the action too – Jonson put down the wine glass which he was holding in his left hand and exposed his bare, splayed palm to the table.

Across the mound at the base of his thumb was etched a dark device. It consisted of a miniature upright and a crossbar. The flesh around this T-shape was pale and puckered. I did not have to ask what the 'T' stood for.

"Not so bad though," said Barton. "You could have had an 'M' which would have taken up more space."

"An 'M' would have been convenient in your case, Martin," said Ben.

"How so? What are you saying? Are you accusing me – "

"Only that with an 'M' you would have carried your own initial around with you in case you forget who you are."

"I think it's you who are forgetting yourself, Ben," said Barton.

"That was not done with any cold iron," I said, unable to take my eyes from the ragged 'T' on Jonson's fleshy palm, and unable too to rise to any half humorous remark. I felt a little shiver inside myself. The taste of the Mermaid's Rhenish wine was suddenly sour in my mouth. Like Cass, I had never seen this mark of Jonson's before.

"Of course it was not done with any cold iron," said Jonson, and again a little pride was detectable. "Do you think the law is kind? I have been through fire – or fire has been through me. Never mind. *Fiat justitia*. Let justice be done. Are we all satisfied now?"

He snapped his hand shut as though he were closing a book. Whether he intended it or not, Jonson's display of the mark left by the hot branding-iron brought a kind of seriousness to the tavern table. We turned to discussing the Somerset House masque and there were no more jokes about the Queen or anybody else.

Over the remains of the wine and oysters, we sorted out who was to play whom, or rather Jonson directed us as to his wishes. The outline of the *Masque of Peace* was straightforward. The figure of Peace would arrive across the sea from Spain, to be greeted on this side of the water by her twin sister. This use of twins was a neat way of suggesting that each country was alike in its desire for Peace. The two Peaces would be attended by Plenty and Tranquillity and other desirable qualities. There has to be a little bit of grit even in the smoothest masques, however, so such figures as Ignorance and Suspicion and Stubbornness would gather on the sidelines, making ineffectual moves to impede the twins' union. But they would be dismissed by the Spanish Peace and the English Peace, and at the end of the action the presiding figure of Truth would descend from above to bless the new-found harmony between the nations.

There was an hour or so of discussion before we all went our separate ways, having arranged a rehearsal for the following day. Giles Cass was left to consult with the Queen's followers as to whether she was content to play the part of the English Peace, other less flattering epithets having been ruled out for Anne of Denmark. Whatever we thought of

Anne, there was a buzz to this part of the conversation. You don't find yourself playing next to a monarch every day.

I stepped out of the Mermaid tavern. It was a fine summer's evening. There was still a feeling of festival in the busy streets, a hangover from the mood of the crowds who'd gathered during the afternoon to watch the arrival of the Spanish.

As I made my way down Bread Street and back to Mrs Buckle's house in Thames Street, my thoughts were still on the masque, whose purpose was to celebrate the end of hostilities between England and Spain. I still wasn't quite sure why Ben had approached me. True, my particular friends like Jack Wilson and Abel Glaze were taking part. We shared a position in the King's Men somewhere between the long-established ones and the newcomers. Maybe Jonson knew that the older, more senior members of the Company would have turned him down.

The crowd in the streets was starting to thin out slightly as evening drew in. Absorbed with my thoughts, I was hardly aware of where I was going. As if on cue, the name of Thames Street swum into my vision. It was halfway up a wall, displayed at the point where Bread Street joined the main thoroughfare. The name was cut into a corner-stone. I halted and looked at the name. City grime had turned solid inside the individual letters. The back of my neck began to itch, as if a rope was grazing against it. The 'T' of 'Thames' seemed to jump out and glare at me, like the T-shape branded into the base of Jonson's left thumb.

The letter on his thumb stood for 'Tyburn', the gallows destination which Jonson had been lucky enough, or educated enough, to escape. Rather than the 'T' he might instead have been branded with an 'M', as Martin Barton had hinted. 'M' for murderer. A few years earlier Jonson had fought a duel with another player up at Hoxton Fields. Ben managed to see off his opponent – a man called Spencer who was said to be a violent, bad-tempered individual – by giving him a fatal thrust in the side. Though the fight was an honourable one, Jonson was arrested and charged with murder.

This wasn't the first time he'd been to gaol but never before had he faced such a serious charge. Jonson might have been ripe for the rope but he was also able to read. He pleaded benefit of clergy and, having selected what the wits call a neck-verse, he read the Bible passage out loud in court. I know all about neck-verses – I'm a parson's son after all, and it was parsons that the neck-verse had been intended to preserve back in the good old days when parson and squire would have been the only ones capable of reading and writing in a village. The murderous parson or squire may escape the noose but, like Cain, they will carry for the rest of their lives a sign of their crime. Unlike with Cain, who was marked by God on his bare forehead, our judges are more humane and allow the murderer to bear his shame tucked away in the palm of his hand.

Once again I felt an itching at the nape of my neck. Perhaps it was the reminder of the gallows fate which Ben Jonson had escaped through his simple ability to read a few lines from the Bible. Or perhaps the itching was due to something else altogether . . .

I moved on a few paces. The itching sensation stayed with me. I knew the symptoms now. There was someone at my heels. I was being watched. I waited a moment before turning my head sharply as though someone had called out my name. Within a dozen or so yards there were maybe half that number of people ambling or pacing along behind me. The street was full of shadows, with the first candles beginning to glimmer in the neighbouring windows. In the half-light it was hard to tell whether anyone averted their eyes suddenly or slowed their pace, as a person will do instinctively if he is caught out following another. I thought I detected a kind of flinching movement in a bearded fellow who was trailing along the edge of the street. He was dressed in a red doublet. And then there was a woman with a pale hat who turned aside and entered a doorway.

I looked to the front once more and walked on down the street, with a show of unconcern. The sense of being watched continued, though it was perhaps fainter now. A couple of hundred yards further on I again turned my head for an instant. There was a glimpse of a red doublet. There was a pale hat bobbing in the twilight. But why not? Why shouldn't these be honest citizens taking an evening stroll, as I was? And why should anyone be on my tail anyway? I was involved in no intrigue of any kind. No one was likely to be dogging my footsteps as they might have dogged the famous players in our Company such as Dick Burbage or Bob Armin the clown.

The discomfort in the region of my neck continuing, I looked back yet again. Still visible were the red-doublet man and the pale-hat woman, despite the deepening gloom. I told myself this was ridiculous. Nevertheless some simple fear of not disclosing where I lived – just in case there really was someone on my heels – caused me to take a little detour away from Thames Street and up towards Candlewick Street. I paused there by the London Stone, which is set in an open area in the middle of this wide thoroughfare and which is said to have been brought to our city by Brutus, who was descended from Aeneas of Troy.

It is a popular place with visitors and, like an out-of-towner, I stopped by the low, square block of stone and pretended to examine it in the dying light. They say that as long as the London Stone is safe the city will flourish. Perhaps they're right. We'd endured the plague and a change of rulers in the last year alone, and unlike Troy we were still standing. There was a faint groove across the upper surface and I ran my finger down it. Was it really so old? Had it stood on the sun-kissed plains of Troy? These speculations were at the back of mind. With the front part, I was keeping my eyes open for signs of anyone, especially anyone wearing a red doublet or a pale hat, emerging into the open area. But all I saw was a handful of shadowy shapes, and no one I could plainly identify.

Eventually, I returned in the direction I'd come from and walked a little further down Thames Street to the front door of my lodgings. I felt a bit of a fool. I could have been home ten minutes earlier.

The moment I opened the door, Ursula Buckle appeared in the lobby. Even by the uncertain indoor light she looked pale.

"Nicholas," she said.

"Mrs Buckle. You are well?"

"Will you join me for supper?"

I'd eaten nothing since that morning apart from the few oysters which were sloshing about in my insides together with the Mermaid tavern's Rhenish, so I gratefully accepted her offer. It was quite late. I wondered whether she'd been waiting for my return before eating. For politeness' sake, I expressed the hope that she hadn't while privately hoping that she had. Where was Elizabeth? I asked. Next door, I was told, visiting with Mrs Morris, another plague-widow but a woman much nearer to Elizabeth's own age and rather better off than her neighbours.

Elizabeth's mother and I sat down at the kitchen table – no formality between us when it came to dining – for some cold pork and bread and cheese brought by the serving-girl with a runny nose. She deposited the platters with a clatter, though not before almost dropping their contents on the floor. I'd grown used to her clumsiness and my landlady never rebuked her. Mrs Buckle was too gentle, and this was another reason why I liked her.

My landlady was a delicate eater. I used knife or fingers while she used a new-fangled fork to spear the occasional sliver of meat and carry it to her mouth. Mrs Buckle had a delicate mouth too, with a quite pronounced indentation running from the base of her nose to her upper lip. The groove reminded me of the line which was threaded across the top of the London Stone and which I had just traced out with my finger. There were a few other lines, less flattering ones maybe, about Mrs Buckle's face but they only enhanced her attractions, to my mind. Nevertheless, I called her 'Mrs Buckle' even though we'd known each other for several months now. She might have been 'Ursula' in my mind, but I liked calling her by her married name for some reason, enjoyed the sound of the words in my mouth. Meantime she called me Nicholas rather than Nick, and I am afraid the name was generally spoken in the way that my mother might have spoken it, although rather more warmly.

We talked a bit about the Spaniards and their arrival in London. Like me, she'd seen them although from this side of the river. But I could tell that there was something else on her mind, not to do with Spain. I could guess what was troubling her.

"There is something wrong, Mrs Buckle?"

"I saw him again, I saw him. Just before you came back this evening."

There was only a scattering of candles in the room but the strain and pallor on her face were clear to see. For the second time that evening I felt a prickling on the nape of my neck.

"Whereabouts this time?"

"The same place as before. Halfway up the stairs. As the light was beginning to fade I was standing in the hall. I was about to do something or go somewhere, I can't remember what now. I looked up and saw the hem of a familiar coat turning the corner where the stairs go out of sight. Then I looked higher up and saw the back of a familiar head."

"But the light was bad. You cannot be certain of what you saw. A flapping curtain perhaps . . . "

She'd put down her fork altogether, was not even making the pretence of eating. I wanted to put my hand across the table and touch her for reassurance but I did not move.

"I am sure. It was him."

"You didn't see his face?"

"No. What difference would that make?"

Because you could have told whether he was happy or sad

from his expression, I wanted to say. But ghosts are unhappy by definition, aren't they? Especially the ghost of a husband who has been snatched away by the plague. If they come back, it must be because they are looking for something. Or if not something, then somebody.

"What difference?" repeated Mrs Buckle.

"No difference probably, I don't know," I said. "Try not to think of it, Mrs Buckle. Tell me about something else."

And I started on my supper once more. I thought it was best not to humour her belief that she was seeing her dead husband. Perhaps I didn't want it to be true, either. She had seen her husband several times before, as a ghost, that is.

"Still bad news," she said. "You know that Lizzie and I are here on sufferance."

She gestured vaguely at the room, meaning to take in the entire house.

"But you pay rent. Anyway the landlord is your late husband's cousin, I think you said."

"He is a cousin to Hugh, yes. And we do not pay much rent. In truth, Nicholas, the money you give us goes quite a long way towards meeting his demands. But now . . . now he is asking for more, much more."

"But why?"

"He says things have changed since the pestilence last year. Enough time has gone by, and property is starting to get expensive again. He can rent more profitably to others. Of course we could stay if we could afford it."

She sounded defeated rather than distressed. I wanted to help her. I would have helped her if I'd been able to but what can a player on a shilling and threepence a day do? Nevertheless my heart went out to her and this time I did stretch my hand across the table and rest it on hers. She allowed my hand to stay there for quite a time before slipping hers out from underneath.

"I nearly forgot, you had a visitor earlier today," said Mrs Buckle.

"I did. Who was it?"

"He didn't give his name. Just asked whether Nicholas Revill the player lived here."

I paused with the knife halfway to my mouth.

"He didn't say why he wanted me?"

"No. He didn't seem inclined to say much."

"But he knew I lived here."

"Is it a secret?"

Now it was my turn to feel a little uneasy although I couldn't have accounted for the feeling.

"What did he look like?"

"Ordinary."

"Wearing a red doublet?"

"Why yes, I think he was. A red doublet. So you have seen him after all?"

"No – I – it's just that I think I know who he might be."

But I had no idea who he was, of course, except that it must be the figure I'd glimpsed behind me in Thames Street.

O *heavy ignorance!*

Ben Jonson had organized a rehearsal of his *Masque of Peace* for the next morning at the house of Sir Philip Blake. Several of the performers would be there (although not the Queen, I assumed). I set off from Mrs Buckle's lodgings and made my way down Ludgate Hill and Fleet Street. A heat-haze was already forming, turning figures in the distance into insubstantial shapes, mere ghosts. I thought of what my landlady had told me about glimpsing her late husband as he climbed the stairs. It was the third or fourth time she'd told me of such a sighting. The detail of watching the hem of his coat, the back of his head, gave a curious truthfulness to the story. But I didn't know whether to believe her. She would not lie – but anyone may be deluded. The dead should stay where they belong, in my opinion, and not indulge themselves in truanting about our world.

Maybe it was the bright morning but I also felt a bit of a truant. There were no activities involving the King's Men scheduled for the next couple of days yet, by participating in Ben's thing, I was somehow mooching off.

I turned my head from time to time and kept my eyes open for a flash of red doublet in the street, especially after what Mrs Buckle had told me about yesterday's caller. But this wasn't very logical. Why should anyone follow me if they already knew where I lived? Anyway, if I had glimpsed a person like the fellow from the previous evening, I would have accosted him. But there was no one who fitted the picture. Instead, I turned my mind to business and this piece of Jonson's in which I was playing.

The idea of the celebratory masque was a shrewd one on the playwright's part. The King's Men were 'in attendance' on the Spanish party at Somerset House only in a ceremonial sense. But it had occurred to Ben that more might be done to mark the occasion than merely having us flounce around the palace in our cut-price red cloth. So he had come up with the notion of a private masque to be played before a select audience. And, more than a select audience, *Masque of Peace* was to be played by a select cast. You can't get much more select than the Queen of England.

The performance was scheduled for a week's time. Our masque was to herald the imminent outbreak of peace, which was a foregone conclusion. In truth the Spanish party was not in London to negotiate – since such a large and grand group would never have set sail from Spain if the outcome was in doubt – but to seal a treaty. I did not need Giles Cass to tell me that. The actual swearing of the peace would be staged at the Chapel Royal in Whitehall in the presence of the King. The performance at Somerset House was to be a first course for that event. I didn't know the behind-the-scenes detail but I guessed that this was Anne of Denmark's way of marking the event, as well as uniting two of her causes. Her partiality both for Spain and for the drama was well known.

By this stage I'd reached Temple Bar by the Inns of Court. Near here, in Middle Temple during the dying days of Elizabeth's reign when we were still known as the Chamberlain's Men, we'd played in WS's *Troilus and Cressida*. Beyond Temple Bar stretched the Strand with its fine mansions, including Somerset or Denmark House, now a temporary nest of Spaniards. The Blakes' mansion stood several hundred yards before Somerset House. It wasn't quite as grand but it would do to be going on with.

I identified myself as a player at the gatehouse and the doorkeeper waved me through. He had a large, hairy wart on his cheek and if you'd asked me afterwards what he looked like or even whether he had two heads, I wouldn't have been able to describe him. Just the large, hairy wart. An ample courtyard extended in front of a fine house-front. Although I wouldn't have admitted it to anyone, I was a little overawed by the scale of the place and so was pleased to see Ben Jonson standing in a shady spot in the yard. He was deep in conversation with another man. Together they were examining a sheet of paper.

Not wanting to disturb them by calling out, I coughed and Jonson looked up. He squinted into the sunlight as I approached.

"Ah, it is you, Nicholas. Wait there an instant."

Obediently I stopped. The other man was a short fellow with a lined face. Jonson nudged his companion and said, "How about *him*, Jonathan Snell?"

The short man looked me up and down.

"Nine and a half, I'd say," he said.

There was a pause.

"Well, Revill," said Ben Jonson. "Is he right? Yes or no."

"I'd have a better idea of yes or no if I knew what you were talking about, Ben."

"We're talking about your weight, man. What do you think nine and a half is? Your age?"

"Is this gentleman a hangman? Why does he need to guess how heavy I am?"

"Do I look like a hangman?" said the man called Jonathan Snell. He sounded amused rather than indignant.

"I can't tell," I said. "The only hangman I ever saw looked like a parson. His real trade was as a butcher, though."

"Never mind all that, Nicholas. Is he correct? Do you weigh nine and a half stone?"

"I can't tell that either, Ben. I expect so."

"Master Snell claims to be able to tell a man's weight just by glancing at him."

"That must be a useful skill."

"It is, sir, it is. See."

Snell held out the sheet of paper which, close to, showed as a mass of lines and circles.

"Oh, you are the engine-man," I said.

Snell beamed. He transferred the sheet of paper to his other hand and held out his right to shake. He had a long thumb which, disconcertingly, seemed to wrap itself round the back of my own hand.

"Jonathan is constructing the chair which will bring Sir Philip Blake down from the heavens like a *deus ex machina*. Sir Philip will be the god who comes down to earth to solve human problems. This is Master Snell's plan of the device."

"I remember now, Sir Philip is playing the part of Truth in our masque," I said.

"Truth must come down in state, though," said the little man. "It wouldn't do if he plunged to earth, wouldn't do at all. You must take account of the sitter's weight in these calculations and I have already assessed Sir Philip's at a glance."

"As long as he has the time to deliver a least a couple of verses while he's descending," said Jonson. "It'll be the best he can do. He's no actor."

"I'll be at the controls myself, Master Jonson," said Snell. "I'll lower him good and steady."

He mimed turning a wheel.

Masques, even relatively straightforward ones like *Peace*, can't be staged in a day and I realized, after hearing Jonson and Snell talk about their device, that this one had been in preparation for some time.

"How is the building going?" said the playwright, jerking his thumb over his shoulder in the direction of Somerset House. I noticed that, consciously or not, he used his right, unbranded hand for the gesture.

"It's going well. We'll be ready inside two days. All ready."

"Good, good. Nothing too elaborate is necessary."

"Nothing that'll overshadow your valuable words, you mean, Master Ben," said Snell.

I glanced at Jonathan Snell with new respect. I didn't know how long he'd been acquainted with Ben Jonson but he had got the measure of the man and his sensitivity, and showed that he wasn't daunted by it. Jonson didn't take offence at the slight irony in the words either (as he might have done with me, for example).

"I must go and check on the waves," said Snell. "One of the cranks has a tendency to stick. Goodbye, Masters Benjamin and Nicholas. What part are you playing by the way?"

"I am Ignorance," I said.

Snell might have made a cheap crack at that point but he simply nodded a further farewell to Jonson and me and walked off towards the gatehouse. He crossed paths with Abel Glaze, Laurence Savage and Jack Wilson who were just entering the courtyard. After we had exchanged greetings, all five of us headed for the house, with Ben Jonson in the lead.

This was a large establishment and, once inside, we were ushered through various chambers by various footmen, all in yellow livery. There was something fish-like about the way they glided from room to room with glassy expressions, being actively uninterested in us. Eventually we ended up in a great chamber overlooking the river. We spent some time examining the view, examining the furniture, examining the tapestries. It was very quiet. The only sounds which penetrated from outside were the cries of gulls or watermen, and they were muted as if out of respect. Our voices dropped almost to a whisper, although not Jonson's. At long last, four people came into the room. I recognized Sir Philip Blake and Lady Blake from the previous day on the south bank of the river. The other two, a man and a woman, I didn't know.

Since all four are going to play quite a part in this story I'll pause here to introduce them, bringing forward what I found out later.

Sir Philip Blake was a courtier, top to toe. He'd been entrusted with a minor part in the current 'negotiations' with Spain, although he had formerly been an opponent of such a treaty, like many Englishmen. Blake was a relatively slight man with quite prominent ears. There was a sharpness to his pointed beard and a touch of severity in his features which was appropriate for the role of Truth in the *Masque of Peace*.

Where her husband was thin and ascetic-looking, Lady Jane Black was plump and amiable. She looked like a tavern-keeper's wife, pleased to see old friends and newcomers equally. (I later discovered that she came from lowly circumstances, being an apothecary's daughter.) In fact, if I hadn't known who she was I would have taken her for the attendant or personal servant to the much more elegant lady who was standing by her side. In reality it was this one who was the servant while the plump lady was the mistress. The tall and graceful woman was called Maria More. As she came into the room she arched her eyebrows and gazed around with a kind of disdain, as if to say 'Oh, so these are the players, are they?'

The final member of this foursome stood a little behind Sir Philip. His name was William Inman. He had something of Ben Jonson about him, a similar air of bustling good humour though with a much redder face. I suspected instinctively that, as with Jonson, the good humour would disappear if he was crossed. Just as I'd seen Cecil whisper in Blake's ear yesterday while both stood near the Queen's carriage, so I now saw Blake turn and whisper into the ear of Inman.

Inman smiled slightly and nodded vigorously at whatever his master had said. This red-faced man stood in the same relation to Blake as the elegant lady did to his wife, somewhere between an assistant and a secretary. And, after a first glance at the four of them, you would've said that the noble lady and gent were closer to their personal attendants than they were to each other. More civil, more responsive.

Ben Jonson strode forward to greet Blake and to incline his head towards the ladies. He trod a nice line between deference and familiarity. This son of a bricklayer always said that he never esteemed anyone just because they had a noble name, and I think it was true. Then, with a sweep of his hand about the chamber, Ben made some remark about great wealth and taste being contracted into a single room. He said this in English before adding some appropriate Latin quotation. The first comment certainly pleased his patrons and broke the ice.

At this point Giles Cass, the go-between, and Martin Barton, the satirical playwright, were ushered into the chamber. Our practice party was complete for the time being, although not all the players were present. Cass was known to the Blakes, of course, and Barton swiftly got familiar with them. For someone who affected to despise the court and all its works, Barton was surprisingly good at getting familiar.

Then it was the moment to begin.

Rehearsing a masque is quite different from rehearsing a play. The action is much shorter, there aren't many lines to learn and no one expects great feats of performance anyway. Despite the engine-man's comment about Jonson's 'valuable words', it is the music, costumes and effects which are more important than the drama. The music and the rest are produced by professionals, which is just as well. Since many of the principal roles are taken by important people like the Queen of England, and since such important people always have much less time at their disposal than we ordinary persons, any rehearsal time is necessarily limited.

Ben Jonson produced a sheaf of papers and distributed them among the company. Each of us in the room had a part in the *Masque of Peace*. I was accustomed to the fat scrolls of the playhouse, especially since I'd started taking bigger parts, and so the couple of sheets which I now held felt like short commons. None of us had many words to say. I wondered about this until Abel pointed out that we'd be playing in front of an audience of whom half would be Spanish. What would be the point, he said, of Ben's penning reams of lines if they were destined to pass over the heads of many of his listeners?

"It hasn't stopped him before," I said.

But Abel was surely correct. Why write a great deal if you're not going to be understood?

Ben had assigned the parts quite artfully – or cynically, if you prefer. On the whole the more attractive roles, such as Peace and Plenty, were given to the part-time actors who just happened to be full-time nobles while the less enticing ones like Ignorance and Rumour were doled out to the proper players.

I didn't have much to do in the part of Ignorance except to look useless (yes, all right, spare the comments). I'd never played a simple, unqualified Noun before, and was quite looking forward to doing it as a change from playing human beings. Looking forward also to wearing my costume, which had been conceived by the Globe tire-man Bartholomew Ridd and which, like all masque outfits, was a kind of walking riddle.

Altogether, this masque should be a holiday from ordinary work. Not much application or effort required.

(Little did I know. I was truly ignorant. Ignorance personified.)

For a flavour of my lines, which cannot have detained Ben Jonson very long in the composition, try the opening:

I know not where I am,
I know not whence I came,
Darkness is my dwelling-place,
Ignorance is my name.

The function of Ignorance was to tremble at the prospect of the arrival of the Spaniards. Along the same pattern, Suspicion was meant to bristle and the figure of Fright was supposed to adopt a threatening posture, while Rumour went running from one ear to another. These 'bad' qualities were intended to be absurd, laughable. But the joke was that this was actually how most of the English felt about the Spanish, and were content to feel. It was probably how the Spanish felt about us too: ignorant, prejudiced, suspicious, hostile.

While we were examining our roles, Sir Philip Blake made a tour of the room, enquiring who we were playing. I told him that I was Ignorance and therefore a kind of opposite to his Truth.

"Truth will prevail," he said, clearing his throat.

"It must prevail. It is written," I said, since I can be just as sententious as anybody else.

"Who are you really, though, behind the mask of Ignorance?"

"Nicholas Revill, sir, a player."

"Revill? Not one of the Revills of Norfolk?"

"No, from Somerset."

"I don't think I've heard of them. Are you connected?"

"If we are, then it's like the connection of one twig to another on the opposite side of the tree."

There was a pause while Sir Philip absorbed this information, at the same time making frequent throat-clearing sounds. Or perhaps he was wondering what I was talking about. I was wondering myself.

"Very good," he said finally, moving on.

The Revills of Norfolk? I made a mental note to ask my friend Jack Wilson, whose family came from Norwich, whether he knew of any Norfolk Revills. Perhaps we were connected. Perhaps they were cousins; perhaps they were rich.

"Nicholas!"

"What is it? Oh, sorry."

It was Ben Jonson, calling me to order. As well as being the author of the *Masque of Peace* he was what's called the 'guider' of the production.

"I wish you to play ignorant now," he said. "Put on an appropriate face. No, not like that. There's a difference between ignorance and idiocy, Revill. You'll be drooling down your front next. Now, my lady, if you would be so

51

good as to take up your position over there. And to cradle the cornucopia in your hands. An imaginary horn of plenty at the moment, I'm afraid. On the night it will be crammed with fruit and flowers."

"I hope it won't be too heavy to carry, Benjamin," said Lady Blake. She had a pleasant voice, with a scarcely suppressed laughter bubbling in it. "I'm not sure how much plenty I can bear."

"The contents will be made of wire and cloth and paper, my lady. Light as air."

If deliberate, it was sly of Ben to have cast Lady Jane Blake in the part of Plenty (one of the blessings of Peace) since she certainly didn't look as though she denied herself very much. I noticed that Ben controlled the members of the Blake household with a looser rein than he did the professional players. With the former it was 'please . . . ' and 'perhaps . . .' He still got his way, though.

During the morning Ben took us through our lines and postures and movements. It was all quite simple after the complicated world of the stage play. A lot of masque-work involves no more than standing up, or sitting down, or lying flat. Also during the morning I made the acquaintance of Maria More, who was playing a handmaid to Plenty. (And where else should More be, but attending on Plenty?) Though she looked more of the lady than her mistress, I'd been mistaken in my belief that she was aloof. Rather she was combative. Combative, tall and graceful.

During a break in the rehearsal, while Jonson was consulting his patrons and the rest of us had split up into chattering groups, Mistress More told me that she'd visited the Globe playhouse on two or three occasions. Then she asked a strange question.

"We're permitted to take part in these masques but we are not allowed to play on your stage. Why?"

"We? You mean, ah, well-born people like the ones here?"

"I mean women."

"Oh, *women*. Women on stage. That wouldn't be proper."

"But some people claim that it's even less proper for boys to dress up as females."

"Such people are general enemies to the playhouse. They object to everything we do. Besides, er . . . I have heard it said that boys make better women than women."

"That is your opinion?"

"Not necessarily my opinion. But I have heard it said."

"Are you always so cautious?"

"I don't want to offend."

"Of course, I forget that it's also a woman's part to be easily offended," she said. "But you still have not answered the question. *Why* should it be improper for us to play our own sex on stage?"

"It is a difficult subject," I said, searching around in my head for reasons and failing to find them. When you came down to it, why shouldn't women act on the public stage? It would not seem right if they did, that's all. Maria More looked at me with a gaze that was half amused, half challenging.

"Difficult indeed," she said after a pause.

I was saved from anything else by the appearance of William Inman, the jolly-faced man who was assistant to Sir Philip Blake.

"Ho hum," he said. "I think I'll turn player. I am enjoying this."

"What part are you playing?" I said (although I knew perfectly well).

"I am the Ocean," said Inman.

There were to be waves in our piece, as I'd gathered from Snell the engine-man and designer. Masque audiences like to watch waves and voyages, and in the *Masque of Peace* there was at least some excuse for a bit of sea since the Spaniards have to get over from their part of the world to ours.

"Be careful you don't sink the Spaniard," I said.

"This isn't '88," said Inman. "They will have a calm

crossing, with a favouring breeze. The favouring breeze will be played by Sir Fabian Scaridge. It is the dawn of a new age. The age of Peace."

This sounded like the kind of diplomatic remark that might have been uttered by his master. I thought Inman was mocking such language.

"Are you wearing seaweed, William?" said Maria More. "Shells and starfish and stuff?"

"I shall insist on a trident. Your man Jonson says the costume man is coming this afternoon to fit us out."

"Bartholomew Ridd is his name," I said. "Ask him for whatever you want. He is very accommodating."

Ridd was just the opposite, very fussy and particular. Let them find that out for themselves though. William Inman went on to expand on the joys of a player's life, as though *he* was the expert and I was the ignorant one. How delightful it must be to travel round the country, how amusing it must be to wear other men's clothes, to speak other men's lines, to play parts that were generally so much above our real station in life. To have so little to do for ourselves.

"Yes," I said, "you're right. We players are hardly required to do anything at all for ourselves. Only to show skill in verse-speaking, and dancing, and fencing, and clowning, and singing. Nothing much."

"Only joking," said Inman. "Don't take offence."

"I'm not easily offended," I said, glancing at Maria More. "I welcome honest comment."

"That's me in a nutshell," said Inman. "Bill Inman speaks things as he finds them."

I don't know why, but I never quite believe individuals who refer to themselves in this detached way. There was no opportunity for any further chat, however, since Ben Jonson summoned us to go over our lines and movements once again. There were various gaps in the rehearsal – for one thing, the Queen was not here to run through her lines as Peace, and there was no sign of Sir Fabian Scaridge who was to play the part of the favouring wind – but we emerged from the Blake mansion with a clearer idea of the action.

And after that nothing much happened for the rest of the day. But the evening made up for this uneventfulness. I went to a brothel and then I got attacked.

O *notable strumpet!*

F irst, the brothel.
I just happened to find myself south of the river after hours. Considering that I didn't have much time for Southwark ale-houses such as the Goat & Monkey or the Knight of the Carpet, it was surprising how often I found myself carousing there with my companions.

And considering how I thought I'd forsworn the delights of the Southwark stews like Holland's Leaguer, it was surprising how often I found my feet straying over the threshold of such houses of pleasure.

Well, not that often, perhaps. I had to balance the state of my purse against my, ah, itch. And some sense of delicacy prevented me from returning to Holland's Leaguer since it was where my old friend Nell had worked and lived – and died. Instead, I went to a less exalted and expensive establishment called the Mitre, also located in the depths of Southwark. Maybe on account of the ecclesiastical associations of the name, the madam of the place – a prim, tight-lipped woman called Mistress Bates – looked severe enough to be running a religious house. The girls also took pleasure in this incongruous title of Mitre, although it was well known that the name referred less to a churchman's headgear than it did to a different appendage further south on the bishop's body.

I was explaining this to the dark-haired girl I was in the habit of asking for at the Mitre. This was the evening of the first rehearsal day for the masque. My dark-haired girl, whom I knew only as Blanche, seemed fresh and innocent, although this was no doubt an illusion. In addition, she was French. So it may be that her grasp of dirty double meanings in English was a bit shaky.

"Oh, Nicholaas . . . " she was saying, "so you mean zat zis 'ouse which we call ze Meeter . . . ?"

"The Mitre, yes."

"Ze . . . mitre . . . eet ees anozzer zing too. It is what a – 'ow you say? – a churchman, 'e put on 'is 'ead, yes?"

"A tall hat with a sort of groove across it which a bishop or a cardinal wears," I said in my best schoolmasterly style. We were lying in bed at the time, not wearing hats or much of anything else.

"And eet is 'ow we call ze name of our 'ouse too, yes? Ze Mitre. Oh, Nicholaas!"

Her pretty eyes wide open, Blanche clapped her hand across her mouth but continued to laugh and shriek. Her laughter was catching. What had been a stale London joke about a dirty name became fresh to my own ears as well so that I started to laugh out loud and then, when our laughter subsided and she asked me *why* the brothel and the bishop's hat should share a name, I just had to explain matters. Better still, I just had to demonstrate the reason why they shared a name with something else. So we turned to other things.

Blanche was a pleasure. I think that she liked me. But with her, unlike with Nell, pleasure was business, strictly business. Pleasure for cash, cash for pleasure. If I wanted to visit her more often then I needed money in my purse, in order that she might put some of it into hers and some into Mistress Bates's, the madam's.

I did not know much about Blanche, knew nothing about her really apart from the fact that she thought she'd been born in Bordeaux. How and why she'd fetched up on the shores of the Thames, she did not tell me. Sometimes these girls in the stews are genuinely ignorant of their very early lives, sometimes they make a little mystery of it so as to entice customers.

It was while I was making my way back after this latest session at the Mitre that it happened. It was another bright summer's evening and my shadow stretched out far ahead of me as I walked along the river bank. I was quite comfortable with the world, not thinking of anything much, lighter in spirits (and a little lighter in my purse).

To my immediate left was the *Hercules*, the barge belonging to the Globe shareholders. Only the day before we'd been crowding its decks to inspect the arrival of the Spaniards. Now the river was nearly empty – most of the day's trade being finished – with only a few watermen plying for hire.

I looked over my left shoulder in the direction of Somerset House. Queen Anne's palace stood out, a pearl even amid the other great mansions on the far shore. We would soon be there, first to practise and then to play out Ben's *Masque of Peace*.

There were only a handful of other people on the river bank behind me. If the red-doubleted individual of the previous evening had been among them I would have noticed, I think, even though it was difficult to see much against the glare of the declining sun.

But there was something about that over-the-shoulder glimpse which caused me to turn my head round once again. Maybe it was a shape moving more quickly than seemed natural on a lazy summer's evening. Maybe it was some sixth sense of danger. I was just in time to see a cloaked figure bearing down hard. I had no chance to react. There was a draught of air to my right and then a jarring blow to the side of my head. Without even knowing that I'd fallen I found myself sprawling on my back on the ground. The evening sky gaped above me, criss-crossed by flashes of light like meteors. The whizzing meteors continued but suddenly the sky was blocked by the cloaked figure who seemed to have grown to the height of several buildings. He moved halfway out of my dizzy vision. I heard someone grunting and a woman's voice shrieking "Kick 'im! Kick 'im!", before experiencing a stabbing pain in my ribs. Then another grunt and another stab, followed by more of both. The bastard was kicking me, as ordered!

It may sound odd, but what I felt most acutely at this instant – over and above the ringing numbness in my head and the sense that all the breath had been knocked violently out of my body – what I felt most was relief. At least my assailant did not intend to murder me, merely to give me a good kicking. If you're going to kill someone then you don't do the deed in a public place, not even in lawless Southwark. Although I couldn't have articulated these comforting notions at the time, they were running through some part of my battered head even while I curled up against the foot thudding into my side. Instinctively I kept my eyes shut but was aware of shadows moving across the lids.

Then there was an indistinct blur of shouting and scuffling feet. The kicking stopped. Moments later I felt someone's hot breath on my face.

I opened one eye, then the other. A trimly bearded male head hovered above me.

"How are you, sir?"

I opened my mouth but nothing more detailed came out of it than a groan.

I made to sit up and fell back on the ground. I tried again, fell back again. Sitting up would take a bit of doing. My new friend squatted down on his hams. He put his arm behind my shoulders for support. It was odd to see the river bank so peaceful and undisturbed, the water still slipping by. The whole episode had probaby taken less than a minute. A handful of other people had stopped to watch the scene.

Eventually I clambered to my feet, clinging to my rescuer. He was plump but solid as a little pillar. I noticed that he was wearing a red doublet which he filled comfortably.

"Did – did you – "

I struggled to regain my breath. My sides were starting to hurt. There was a cloudiness over my right eye, near where I'd been struck at the beginning of the attack.

"They ran off," said the other, answering one of the questions which I hadn't been able to ask. "They ran off when I came near."

"Did – did – "

"No more now, sir. Let us get you to some comfort. Here is the Pure Waterman close at hand."

Still holding tight to the stranger, I limped across towards the tavern. The few bystanders strolled on. We entered the tavern. The Pure Waterman, which stands four-square on Bankside, was named either in irony (since watermen are almost always impure, at least in their speech) or in propitiation of its customers, most of whom are ferrymen and don't care for outsiders. Nevertheless it was welcome as a place to get my breath and wits back. Tactfully, the Samaritan in a red doublet, steered me towards an obscure, smoky corner. I stared about, still slightly dazed. The tavern was crowded. Instead of waiting for a drawer to notice us, my rescuer went off in search of refreshment.

Quite soon the plump man returned. He placed a little pewter mug in front of me and I gulped from it straightaway, then wished I hadn't. I coughed and gasped for air. He looked concerned.

"Be careful, take it slowly. I have the landlord's word for it. That's his best aqua vitae."

The fiery liquid prickled in my throat before it began to glow lower down in my guts.

"I asked him for something restorative," said the other man, sitting down and taking a more modest swallow from his own mug.

"I feel – ah – better – already."

I did too. Normal vision was returning to my right eye. My sides would ache for a good few days, and I could visualize the bruises taking shape like little thunderclouds even while I was sitting here, but some experimental shifts and turns told me that nothing was broken, most likely.

"That was a vicious attack," he said, gesturing in the direction of the river.

I made to shrug manfully and felt a sharp pain in my side.

"Do you know who it was?" said my rescuer.

"Who?"

"Your attacker. There was a woman there but it was a man doing all the work."

"No, I don't know."

"Did you see his face?" he persisted.

"No. Did you see it?"

"They ran off, like I said. *He* was wearing a cloak which he kept about his face, thus."

Suiting the action to the word, my rescuer lifted up his arm so that it obscured the bottom half of his face. He gazed at me over his crooked elbow. He had brown eyes and a steady gaze, and he seemed to be assessing me somehow.

"An enemy?" he said.

For an instant I thought he was referring to himself but then realized he was talking about the person who'd set on me. I took a more cautious sip from my mug of aqua vitae and said, "It looks like it. Sir, I have been guilty of discourtesy. You must put it down to the, ah, surprise I have just received. But I do not know the name of my rescuer."

"While I do not know the name of the person I have rescued."

"I think you do," I said.

He did not reply.

"For form's sake then, I am Nicholas Revill. A player, a member of the King's Men in fact."

This gentleman showed no sign of recognition but nor did he ask why I supposed him to already know my name. Rather, he continued to gaze at me with those shrewd, assessing eyes. There was a silence. Eventually it was my nerve which went.

"Well, sir, if you won't tell me to whom I owe my gratitude, there is at least one piece of information which you could give me."

"What is that, Master Revill?"

"Tell me why you've been following me for the last couple of days. Tell me who you are."

Put money in thy purse

S o we talked, my rescuer and I, and eventually I found
myself listening to a proposal. Then I found myself
agreeing to the same proposal, uneasily.

By the next morning I'd more or less forgotten the attack,
despite the bruises and the pang in my side if I turned sharply.
Instead I was preoccupied with the conversation we'd had in
the Pure Waterman. I could not rid myself of the idea that
this might be a dangerous undertaking, although it looked
straightforward enough on the surface.

From one aspect I was doing my duty by my country.

From another, I was storing up favours with powerful
people, wasn't I?

And then, apart from the duty and the favours earned, there
was the money.

Ah, the money . . . I patted my pocket and felt the unusual
bulk of my purse. As a token of his good faith, the gentleman
in the Pure Waterman had given me three sovereigns, with
the promise of more to follow. Three whole sovereigns.
Count 'em – not one, not two, but three weighty circles. This
was the equivalent of almost two months' pay to me.

Money is serious, it should be listened to.

This was how my conversation with the gentleman
unfolded.

Nicholas Revill: Tell me why you've been following me for
the last couple of days. Tell me who you are.

The Other Man: My name is John Ratchett. I have not been following you exactly, Master Revill, but waiting for the opportunity to speak with you.

Nick Revill: You called at my lodgings recently?

John Ratchett: You were out.

NR: And you pursued me down Thames Street yesterday evening, I think. What is it you want with me?

JR: A word or two.

NR: Well, I am indebted to you and so must listen.

JR: We hope that *we* may be indebted to you shortly.

NR: We?

JR: Nicholas – may I call you that? – I speak on behalf of a certain group which is interested in the King's Men.

NR: If you want to hire us for a private performance then you should be speaking to one of the Burbage brothers. I believe our rates are very reasonable.

JR: More precisely, we are interested in the masque which your man Jonson intends to put on at Denmark House.

NR: Ben Jonson would be gratified.

JR: The purpose of the masque is to celebrate the peace between the English and the Spanish?

NR: That's no secret.

JR: You've been rehearsing for it in the house of Sir Philip Blake?

NR: Yes.

JR: What is your opinion of the Spaniard?

NR: I do not concern myself with affairs of state. The Spanish were our enemies once, is as much as I know. What is the nature of this group which you speak for, Master Ratchett?

JR: We are interested in establishing the nature of the ties between England and Spain.

NR: England and Spain are about to become fast friends, aren't they? Now I remember, it is to be written down in a treaty so it must be so.

JR: To get to the quick of the matter, there are others who are interested in breaking those ties.

NR: Old enemies of Spain, I suppose. This is dangerous territory, Master Ratchett.

JR: Do not worry, you are well protected.

NR: 'Protected.' Now you do worry me. How? Why? Who do you speak for?

JR: I . . .

NR: Do you speak for . . . ?

JR: I cannot say it.

NR: Then I shall say it . . . it is the Privy Council, is it not?

JR: Please lower your voice a little, Nicholas.

NR: All right. But now I do refuse. Whatever you're suggest-ing, I refuse. I have worked before for Master Robert Cecil, or rather I have followed his instructions while he was digging into plots. I remember well what danger those instructions led me into. If you'll excuse me . . .

JR: Sit down again, Nicholas, and wait until I've told you what we require. Sit down. Thank you. What we require is nothing – or as good as nothing.

NR: Then why are you asking?

JR: You mentioned plots but there is no plot here. There are rather . . . directions and tendencies. Shades and shadows.

NR: In plain English, please.

JR: We are interested in the precise – colouring – of certain individuals with whom you are in touch. For example, Sir Philip Blake and his wife. And there is a person called Giles Cass. We wish to be more precisely informed of their senti-ments, their talk.

NR: And the Queen too? Should I inform on her? You know that she is to participate in the masque?

JR: Her presence is one of the reasons why it is so important that we are kept informed, thoroughly informed.

NR: Why me?

JR: Because you have worked for Secretary Cecil before. You said as much.

NR: But Secretary Cecil has direct connections with such people. I saw him talking to Sir Philip Blake only yesterday. Why on earth should he want to recruit me?

JR: The more eyes the better. Listen, Nicholas. We require you only to look out and to listen in. Then to write for us – to write a kind of report – on the preparations for this *Masque of Peace*, material which would be read only in the highest circles. To describe the people, the little events, that occur in the Blake household or in Denmark House, as you see them. Giles Cass, for example, he would bear watching . . .

NR: Cass? I thought that he worked for Cecil.

JR: There are outer circles and inner circles.

NR: Circles, shadows, tendencies. Haven't you anything more solid, Master Ratchett?

JR: Can I put money in your purse, Nicholas? Will this be solid enough? These coins are a kind of circle after all.

Well, all I had to do was to pen a couple of reports or three on the goings-on surrounding the production of the *Masque of Peace*. Nothing much. As I said earlier, it seemed pretty straightforward. John Ratchett also insinuated that I would be doing the state – or the Privy Council at least – some service. I'd be working under their 'protection'. I should have known better.

The stuff about the state sounded quite plausible. at the time. Although I'd claimed ignorance when he was speaking to me, I knew a bit more than I let on. For example, when Ratchett claimed that there were people who'd like to break the ties between England and Spain, he was only speaking the half of it. There were many more people who were fearful of the Spanish than ready to befriend them. Indeed, under the old Queen, it had been the duty of all right-thinking Englishmen to regard them as the enemy. If we weren't engaged in open warfare, then there was a hidden struggle proceeding all the time. Why, only a few years ago, there had been a mad plot to assassinate Queen Elizabeth by smearing the pommel of her horse's saddle with poison. And now we were all meant to whoop and throw our caps into the air when we witnessed the Spaniards sailing up the Thames.

Yet who was I – playing the part of Ignorance in Ben's masque – to question the wisdom of our councillors and statesmen? Peace was a blessing, wasn't it? If I could play some tiny part in furthering an accord, then wasn't it my duty to play that part? This was the sort of inflated notion that swelled up and filled my head.

And then there was the money. "Can I put money in your purse, Nicholas?" he'd asked, as if I was the one doing him a favour by accepting it. John Ratchett was prepared to pay me three pounds for each account I provided. I never knew that writing might be so lucrative, but then I supposed that the Privy Council had a deep purse.

The prospect of cash didn't altogether blind me but, mixing metaphors, it added the cheese to the mousetrap. And when it came to money, I wasn't only thinking of myself. For instance, Ursula Buckle needed money to stay in her Thames Street house. Gaining a little extra cash, which I might hand over to her with a careless flourish, could buy her a bit of time with the unfeeling cousin who wanted to kick her and her daughter Lizzie out on to the streets. It might even be the way to her heart. (But probably not, she wasn't that sort.) While as for me, if I wanted to go on visiting my French friend Blanche in the Mitre, that certainly required a nice fat purse.

And besides all this there was that little implication – the fatal, flattering little implication – that Sir Robert Cecil himself would be reading what I wrote. In spite of what I'd claimed to Ben Jonson on the quayside, about having no wish to meet the Secretary again, the truth was that I was no more immune to a request from on high than most men would be.

So I said yes to Ratchett. Yes, I will report on the masque preparations.

Fool.

Did you not hear a cry?

I discovered it wasn't just the red-doubleted Master Ratchett who was interested in the *Masque of Peace*. I was soon approached by William Shakespeare.

"Ah, Nick, good morning," he said, his tone telling me that something else would follow on from the greeting.

I was standing on the open stage of the Globe playhouse. WS had just emerged from the stage-left entrance. If he'd been making an entrance in a real drama, the style of his approach would have been somewhere between casual and purposeful. The stage floor, not covered with rushes as it usually was for performance, resonated to the playwright's tread.

The Company wasn't playing at the moment. These dog days of August can be dry and dusty for business. Also the energies of the King's Men were officially directed towards playing the Grooms of the Outer Chamber for the duration of the Spanish visit. We had become 'grooms of the chamber', you see, at about the same time that we received the royal patent. From this court position we earned almost no money, only prestige. But it's customers, not prestige, that pay the rent. And customers need to be drawn to the playhouse, especially since the excitement of our return to town after the plague had worn off. Customers – or the better class, at any rate – enjoy bright, fresh surroundings. So the shareholders were taking the opportunity of the August dog days to smarten up the playhouse.

There were ladders and scaffolding about the stage. Perched twenty feet or so above us were a couple of craftsmen touching up the gilded ribs and the stars of the stage ceiling. One was sitting astride a plank while the other was lying on his back. Only one of his legs was visible, carelessly dangling over the side of a platform as if he had no further to fall than from a truckle-bed.

I turned towards Shakespeare and gestured overhead.

"Look you: a brave overhanging firmament – or it will be again soon," I said, quoting him, at least in the first few words.

"Fretted with golden fire," said WS, quoting himself.

"I wouldn't choose that job," I said.

"No head for heights?"

"I'd be afraid all the time of losing my head."

"Once you'd been up there for a day you would forget your fear," said WS.

"I hope Sir Philip Blake has a head for heights," I said quickly. "He is playing the figure of Truth in Ben's masque, and has to be lowered from the ceiling in a chair."

WS smiled slightly. I had brought up the subject of Jonson's *Masque of Peace* because, in truth, I was a little uneasy about my participation in it. I suppose I wanted WS to endorse me. Even though the seniors must have given their approval for the Somerset House presentation, if only tacitly, I couldn't escape the notion that Ben Jonson was setting up a little company of his own within the larger Company. It was gratifying to have been asked by Jonson to take part, but I would not have sacrificed the good opinion (as I believed) of the Globe shareholders.

Perhaps WS read something of my anxiety in my face for he put his hand to my shoulder. It was a firm grip but quite different from Jonson's bear-like grasp.

"You have hit on the subject I wanted to talk about, Nick. How do the masquers do?"

"We've only had one rehearsal."

70

"Even so . . . ?"

"I think that a noble audience will have to learn to be less, er, fastidious than the groundlings."

"They are less fastidious already. You've played often enough at court to realize that. They have not paid good money for one thing. The spectators are not really watching us most of the time, anyway. They're watching the King or the Queen."

"Or they're pissed or asleep," I said, entering into the spirit of the conversation.

"We are to present *Othello* at Whitehall in a few weeks," said WS. "I hope they'll have woken up in time for that – or sobered up."

I thought of *Othello*, the play about the Moor of Venice. If anything could wake them up, that should. The King's Men had presented this piece of WS's soon after our spring return to the Globe. We'd drawn good audiences for it. My own parts hadn't exactly been large – a Venetian senator (white beard), a drunken soldier on the isle of Cyprus (black beard). I wondered whether I'd get something a bit bigger next time around.

I sensed that we still hadn't reached the end of our dialogue, WS and I. Overhead the scaffolding and planking creaked and groaned as the painters shifted position. One of them was directly above us. Instead of a leg, all I could see now was an arm waggling across those 'heavens' which, with their moon, stars and zodiac, provide the roof of our stage-play world.

"Nick," said WS, "if I were to ask you to report on anything – untoward – which occurs while you are preparing for Ben's masque, you must not suppose that I am asking you to turn into a spy."

"Untoward?"

I probably looked confused. This was the second time such a request had been made of me within twelve hours. What was this one about? I made a stab in the dark.

"Is the good name of the King's Men at stake here?"

"Not yet but it might be. Ben is one of our number – at least some of the time he is. And you and several others are taking part in his masque."

"Abel and Laurence Savage and Jack Wilson," I said, as if I was trying to show that this wasn't my enterprise alone. Or perhaps I was hinting to WS that he could have asked any one of *them* to be his non-spy.

"An unfortunate outcome would not reflect well on the Company," said Shakespeare.

'An unfortunate outcome'. The phrase sounded round-about, almost diplomatic. So I asked WS whether he had any reason to expect trouble.

"This situation is like a cauldron into which all sorts of odds and ends are being thrown," said WS. "Ben's patrons now, Sir Philip and Lady Blake. There is coldness between them. And Jonson has connections with the man Giles Cass, who is a weathervane. He once veered towards Raleigh. Now he veers towards Cecil."

"I know. I don't trust him."

"Then there are the Spaniards at Somerset House. I would be interested to have your account of them."

"I'll keep my eyes open – though I hardly know what it is I'm looking for," I said.

"Thank you," said WS, making to move off. I sensed that he was a little uncomfortable with the request he'd just made. Then he suddenly stopped and looked down, as if deep in thought.

"Have you cut yourself?"

"What? No, I don't think so."

Shakespeare was gazing at the bare boards. A spatter of blood-red drops had appeared on the floor between us. Instinctively we stepped back. Even as I watched, another drop fell to leave its mark on the stage. I looked up. So did the playwright.

"Hey. You there!" WS called. "Take care with your brush."

After a moment a gargoyle of a face thrust itself over the side of the aerial platform and leered in our direction.

"Whassat, mate?"

"Be careful, man. You're covering us with red paint."

"Red paint?"

The big-nosed visage vanished from view. When it reappeared it was accompanied by a hand clutching a brush.

"No red paint 'ere."

Even from our position on the ground, we were able to see that his brush was tipped with a dark blue colour. Not surprising really if you're painting the sky.

"Only blue up 'ere, see."

As if to confirm this, a couple of blue drops now flew down to join the scatter of red ones on the floor.

"You're right," said WS. "Sorry to have interrupted you."

"'sallright, mate."

The head vanished again.

"And it cannot be that other fellow now," I said, pointing to the second painter who was still sitting astride his plank at some yards' distance and who was carefully running his brush along one of the ribs or frets which divided the ceiling into segments. "He is using gold paint."

"It's a mystery. You like mysteries, Nick," said Shakespeare, gazing down once more at the cluster of red drops. Already the wooden flooring seemed to have drunk them up, and they had lost some of their brightness. WS spoke lightly and turned away. A man used to dealing with the higher mysteries, perhaps he was not over-concerned with little ones.

Nor was I, much.

But the blood-red drops on the playhouse stage, if they were no great mystery, were certainly an omen.

That night I woke up with a start in the widow Buckle's house. I sat up in bed. What had woken me? Some sound? No. The house was quiet apart from the tiny creaks and groans which you never notice during the daytime. A bad dream? Maybe. I couldn't recall what, if anything, had been going through my head beforehand.

Nor could I get back to sleep. Instead I lay down and returned to the conversation with John Ratchett in the Pure Waterman. I'd attended another practice for the *Masque of Peace* and, in a somewhat half-hearted fashion, had begun to write down my observations on the event. I felt uncomfortable, spying. I was doing this for money, wasn't I? But I was also doing the state some service, wasn't I? Duty and profit. Where was the harm?

And then Master Ratchett's expression came back to me. *Can I put money in your purse, Nicholas?* (Why yes, you can, John Ratchett. Feel free to load it with as many sovereigns as it will hold. I will be able to carry them, however many.)

Put money in thy purse.

These are the words of the villainous Iago in WS's *Othello*, the play which Shakespeare had mentioned to me on the Globe stage. Although I'd had only a couple of small parts in the previous performance, I was familiar with the story of *Othello*.

Ordinary players don't normally get an overview of the works they're acting in unless they have meaty parts like the ones that go to Dick Burbage. But back in the spring of this year Geoffrey Allison, the Globe book-keeper, had asked me to pick up the fair copies of Shakespeare's latest from our scrivener, a gent in Paul's Yard who spends his life bent over other men's scrawlings and who looks up at you with the wide-eyed surprise of an owl. WS must be comparatively easy to copy out, however, since I'm told he doesn't blotch or cross through his lines. Anyway, before I returned to the Globe with my precious cargo of fair copies, I ducked into a quiet corner of St Paul's and had a quick read-through of the play. Naturally, I imagined myself in one or two of the principal roles.

But I knew I'd never get them. *Othello* is a duel of wits between the Moor and his wicked lieutenant Iago, who tempts and seduces his commander into the belief that

Othello's new wife Desdemona is unfaithful. Only three people – Othello, Iago and Desdemona – are of much importance in this vicious triangle. Dick Burbage was bound to play the part of the Moor, while the voluble villain would be taken by one of our other seniors (as it turned out, Iago was played by Henry Condell), and Desdemona could only be the property of one of our boy-players. The rest of the characters hardly mattered since they were so much clay in the hands of Iago. I wouldn't have minded playing the dashing Cassio, the honourable ladies' man. I could have dealt with the dupe Roderigo. In the event I wound up with the white-bearded senator and the drunken soldier.

Lying sleepless in my chamber in the house of Mrs Buckle, I wondered about purses and the putting of money into them. Wondered whether John Ratchett, who was paying me to give intelligence on Jonson's *Masque of Peace*, had seen *Othello* when we'd first staged the play at the Globe in the spring. Had he picked up Iago's phrase and, forgetting its origin, used a version of it when he was trying to tempt me? *Put money in thy purse.*

Perhaps I should return the three sovereigns and refuse to write any spy-reports, should have nothing more to do with John Ratchett. That would be risking the displeasure of the Privy Council. But what could the Council do to a free and guiltless Englishman? The answer was, they could do a great deal. A great deal to make life uncomfortable, and worse than uncomfortable.

These were my night thoughts. Now I wished that I'd never listened to Master Ratchett. True, he had saved me half-way through being beaten up on the river bank. I could feel the bruising down my sides, worse at night. The arrival of the man in the red doublet had been opportune. Very opportune. What if – ?

But I got no further in my speculations because the night silence was suddenly disturbed by a noise somewhere between a cry and a groan. It came from outside my room.

Without striking a light, I got out of bed, crossed the floor and opened the chamber door. My room was on the top storey. Mrs Buckle and her daughter Elizabeth had their bedrooms below. The runny-nosed girl slept somewhere off the kitchen. I saw my landlady where she stood in the open area at the top of the stairs leading to the ground floor. She was in her night-clothes, holding a candle and staring fixedly at the uppermost corner of the stairs. Her eyes were wide open, but I am not sure whether she was really seeing anything.

In a tavern near the Bristol docks I once witnessed a young woman being put into a trance by a man who came off a ship. The woman had gazed about with the same blank vision as Mrs Buckle's, until the sailor had restored her to herself by snapping his fingers and whispering some words in her ear. Uncertain what to do next, I had half a mind to leave Mrs Buckle alone. There was no sign of Elizabeth. Then a low moan emerged from the widow's lips and the hand holding the candle became agitated. The light fluttered and I suddenly grew afraid that the flame would set fire to her nightdress. Almost before I was aware of it, I was down the narrow stairs connecting the first and second floors.

Mrs Buckle gave no sign that she'd heard or seen me but the candle stopped weaving about. Now she was standing like a statue once more, and her gaze had returned to the vacant corner by the top of the stairs. The candle illuminated a curiously placid expression on her face, still as a mask. We were only a few feet apart.

Gingerly, I stretched out an open hand. Light spilled on to my palm from her candle, and the shadows shifted around us. At once, Mrs Buckle seemed to come to herself. I can't think of any other way to describe it than to say that her eyes, which had been empty, became full. It was like pouring wine into a glass.

"Nicholas, it's you. What are you doing?"

"Are you all right, Mrs Buckle?"

"My husband was telling me . . . telling me . . . "

"Your husband . . . "

"He was telling me . . . something."

"When?"

"Just now."

"He is dead, Mrs Buckle."

"Why, so he is."

She looked down, as if conscious for the first time that she was dressed in her night things, and then looked at the space between us. After a time she said, "I shall return to my room now."

And she turned about and entered her chamber, her candle lighting the way to bed. She shut the door. I clambered up the ladder-like stairs to the second floor and shut my own chamber door. I lay down on my bed.

I don't know whether Mrs Buckle found it easy to get back to sleep but I was thoroughly awake by now. Dawn was a good few hours off.

I struck a light and examined the notes which I'd made on that day's practice for the *Masque of Peace* in the great room in the Blakes' mansion overlooking the river.

The notes were scrappy – and not very revealing. I wasn't sure how I could work them up into a 'manuscript' which would be worth three pounds to Master Ratchett and the Privy Council. All I had were a handful of gobbets picked up in overheard conversations or jibes thrown about the room during gaps in the rehearsal. There were other individuals in the practice room, like the Scaridges and the Fortunes. (It's odd how easily one gets used to throwing off these noble names, as if one was mingling with them every day.) But I will concentrate here on those who are relevant to this story.

For example, I had picked up an anti-Spanish comment from William Inman, secretary to Sir Philip Blake. Yes, an anti-Spanish comment, such as you may hear a dozen times over standing on any street corner in London for half an hour. In his bluff, hearty manner, Bill Inman had said something about preferring a Spanish *piece* to peace with Spain, although both were likely to prove poxy and rotten. He accompanied the remark with a rude gesture. Then he'd caught Mistress Maria More looking reprovingly at him. This was important information, and certainly worth reporting in a despatch to Robert Cecil.

Martin Barton, the red-headed satirical playwright, was talking about art. He had been boasting to Abel Glaze and Maria about the gratifying reception given to his recent tragedy *The Melancholy Man*. But I think he was doing this to needle Ben Jonson, who was in earshot and whose own late attempt at a court-tragedy had flopped so lamentably in a play called *Sejanus*. Barton was not a player – there was something about his combination of red hair and spindly little legs which would have made him suitable only for clown's parts – but Jonson had given him a part as Poesy and Drama in the masque. Maybe mischievously, Jonson had written almost no words to go with this role. Barton seemed content, however, drinking up his surroundings. I reckoned he was storing up material for his next satire and thinking how much better he could have managed the whole business. He was one of those people who are happiest feeling superior.

Giles Cass, the dapper go-between, was also talking about art. He was praising Queen Anne, assuring us that we professional players would find in her a woman of taste who – had destiny not called her to the supreme role in public life as a king's consort – might have excelled in any of the arts. He dabbed at his mouth while he mentioned the Queen, as if he could only do so with clean lips.

I enjoyed a chat with Sir Philip Blake which, after he'd cleared his throat, went in its entirety as follows:

Sir Philip Blake: Oh, er, Ignorance!

Nicholas Revill: Ah, Sir Philip.

Sir Philip Blake: Very good.

In fact I saw and heard nothing of any significance during our time with the Blakes. Nothing except for a couple of exchanges. One was harmless, I think, or at least predictable. And I hardly knew what to make of the other.

Martin Barton accosted me at one point. He waved his hand about the room and said, "What do you think of all this?"

"Think of it?"

"Is there honesty here?"

"As much as anywhere," I said.

"I tell you there is more honour and honesty in the thumb of a single craftsman than there is in all these finely swathed corpses."

"If you say so."

But Barton wasn't interested in agreement or disagreement. He'd approached me only in order to unburden himself. Perhaps he'd had enough of being struck virtually dumb as Poesy. I was treated to a rant about the corruption of the court and the age which might have come from one of his plays. Everything was foul and decayed. It might look fine on the surface but poke your finger through, and it was all seething rottenness underneath, food for worms. I nodded politely, not wanting to spoil the satirist's enjoyment, but eventually I just had to excuse myself. A call of nature, you know.

I was out of the room for a few moments answering nature's call. In less grand surroundings I might have pissed in a randomly chosen fireplace, as one would in an inn, but somehow I didn't think they'd approve of that sort of behaviour in this sort of place. So I dropped in on the servants' privy in the back quarters of the establishment. Even here the buckets seemed to have an extra sheen, no doubt on account of the reflected nobility of the retainers' gilded waste. In the main bedrooms upstairs the chamber pots were most likely silver.

I was making my way back to the principal room where we were rehearsing. A man and a woman were standing just outside the door, deep in conversation. It looked to be one of those discussions at which a third party would not be welcome. I was about to cough to alert them to my presence, then paused. The woman was Lady Jane Blake. The man had his back to me but there was something familiar about him.

The light was dim in the passageway outside the practice room and there was a great tapestry hanging from the wall next to me. I've always had a hankering to eavesdrop from behind a tapestry or arras. (It's what Polonius does with fatal results to himself in WS's *Hamlet*.) I stepped into the shadow of the arras but without concealing myself properly behind it. I wasn't so much an eavesdropper as a passer-by. Then I listened. There was the rustle of paper.

"And the seat," said the voice of Lady Blake. There was that suppressed laughter in her tone. "You are sure about the seat?"

"Absolutely, my lady," said the other.

I recognized his voice. Had listened to him lately. Who was he?

"But will it hold up under the weight?"

"It will hold up. We wouldn't want anyone falling off the device accidentally, would we?" said the man.

The man and woman almost giggled in a manner that seemed to me, loitering in the folds of the arras, somehow improper. As if they were children sniggering over adult matters. I risked a peep around the edge of the hanging. Heads together, the couple were examining a sheet of paper. I recognized the man now.

"Then this will come down," said Lady Jane, stabbing a plump forefinger at the sheet.

"Oh, it'll come down all right," said Jonathan Snell. "It will all come down."

Jonathan Snell, the engine-man who was designing machines and effects for Jonson's *Masque of Peace*. The gentleman who'd been invited to guess my weight in the courtyard. Now he was demonstrating something to Jane Blake, with the same confident style in which he'd shown off the diagram of the *deus ex machina* chair. He was surely talking about a device of his own making, but what was it?

My impression that there was an underhand aspect to this meeting was strengthened by the way in which the two of them – the noble lady and the engineer with the long thumb – responded when one of the household footmen glided by. Luckily this yellow-liveried gent came from a different direction to the place at which I was standing. The Blake footmen were very silent and this, combined with their glassy stares and golden costumes, gave them the indifferent quality of fish in a big pond. This particular fish was almost on Lady Blake and Master Snell before they spotted him. When they did, the couple seemed to spring apart and Snell hastily folded up the sheet of paper. The footman glided on, far too well-bred to observe the behaviour of his betters. If he noticed me while I was loitering he gave no sign of it. After a moment Lady Blake returned to the practice room, and shortly afterwards Snell followed her inside. I had the distinct impression that they didn't want to be seen entering together.

Putting on my best just-wandering-around air, I stepped out from the shelter of the arras and went back to the masque rehearsal. There wasn't much for me to do since I had my lines as Ignorance off pat – no great feat considering there were so few of them – and Ben Jonson's energies were largely directed at polishing the performances of the non-professional players. Lady Jane Blake disposed herself as Plenty, clutching a jug instead of a cornucopia to her ample chest. Sir Philip hummed and cleared his throat and just about got through his few verses as Truth, although he could not resist slipping in a 'very good' from time to time. Maria More was a graceful handmaid to Plenty, while Bill Inman billowed about as the Ocean. Giles Cass was playing Suspicion – he had asked Jonson for the part, I gathered.

Jonathan Snell sat at a desk to one side of the room, sketching and scribbling on sheets of paper and from time to time coming across to consult Jonson. I guessed he was working out the final details of the masque machinery. He nodded towards me, acknowledging our meeting from a day or two before. He seemed a straightforward fellow but I was puzzled about why he and Lady Jane had been conversing so secretively outside the door and why they didn't appear to want to have anything to do with each other inside the room.

The light in the passageway had not been good but, from what I'd glimpsed, the sheet of paper was covered with lines and circles. It looked very similar to the one which Snell had shown to Jonson and me in the courtyard. The fact that the two had been talking of 'seats' and 'weights' tended to confirm that the engine-man was explaining to Lady Jane the device intended to lower her husband to the ground during the *Masque of Peace*. These chairs, on which gods and other elevated figures are brought down to earth, are standard features of modern stages. We've got the mechanism for one at the Globe. It is housed in a little hut or cabin on top of the 'heavens'.

Perhaps, as a loving wife, Lady Jane was concerned for her husband's welfare as he sank to earth. *Then this will come down*, she'd said, and *Oh, it'll come down all right*, Snell replied. But the sniggering, conspiratorial tone of the dialogue somehow made a less . . . innocent . . . interpretation more plausible. And hadn't Shakespeare said that the relations between the Blakes were cold?

But what was I meant to put in my report to John Ratchett? That I'd heard two people talking secretively about a *deus ex machina* device? That William Inman had cracked an anti-Spanish joke? That Giles Cass played the part of Suspicion rather well?

I was not exactly happy in the role of intelligencer. More to the point, I was not exactly successful, having little to report. I decided that I would wait until the next practice, which was to take place at Somerset House, and hope that something more significant would occur to earn me my three pounds from the Council.

O, *a chair, a chair!*

"Ah, Nicholaas, come 'ere. You look so fatigay, *mon chéri*," said Blanche, the girl in the Mitre brothel. "So tired."

"It's been a hard day," I said.

"Come 'ere and be soozed by your Blanche," she said, grasping me firmly by the arm.

I don't know how she could tell that I was tired, since she kept the light in her little chamber so dim, but I was more than ready to be soothed. Later, when my tiredness had disappeared after a vigorous soothing, I lay stroking her dark hair where it fanned out over the pillow and thinking of nothing.

"What's that?" I said.

"I 'ave found out sumzing about you, Nicholaas," said Blanche.

"'ave you?"

"Now you make fun of ze way I speak. Zat is not fair."

"And why is zat, Blanche?"

"Because it is you who teach me."

"Me?"

"I learn from ze gen'lemen of England."

This was a nice way of referring to her customers, so I said, "But I like the way you speak. Honestly, Blanche. Tell me what you have found out."

"*Non.*"

83

The pout and the shrug which accompanied this were more expressive than her refusal.

"All right, don't tell me," I said.

"Now I will tell you. You live wiz a – 'ow you say? – *une veuve* . . . "

"If that means widow, yes, I lodge with a widow."

"I knew it!"

"How did you know?"

Pleased with herself, Blanche tapped the side of her nose.

"I 'ave a little bird, 'e tells me zings."

"Well, your bird's got it right this time."

"A young – widow – *elle est belle*?"

"I'm sure your bird could tell you that as well."

"Perhaps she likes you, *la veuve*?"

"Jealous, Blanche? 'ow you say *that* in French? *Jaloux*, is it?"

For answer she looked across to the sand-glass which measured time in this place. Now my time was up. So I rose from the bed and settled up with Blanche, using part of the money given me by John Ratchett. There was a small pleasure in using Privy Council cash in a Southwark stew, but I don't imagine I was the first. Blanche's hand closed round the coins. She didn't bother to conceal the business aspect to our transactions or make any play about being surprised to get cash.

To be frank, I was happier keeping things on this business level with the Frenchwoman. Nevertheless I wondered how Blanche had found out where I lodged. Not too difficult, perhaps. Some other players frequented the Mitre. I knew that Laurence Savage did, for one. He must have been blabbing. Perhaps he too saw Blanche. The thought was unwelcome and I put it away.

Blanche had said that I looked so *fatigay* when I arrived. If I did, the reason was the dramatic day which I'd just spent at Somerset or Denmark House, where we had assembled for an on-the-spot rehearsal of the *Masque of Peace*.

We arranged to arrive as a playhouse group, Laurence Savage, Jack Wilson, Abel Glaze and I, uneasily aware that we were entering enemy territory when we passed through the gatehouse.

Inside, we expected a nest of Spaniards. What we discovered was a crowded establishment in which control was uneasily split between the natives and the newcomers. For when Queen Anne had withdrawn to Whitehall so as to give the Spanish embassy a place to stay in London, some of her household had remained to look after the guests. And, as we'd seen from their display on the river, the Spanish party had brought with them a considerable retinue of their own. So every corner of this palace seemed stuffed with exotic strangers, while pale-faced English officials flitted about.

Giles Cass greeted us and ushered us down passages and through waiting areas. He put on an air of being absolutely at home in Somerset House, nodding to individuals and even exchanging greetings in Spanish, *buenos diassing* (if I have it right) like mad. He seemed to have swallowed that resentment of the Spanish presence which he'd shown in the Mermaid tavern.

We overheard incomprehensible snippets of conversation emanating from huddled groups, we heard low throaty gabbles and a style of laughter that was definitely unEnglish. We fetched up in one of the audience rooms – not the place for an audience in the playhouse sense, but a chamber for the reception of important visitors. All five of us paused on the threshold for a moment. I didn't know what this great chamber usually looked like, but it was evidently in the process of transformation. It was as if a wooden house was being built within the walls of the room. There was scaffolding everywhere, both for the seating and to support the masque scenery and machines. The sounds of hammering and sawing filled the dusty air. Painters were at work on a great canvas sheet spread out on a vacant area of the floor. I spotted Bartholomew Ridd, our tire-man, pinning up an elaborate-looking costume on an elaborate-looking lady whose name was Sybil Fortune. She was playing the part of Hope, and her outfit was covered with hope's symbol, the anchor.

"So will the Queen be appearing today?" said Abel to Giles Cass.

"I believe not."

"Oh, that's a pity," said Laurence.

I think we all felt slightly relieved, however. There's something intimidating about attending a rehearsal with the Queen of England, even if we'd eventually be playing alongside her.

"She will be word-perfect, never fear," said Cass.

"She's only got a single verse," whispered Jack.

"Two verses at least, Master Wilson," said Cass.

Jonathan Snell suddenly materialized in front of us.

"Well timed, gentlemen," he said.

The long-thumbed engineer shook hands with each of us. He was wearing a mechanic's apron, grease-stained. There was sawdust in his hair and even in the lines on his face.

"I am looking for an assistant," he said, casting his eyes along our little group. "How about you, Nicholas? You'd be about right."

"What for?"

"You'll see."

He reached out and took me by the shoulder, giving me little choice but to accompany him. I looked round and raised my eyebrows at the others.

"The thin fellow's too light," said Snell. He had to speak up, over the din of hammering and sawing.

"Too light? Abel Glaze?" I said, starting to feel uneasy.

"If he's the thin one. While the others look a bit on the heavy side. But you, you do look about right."

Distinctly uneasy now.

We skirted planks and ducked under swags of satin hanging from makeshift supports until we came to a shadowy area at the rear of the dais on which the masque would be staged.

Master Snell gestured at a ladder which was propped against a trellis-like arrangement of scaffolding.

"You want me to go up there?"

"If you would be so good, Nicholas. We've enough time before the practice begins."

I looked up, looked down again quickly. The ladder tapered into darkness, the topmost rungs invisible.

"What do I do when I get up there?"

"You come down again. In the chair."

"You want me to be the *deus ex machina*?"

"I need to try it out but only for practice on weights and tensions," said Snell. "The body in the chair is immaterial, so to speak. Sir Philip Blake will be doing it for the actual performance. He is Truth, you know."

"While I am merely Ignorance, and so expendable."

This was intended as a throwaway comment but I was nervous and it emerged as resentful instead.

"Oh, I see," said the engine-man, sounding surprised. "You're worried that it's not safe. It's perfectly safe. I made it myself and I've ridden the chair myself several times. It would be an advantage to put you in it though."

"Advantage?"

"You and Sir Philip are about the same weight."

"I'd say that he was a bit lighter."

"Not much in it, I'd say," said Snell, gesturing once again at the foot of the ladder.

"Oh, well," I said, slowly reaching out a hand to grasp at the nearest rung, and hoping desperately that something – the end of the world, for example – would intervene and prevent my having to scrabble up the ladder.

"Naturally, if you'd rather not . . . "

Snell left the sentence dangling. Clever of him. I could not back out without losing face, losing face badly. This was a choice which was no choice. Anyway what was the worst that could happen? (The worst that could happen was that I would fall down and break my neck.)

"I'll be down here, minding the windlass."

In my distraction I had not noticed an elaborate device which stood a few feet away from the ladder. It was like a great barrel wound about with hemp rope and with long spokes projecting from each end. Up in the gloom were more ropes, some of them slack, some taut, together with various pulleys. I couldn't see how any of this worked.

"Made of the best English elm," said Jonathan Snell, going across and patting the windlass as if it were a horse. "It took six men to put this in position."

"And just one to operate it."

"It requires a light touch only. You will provide the motive force, Nicholas. That is the beauty of it."

"Beauty?"

"Some people find beauty in a face or a figure or a flower," said Jonathan Snell. "But I find beauty in an engine in which each part co-operates with its neighbours, and where nothing is superfluous. Specifically, Nicholas, your weight in the chair will bring it down. My job is to make sure you come down at the right speed."

"My life in your hands," I said, putting my foot on the lowest rung and starting to haul myself up the ladder.

The engine-man called after me. It was some words about finding Jonathan up on the top, but I must have misheard because he, Jonathan Snell, was waiting at the bottom, wasn't he? He was going to operate the windlass and safeguard my life, wasn't he?

No head for heights? WS had said to me recently, and I'd made a light reply. But it was true. I did not much like heights. I glanced down. Already I seemed a long way above the ground. Snell, holding the bottom of the ladder, nodded at me encouragingly. The ladder swayed and shivered under my weight. My hands were slick as they took hold of each rung. As I climbed I entered into a more obscure region, one which was cloaked with curtains and screens. A web of uprights and diagonals, of beams and ropes, criss-crossed in the darkness. I risked a glance upwards and almost fell off the ladder in surprise.

A spectacled face was hanging over the edge of a kind of gallery or platform where the ladder terminated. One hand was holding firm to the top of the ladder while the other was extended to help me up the last few feet.

"Welcome to paradise, sir."

I stepped warily on to the railed gallery, holding on to the arm of the man at the top.

"Your father sent me, Jonathan," I said. I was pleased that, all things considered, I had my voice under reasonable control. There wasn't much illumination up here in the realm of the gods – only a few oil lamps, doubtless safer than naked candles – but there was enough for me to detect the likeness between the man at the bottom of the ladder and the younger, unlined version of him at the top.

"He said he'd send someone up."

"Well, here I am."

"Come this way, er . . . "

"Nick."

Jonathan Snell the younger picked up one of the oil lamps. Like a nightwatchman, he turned and led the way across the gallery. His spectacles gave him an old-head-on-young-shoulders appearance, and he walked with a slight stoop as though feeling his way forward. But he must have known this floating platform well, for he moved with assurance. It was more stable underfoot than I'd expected, but then after the swaying ladder anything would have seemed so. I observed a pack of fleecy clouds, made of canvas stretched over wooden frames and stacked to one side of the gallery. Next to them was the pale orb of a full moon, more than a yard across.

"The figure of Truth will come down with these clouds?" I said, indicating the painted effects.

"No, they're for the sea-crossing of the Spaniard," said young Snell, miming waves with his free hand. He had his father's long thumb, proof of paternity. "Be careful, Nick."

I hadn't really forgotten that we were the best part of thirty feet above the ground, but the novelty of our surroundings had enabled me to push the fact aside for an instant. Now it came rushing back as I stood on the far edge of the platform next to Jonathan junior. Below was an unimpeded drop to the floor of the dais or stage. People bustled about, carrying objects, chatting together, whistling while they worked, quite oblivious that we were peering down at them.

Fastened alongside the exterior rails of the gallery was a chair – a simple wooden chair attached to ropes disappearing into the darkness overhead. The chair had a seat and a back, it had arms and legs, but no more.

"I know it looks a bit plain," said Jonathan, "but believe me, on the night it'll be fully decked out. Gilded and richly draped."

If I looked surprised, it wasn't because of the plainness of the chair but because of its flimsiness. Was this fragile contrivance meant to bear someone's weight while he descended to the bare boards below? Meant to bear *my* weight?

"Aren't you afraid of, er, losing Sir Philip Blake if he rides in this device?"

I meant, of course, aren't you afraid of losing *me*?

"He'll be strapped in, discreetly strapped in. No one'll notice. But the straps haven't been installed yet. So *you* will have to hold on. I'll help you in. Step over the rail here and swing yourself around."

He put out an arm to steady me.

It was like being requested to walk off a cliff. If I could have thought of an honourable way to refuse I would have done. But my head was empty. I straddled the rail and by some sideways shift got myself into the seat, which quivered. (Or maybe I was doing the quivering.) I placed my feet on the cross-piece between the front legs. I gripped the arms of the chair and stared out straight in front of me.

"Take it easy, Nick. You might even enjoy it," said Jonathan, untying the cords which secured the chair to the rails.

I grimaced. Jonathan stepped across to the other side of the aerial platform and tugged on some ropes as a signal. Moments later I experienced a mild jolt, and the chair began to move downwards. I kept my eyes shut for several seconds. The only thing that persuaded me to open them was the thought of how I must appear – that is, scared enough to piss myself – to anyone looking up from the ground.

So I opened my eyes. I was on a level with the top of a wide window at one end of the audience chamber. It was a slow but surprisingly steady descent. I had time to wonder why it was that, instead of spinning around in space like a top, the chair stayed more or less angled in one direction, facing out towards the prospective audience. I attributed this to the mechanical skills of the Snells. Then at once the chair stopped dead.

I glanced down. Between my splayed feet the floor seemed to rock slightly. It wasn't the floor which was rocking. There were creaks and groans from up above. I did not want to see what was causing them. Down below, the painters and carpenters had broken off from their work to watch a man coming down, or not coming down. And then there were a couple of gents wearing elaborate ruffs and standing with Giles Cass by the dais. They were holding their hats in their hands, so I was able to see their heads from above. One balding, one black-haired. Spanish, weren't they? Cass was pointing at me, or more precisely at the chair which dangled from the heavens. He leaned over and confided something in the ear of one of the gents. The gent grinned. This did not make me feel any better. I put on a brave face in front of these foreigners. Still at least twenty feet from the ground, I estimated. Quite enough of a drop to ensure fatal damage.

Then, all at once, a strange mood overtook me, a resigned mood. What could I do, anyway? I was absolutely in the hands of others, at the mercy of their ropes, windlasses and pulleys. From what I'd seen of the Snells, father and son, they were skilled engine-men. Snell senior had talked lovingly of his engines. I might as well take up the younger Jonathan's suggestion and enjoy myself. Who hasn't dreamed of flying? Well, here I was hovering above the ground like a skylark!

This new state of mind, carefree or reckless, was only a little disturbed by the sight of Snell senior strolling round the corner of the scaffolding.

Wait a minute, though. If he was here, who was looking after the windlass?

"Don't worry, Nicholas," called up the engine-man. "It's only a question of soap."

Soap? I must look more ragged and dirty than I feared. Had I pissed myself after all?

"I told my son to make sure to put more soap on the ropes," said Snell to Cass by way of explanation. "Does he listen?"

To the trio on the ground, he mimed pulling a cord through a furled fist. There was a barely concealed irritation in the gesture. He didn't like mistakes or the fact that English incompetence was being shown up in front of foreigners.

Giles Cass nodded and spoke again to the Spanish grandees, who continued to look more amused than bothered at my plight.

Snell senior disappeared behind the scenes again. I hung about for what seemed like an eternity. The little knots of workers, understanding that nothing really interesting (such as a death-plunge) was likely to occur, had resumed their labours. The chair jerked once more and started to *ascend*. Fortunately we went upward for a moment only before resuming our downward course.

By the time I'd landed on the dais, I was beginning almost to enjoy the experience of flying. Why, if one of the Snells had indicated that the device required another test, I'd probably have volunteered.

I got to my feet, a bit shakily. There was some ironic clapping from those good friends of mine, Abel Glaze and Jack Wilson and Laurence Savage. I bowed to them and inclined my head towards Giles Cass. He returned the gesture while the two grave gents at his side made the slightest of movements. Their ruffs were so large that it looked as though their heads were sitting on two platters.

"Ah, Master Ignorance," said the dapper and witty Cass. "We can never expel Ignorance for long from this world. We can't do without him. He will always land on his feet."

I was glad that the part which I played in the masque was making for so much amusement. If Cass hadn't been accompanied by these imposing Dons I might have given him a rough answer, important as he was. Instead I said nothing. Then he turned towards them and uttered some foreign words, among which I could pick out only one. It sounded like *ignorancia*. Now I'm no expert in the Spanish tongue but I'd guess that he was referring to 'ignorance', wouldn't you?

Then Ben Jonson turned up with Martin Barton and the Blakes and others, and our first Somerset House practice for the *Masque of Peace* began.

"Two Spanish gentlemen," said John Ratchett.

"Yes. Grandees from their appearance."

"Please describe them, Nicholas."

We were sitting in the Pure Waterman tavern in Southwark. The plump agent for the Privy Council was wearing his customary red doublet. He had tried to ply me with aquae vitae once again but I insisted that beer would do.

"It's all written down here," I said, patting the pocket which contained my 'report'.

"Even so."

"Well. The older one was almost bald. He made up for it with a beard which was about the width and length of a man's hand. Grey-white at the edges, the beard that is. A bulbous nose. Maybe there was a touch of humour in his eyes, but mostly he looked serious."

"That is Juan de Tassis. The Count of Villamediana."

"Ah," I said as though the name meant something to me. "And the other one?"

"He was younger. Shorter than Count Whatsisname. This one's hair was still dark but receding at the sides. He had a sallow face with a hooked nose. Eyes close set. A direct gaze."

"Hawk-like, even?"

"You could call it that."

Master Ratchett drained his beer mug.

"You're describing Señor Alessandro Rovida," he said. "He is a lawyer, a very learned lawyer."

"Why doesn't that surprise me?"

"Giles Cass was with them and talking in Spanish, you say?"

"Yes."

"Well, there's no law against learning other men's languages."

Yes, anyone may learn another's language. There's no law against it. An image of Blanche flashed through my mind. Blanche, who had learned our language from what she called the 'gen'lemen of England'. In her bed I had spent a portion of the money which Ratchett had given me earlier, spent it before it was properly earned. But it was all right. He was willing to give me more cash for the report which I now fished out of my doublet pocket and placed on the table between us.

I'd done my best to work up some fairly trivial observations on the handful of practices for the *Masque of Peace* into a proper despatch. I didn't mind reporting on Giles Cass in particular, since I did not like him. Anyway I was only writing down the truth. He had been speaking in Spanish, he had been on good terms with Count This and Señor That. And yet Cass was the man who'd tried to entice us with his anti-Spanish remarks in the Mermaid tavern. I was fairly sure he'd been gabbling at the time in order to draw us out.

But there was something else which had been puzzling me.

"Tell me, Master Ratchett, could you not obtain this information directly from someone else, from Giles Cass for instance? He would be able to tell you about the Spaniards, much better than I can. Both of you have the same, ah, employer. The Privy Council."

"There you show your ignorance if I may say so, Nicholas," said Ratchett, looking round before picking up the report, which I had folded and sealed in letter-fashion. He slipped it inside his red doublet. "The Privy Council is like the cuttlefish."

"It is?"

"Both the Council and the cuttlefish have many arms . . . and it may be that only the head knows what all of those arms are doing."

"Oh."

"Sometimes the cuttlefish shoots out an inky cloud to baffle an enemy. In the same way the Council seeks to obscure its purposes from its enemies."

"What about its friends? They may be confused as well."

"The Privy Council has no friends. It has those who are useful to it, and those who would try to undermine it."

This all sounded suitably impressive. Ratchett's description of obfuscation and hidden purposes fitted what I knew of Sir Robert Cecil. However, I wasn't sure I wanted to hear any more about the Privy Council and the cuttlefish. There are some illustrations which make matters clearer, and others which have the opposite effect.

Our business in the tavern was almost done. Ratchett slid three sovereigns across the table, keeping them concealed under his hand. I quickly pocketed them. We were in a dark and smoky corner of the Pure Waterman but you never knew what prying eyes might be watching. I didn't want to get knocked down outside the door for a second time.

We parted, agreeing to meet in a couple of days' time. I was more than satisfied with the money but was unable to see how the 'information' which I had given to Ratchett could be worth three pounds. Still, if he didn't consider that he was getting his money's worth, why was he eager for another meeting and for more reports?

Like the enemies of the cuttlefish, I was baffled and confused.

Some swift means of death

If I was baffled and confused on that day, things got much worse on the following one. I found out what a fool I'd been in agreeing to take cash from Master Ratchett. More importantly, the *Masque of Peace* turned from what it ought to have been – a celebration of order and tranquillity – into a display of disorder, fear and suspicion. As well as murder, although at first it did not seem so.

It began promisingly enough. We were back in Somerset House under Ben Jonson's direction for yet another run-through of his piece. More time and care were being expended on this production, which would last for about half an hour, than would go into a two hours' performance on the Globe stage. But then you don't get the Queen of England playing alongside you every day. Not that we had her playing alongside us on this occasion. If we weren't blessed with the presence of the English Peace, we did have in compensation her Spanish twin, a beautiful lady by the name of Doña Luisa de Mendoza (if I have it right). She had no English, but Jonson had written some words for her to say which had been translated into her own language.

The Snells, father and son, together with their carpenters and painters, had been toiling mightily to transform the audience chamber into a theatrical space. The seating was in place. The dais was done. All the apparatus for shifting and

97

lifting was concealed behind screens and curtains. The whole cast, with the exception of the Queen, was present.

I had one more encounter with Sir Philip Blake. We bumped into each other behind the dais or stage. The back-cloth was up now, representing the shores of England with a scene of blue sky and white cliffs. Perhaps these were the cliffs of Dover, of which I had heard.

"Ah, Ignorance," said Sir Philip. "Very good."

This had evidently become his standard greeting to me. He was decked out as Truth, his costume glowing with minia-ture suns.

"I am told to go aloft," he said, "but I am not sure where."

"Then perhaps Ignorance can help you," I said.

I led him to the ladder where, a day or so before, I had clambered up into the heavens. The climb looked less daunting now. Blake paused and took a flask from somewhere under his cloak. He unscrewed the cap and took a swig from the flask. Dutch courage perhaps.

"Follow me, sir," I said.

I sprang for the bottom of the ladder and started to climb. I was showing off a bit, I must admit. I arrived at the top and swung myself over the railing. I turned round to give Sir Philip a helping hand but he was right behind me and did not need any assistance. I was surprised at his dexterity, al-though he must have had more than ten years on me.

"Your chair is over there," I said, gesturing to the far side of the platform. "I rode in it the other day."

"Very good."

There seemed to be three or four other people up here in these shadowy heavens, including Jonathan Snell the younger. I presumed that the other figures were men from his father's workshop. They were moving about, making final adjust-ments to ropes and pulleys. The fleecy clouds were now dangling over our heads. It was fairly dark, although a scatter-ing of oil lamps threw out small circles of light. The planking creaked under our feet. The whole structure must have been very tough to withstand the demands put on it. I felt quite confident in these heavens now and was almost sorry to have to climb down again to join the people on earth.

I had reason later to remember who was present at this fatal practice. So I might as well give here an indication of the *dramatis personae* of the *Masque of Peace*. Arranged in a kind of hierarchy, we were:

The English Peace	Anne of Denmark (not present)
The Spanish Peace	Doña Luisa de Mendoza
The Spirit of Truth	Sir Philip Blake
The Spirit of Plenty	Lady Jane Blake
Plenty's Handmaids	Lady Agnes Scaridge & Maria More
Tranquillity	Margery Howard
Hope	Lady Fortune
Resolution	Lord Fortune
The Spirit of Poesy	Martin Barton
Suspicion	Giles Cass
Rumour	Abel Glaze
Stubbornness	Jack Wilson
Fright	Laurence Savage
Ignorance	Nicholas Revill
Oceanus	William Inman
A Favouring Wind	Sir Fabian Scaridge

This wasn't the end of it because there were various nymphs, attendants, dancers, & cetera also participating in the masque. As you can see, the 'good' parts were restricted to the nobility while the 'bad' qualities, with the exception of Giles Cass's turn as Suspicion, were played by the professionals.

There were plenty of people in the audience room. Ben Jonson was present of course as the 'director', standing on the little raised space which would eventually accommodate the King if he condescended to attend the performance. Costume-maker Bartholomew Ridd was assisted by a couple of helpers, or tire-boys, whom he was training up. There was a band of musicians, and the air was full of noises, most of them pleasant ones. Both versions of Jonathan Snell were busying themselves with last-minute adjustments to the backstage machinery. There were some Spanish in attendance, including the two senior Dons I'd seen the other day, the ones with the platter heads. They were plushly dressed, in white and gold and purple. And there was the usual gaggle of other folk who seemed to have no particular business being there, except to watch the spectacle. Spectacle was what they got.

Everything went smoothly at first. In itself this was worrying. If matters go well in the beginning they end less well, in my experience. I don't know why this should be so.

Anyway, after an introductory song (*Sound, O sound aloud the welcome*) and a bit of dancing, the Spanish Peace came wafting across the waves, ushered on her way by William Inman as Oceanus. The Spanish Peace – or *la Paz* – was indeed something of a *piece* and was wearing a costume which demonstrated that she didn't feel the cold. Oceanus could hardly take his eyes off Doña Luisa – nor could several of us – and had to be called to order by Ben Jonson. I wondered whether he remembered his crack about a Spanish 'piece'. Inman was wearing a weighty costume embossed with seashells and, as he'd requested, was toting a trident which waggled whenever *la Paz* drew near. He did not like being told what to do by Ben Jonson and I sensed the temper that underlay his bluffness. By contrast, Sir Fabian Scaridge, who played the wind which blew Peace across to our shores, took direction easily. Sir Fabian puffed to great effect.

The waves, long scallop-edged sheets of painted canvas and wood, slid a few feet in one direction then back in the opposite one. Arranged in rows, they were operated by cranks which were hidden by screens on either side of the dais. The cranks in turn were operated by men from the Snells' workshop. The noise of the machinery was covered by the sound of the musicians. The illusion was impressive, especially if you stood at a little distance. And this striking effect was achieved by the light of day. When the *Masque of Peace* was performed for a proper audience it would be at night, by candlelight, which favours certain colours such as sea-green. And it would be watched with all the drink-induced blurring of vision that accompanies an evening performance.

And so it went. More singing and dancing. *La Paz* arrived to be greeted by the English Peace, a lady-in-waiting who was standing in for the absent Queen, and more covered up than her Spanish counterpart. On the sidelines were Tranquillity and the Spirit of Plenty. The ample shape of Lady Blake thrust herself forward, carrying a cornucopia of fruits which was bigger than her bosom but almost lighter than air. (I knew this, because I'd earlier picked it up and marvelled at the ingenuity of the Snell workshop when it came to fashioning wire and coloured paper.) Lady Blake was attended by Lady Agnes Scaridge and Maria More, the latter looking much more blue-blooded than the real noblewomen. At some point Martin Barton as the Spirit of Poesy delivered himself of a couple of lines, all about how inadequate he was to celebrate this occasion. Jonson must have enjoyed writing those, if he'd always had Barton in mind for the part.

Then, in a flurry, those of us playing the negative qualities – of Suspicion and Rumour and Stubbornness and Fright and Ignorance – had to creep and crawl on stage to engage in an antic dance. We were destined to do our turns, and to cast doubt on this outbreak of peace and goodwill between two old enemies. It wasn't like a proper drama. There was no ding-dong to it, no bite. We said, or rather declaimed our lines (*I know not where I am*, and the rest of it) until Hope and Resolution – the husband and wife duo with the title of Fortune – stepped in to assert that history would be different this time. As a sign of this, Hope and Resolution intended to summon from on high the figure of Truth, who knows all things past, present and future. Truth would testify to the amity that must evermore exist 'twixt these two great nations, Spain and England.

The action of the *Masque of Peace* didn't unfold as smoothly as I've described it here. Since it was a rehearsal, there were frequent pauses while people forgot their lines (not that there were many to forget), forgot their dance steps, forgot their entrances, or forgot the bits and pieces they were supposed to carry with them on stage. We proper players, of course, did not make such mistakes – or not so often. But the noble participants went wrong about as frequently as they went right. Lady Agnes Scaridge, one of Plenty's handmaids, was supposed to enter clutching a globe. But Lady Agnes, evidently unable to lay her hands on the correct prop, appeared wielding a chamber pot or jordan. She didn't realize what it was until she got on stage. Someone – mischievously? unawares? – must have thrust it into her hands as she was entering and, in the confusion, she'd seized it. It was a Somerset House chamber pot and therefore a fine version of that universal item. But it was still a pot, and when she realized what she was holding she almost stuck her head in it for shame. Quick-witted Ben Jonson made some remark about it not yet being time for her to cross the Jordan.

Her husband, Sir Fabian Scaridge, was no more impressive. He was one of King James's new knights. Sir Fabian was reputed to have been a barber. Well, if a barber may get knighted, then there's hope for a player. At least a player may get *inside* your head with his lines . . .

The Fortunes, Lord and Lady, were amiable enough but not over-endowed with brains either.

I mention these characters to give you the flavour of our noble associates. By contrast with them, I had started to warm towards Sir Philip Blake. And it was Sir Philip we were now waiting for.

The two Peaces, the English and Spanish ladies, were standing patiently side by side. Hope and Resolution had banished Suspicion, Rumour and the rest of us to the corners of the stage. There we cowered.

The green-garbed Hope waved her garland of flowers in the air and gazed expectantly upwards.

Resolution, or Lord Fortune, looked suitably determined while he delivered his couplet:

Come down, O Truth, and show the eyes of man
The gods' design and heaven's chiefest plan.

I glanced up into the dark area above the stage. I thought I could glimpse the chair in which Truth was due to ride down but it was hard to see if it was occupied or not.

I looked round at my immediate companions. There was Abel Glaze dressed as Rumour in an outfit painted with tongues and ears. Laurence Savage as Fright sported a gold helmet and carried a short sword, although from his posture it would have been difficult to say whether he was meant to be frightened or frightening. Then there was Jack Wilson dressed up as Stubbornness in a gown on which were depicted coils of ivy (to show that Stubbornness takes hold of the mind and pulls it down, as ivy does a wall – I said that these masque costumes were like walking riddles). Meantime, as Ignorance, I was garbed in a costume that was black and rather rustic. I wore a kind of blindfold that was very gauzy and easy to see through.

The parts we were playing, and the costumes we were wearing, might have been designed by Bartholomew Ridd to make us look silly. But not much sillier than our noble patrons parading about as Hope or Peace or Truth.

And talking of Truth, where was he?

The band of musicians, cued by Ben Jonson, had already played – already played twice over – the flourish which was to herald the descent of the *deus ex machina*. I glanced up once more.

At last the chair was on its way down. It was no longer the plain item which I'd ridden in, but decked out with gold hangings and surmounted with a sunburst device. Even the cables which supported it were concealed with green and gold ribbon. It was a flying throne. From our corner at the edge of the stage I could make out only the legs of the occupant of the chair. I wondered if Sir Philip was as apprehensive about the descent as I had been. That was unlikely. He'd seemed quite at home in the 'heavens'.

And now the music was tootling in triumph. The figures of Hope and Resolution were moving to positions on either side of Truth's landing-point. We naughty characters cast our hands over our eyes or shrank into ourselves, to show the conquering authority of this figure from the sky.

Then all at once the chair quivered and came to a halt. As far as I could tell, it was stuck at a point even higher from the ground than when I'd ridden in it during practice. Well, this was still a rehearsal. They'd get it working properly for the real thing. I imagined Jonathan Snell the younger frantically checking the pulleys up above, tugging at cords and cables. No doubt he'd receive a dressing-down from his father afterwards. Not enough soap on the ropes, maybe.

The chair swayed slightly. Jonson shushed the musicians. Perhaps he could observe something from his position out in front which wasn't apparent to us.

I saw the face of Sir Philip Blake peering out and down. If he hadn't been alarmed before, he certainly looked so now. His mouth was a gaping O. His face was white against the elaborate sunburst that crowned the seat. Something was wrong. A silence suddenly fell over the entire room.

This flying chair was the crowning effect of the *Masque of Peace*. Running smoothly, it should elicit *oohs* and *aahs* from the audience. Getting stuck, it would provoke laughter.

But there was another possibility, a much worse one which would produce neither delight nor laughter. And it was this other possibility that happened next.

With a strange sound, like an axe-stroke, one of the cords holding up the chair snapped. The chair tilted forward and downward. Sir Philip would have fallen out had he not been grasping hold of the arms very tight. Evidently he wasn't strapped in. One of his legs slipped instinctively as if seeking a foothold in space The chair, off balance, started to sway on its three ropes, making his position even more precarious.

There were several gasps and cries from the watchers but no one spoke a word. No one moved an inch.

Where were the Snells? If they were up above, did they even know what was happening? If they could get the ropes running and the chair moving once again, Blake might reach the ground unharmed. But they would have to act quickly.

Then, with a second thunk, a second cord severed. By bad fortune, it was the other of the pair of ropes securing the front part of the chair. The immediate effect was to pitch the occupant violently forward.

His cloak billowing behind him, his arms outstretched, the figure of Truth tumbled head-first from his aerial seat. It was as if he had launched himself into the air, rather than being flung.

It must have taken Blake less than a second to reach the ground but I have known hours pass more quickly. There was a horrible crack, like a walnut being split with a hammer. His imposing cloak – embroidered with suns to signify the dazzling light of Truth – wafted up in the air before falling forward and obscuring the top half of his poor body. He lay still, arms spread wide. After a few moments, blood began to pool from underneath the cloak.

I turned away, feeling sick and cold.

I thought, it might have been Nicholas Revill up there.

Still, no one moved.

Fragments of gold ribbon from the supporting ropes fluttered down on to the stage. The chair, empty but still held up by two cables, creaked backwards and forwards like a giant swing.

Some time went by, it seemed, before a woman screamed from the back of the chamber. I noticed that Lady Jane Black had fallen down in a faint. Her paper-and-wire horn of Plenty had tumbled on the ground beside her. Hope and Resolution stood as if turned to stone.

Then, gingerly, several people moved towards the prone figure even as others were starting to edge away from it. Jonathan Snell the elder emerged from behind the backdrop. His face was ashen, the sawdust standing out lividly in the lines of it. Ben Jonson stepped up on to the stage from the place where he'd been conducting operations. My friend Abel Glaze walked in the direction of the corpse. It occurred to me afterwards that both he and Jonson must have been accustomed to death on the battlefield. Snell got there first. He dropped to his knees by the corpse. The only sound was that of his knees striking the wooden boards.

He reached out his hand to lift the obscuring cloak but I did not see anything more because a cluster of figures now obscured the shape. There was some subdued, broken talk. I moved a little distance off.

This accident was nothing to do with me. Others could take charge.

As if the thoughts inside our heads were running together, Jack Wilson said to me, "There can be no more playing today. There is nothing left here for us. We might as well go."

"We ought to wait for Master Jonson to dismiss us," said Laurence Savage.

"He has other things on his mind," said Jack.

A different kind of bustle now filled the audience chamber. People were scurrying to and fro, as if to make up for their previous immobility, and the room was filling up with grandees and their attendants. Bursts of Spanish exploded from various quarters like volleys. Some of the noble on-lookers looked as white and clammy as I felt, but in others there was detectable that taste for disaster which lurks inside quite a few of us.

Before we knew it we were outside in the courtyard of Somerset House. It was a heavy August afternoon. Even so, being out in the air was preferable to being shut up inside a chamber where a death had just occurred. Then we looked at ourselves and realized that we were still wearing our costumes. We could have slunk through the streets as Stubbornness and Fright and Ignorance, I suppose, at the cost of a few jeers. But if Bartholomew Ridd discovered that we'd removed our costumes from the premises we'd be fined, whatever the circumstances. Anyway we had to retrieve our own street clothes.

So we turned round and re-entered the palace and deposited our gear with one of the tire-boys, who was confined in a small antechamber (small by Somerset House standards yet much larger than its counterpart at the Globe). The tire-boy, not having witnessed the accident, seemed eager to examine our stage clothes for any drops of blood spilt by the dead man and, failing any marks of blood, to hear a detailed account of Sir Philip's fatal plunge to earth. Laurence rebuked him for his lack of feeling and Jack promised to tell him more later. I was silent because I'd just seen Master John Ratchett slipping past the open door. I was alerted by a flash of red doublet. He turned his head and caught my eye. What was *he* doing here?

I failed to discover the reason for John Ratchett's presence in Somerset House, but I soon found out that he expected me to work very hard for my next three sovereigns. Events had taken a sombre turn with the death of Sir Philip Blake; now they took a dangerous turn.

Ratchett did not wait for our next assignation in the Pure Waterman tavern on Bankside but accosted me as I was walking into the Strand. I had separated from my companions. The violent death of Sir Philip had put a dampener on our spirits and we had little to talk about. It must be doubtful now whether the *Masque of Peace* would go ahead. I looked round to find Master John Ratchett walking beside me.

He knew everything that had occurred inside Somerset House, he said without preliminary. Good, I thought, you won't require another 'report'. I can get free of you.

But I knew I was still under an obligation. I'd been paid. Like Judas, I had accepted my thirty pieces of silver. Or my six pieces of gold. Had even spent a portion of them (on Blanche, the French girl in the Mitre).

So, when Master Ratchett went on to suggest that I should look into – that was his phrase, 'look into' – Blake's death, I experienced a growing sense of unease. It was an accident, I said. What was there to 'look into'? Anyone could see that those ropes weren't strong enough to sustain the weight of the heavily adorned chair and its occupant. The weakest rope snapped, to be followed by the next weakest, and that was sufficient to send the unfortunate knight plunging to his doom.

"How convenient this death is!" said John Ratchett.

"How so?" I said.

"Convenient because it might well have a disastrous effect on the negotiations with Spain – and that would suit many people," explained Ratchett as we paced down the Strand.

"But the Spanish party is already in London and the deal is as good as done, isn't it?"

"No treaty is worth the paper it's written on until it's signed and sealed. Sir Philip's sudden death might give the Spaniards second thoughts if they grow suspicious about it."

"That's not very likely," I said.

"Or at least it might slow down the process, turn it sour. It is vital to ensure that Sir Philip's demise was as accidental as it appeared. You must investigate, Nicholas."

"Why me?"

"You were there when it happened. You know your way round the – what do they call it? – the back of the stage. You can ask the right sort of questions."

"If I refuse?"

"Why should you refuse? You will be paid, rest assured of that. Your reports are already being read with interest."

"Read by the Privy Council?"

"Who said anything about the Council?"

I stopped in the middle of the street. I almost seized the fellow by his red doublet.

"What's going on here, Master Ratchett?"

He fixed me with his shrewd brown stare.

"Nicholas, you leapt to conclusions. You assumed I worked for the Council."

"Because you said you did."

"No, *you* said it. I didn't."

My brains were too scrambled to think straight. Hadn't Ratchett claimed to work for the Privy Council at our first meeting – or had I put the words into his mouth? I couldn't be sure.

"Then there was all that stuff you spouted about the Council and the cuttlefish."

"That was no lie, the Council *is* like the cuttlefish, many-armed but with a single head."

"And going about deliberately confusing friends and enemies with its inky blackness, to say nothing of honest men!"

"Calm down, Nicholas. I have nothing to do with the Council . . . "

"Then I want nothing to do with you!"

" . . . but I am with another, ah, group which has this country's welfare at heart."

"How do I know that? Why should I believe a word you say?"

"I swear to you that what I'm requesting now is an honest and honourable business. It is simply to delve into the circumstances of Sir Philip's death."

"And if I say no?"

"You are fond of saying no."

Very well, I thought. So now I shall say nothing.

I made to walk away.

"You cannot back out now," said Ratchett softly, creeping up behind my back. "If you do, the Council may well be interested in why you have been writing reports for a certain gentleman in Salisbury Court."

I turned round.

"A certain gentleman? In Salisbury Court? More obfuscation. Means nothing to me."

"If you want to find out, you only need to ask, Nicholas. Three days' time at the Pure Waterman. Come to me with some discoveries."

And with that he strode off, his doublet glowing. I could have strangled the man. If my brains had been scrambled before, now they were buzzing. I was in deep trouble and, like the man in a quaking bog, any attempt to extricate myself was causing me to sink even further down.

I had unwisely consented to report on the *Masque of Peace* preparations for Ratchett in the mistaken belief that he was employed by the Privy Council. I'd been stupid in jumping to conclusions. Very stupid. Now it appeared that he worked for a different 'group'. For 'a certain gentleman in Salisbury Court'. This court was situated not far from where Ratchett had left me. It lay beyond Temple Bar and towards the end of Fleet Street, a prosperous enough area even if it was close to the Bridewell house of correction.

The simplest thing would be to go and enquire in the neighbourhood. I was close by. I wouldn't have to go and knock on the front door. I could probably find out who lived in Salisbury Court by a casual enquiry.

It turned out to be easy. The very first person I asked was able to tell me. This was an individual who looked as though he might have spent a bit of time in Bridewell himself. He was leaning against a wall lopsidedly. He didn't move from the wall during our brief exchange. He repeated my words slowly, chewing them in his mouth.

"Salisbury Court?"

"Yes. Who lives there?"

"That'll be the Mon-sewer."

"Monsewer? A Frenchman?"

Nothing too unusual in that. There were quite a lot of French people in London (like Blanche of the Mitre).

"Yes, a Mon-sewer like I said. His name is . . . let me think . . . let me think now . . . his name is . . . "

"Perhaps this'll refresh your memory."

My penny saw the light of day for only the fraction of a second.

"Mon-sewer La Boderie is his name. It comes back to me now. It's a French name."

This name meant nothing to me either. I shrugged.

My lopsided friend said, "He's the leg-it, La Boderie."

The leg-it?

Ah, the legate.

La Boderie was the French ambassador in London.

Thou hast set me on the rack

I cursed myself, profoundly. I'd turned into a spy. Partly out of gratitude – because John Ratchett had rescued me from a pair of assailants on the river bank – and partly out of greed, I had turned into a spy. Or been turned into one. True, I'd been led by the nose, believing that I was working for the Council at two or three removes. But that was my fault too. Ratchett had chosen not to enlighten me, and so allowed me to sink into a quagmire of my own making. I was more angry with myself than with him. And, more than being angry with both of us, I was frightened.

What did La Boderie the French ambassador want? I hardly had to ask myself the question. The answer was simple. If the English were coming to an accommodation with their old enemy in Spain, then this was naturally of concern to the French. No doubt Monsieur La Boderie had quite a few eyes and ears at his disposal out on the streets of London and inside its grand houses. He'd want to be kept informed. He might even want to interfere.

What did Nicholas Revill want? The answer to this was also simple. To get out of the situation with a whole skin.

As far as I was able to see, I had no choice but to do as John Ratchett had instructed. That is, to enquire into the circumstances of Sir Philip Blake's death. With luck, I could present Ratchett with an account that showed it was a straightforward accident, even if an unusual one, and so finish with the whole affair. The plump red-doublet had a hold over me – the threat to inform on me as a spy to the Council – and my only defence would be that I'd acted in ignorance. Ignorance might have been my part in Ben's masque, but even I knew that it wasn't much of a defence in law.

Best not to think about what might happen. Best to hasten back to Somerset House and attempt to sweep up a few fragments of evidence which I could assemble into a 'report' for Ratchett.

It wasn't very far to Somerset House from the spot where I was presently standing near Salisbury Court. The afternoon – still only the afternoon despite all that had happened! – was hot and heavy. As I strode back towards the Strand, sweat broke out all over my body, partly brought on by thoughts of what dire consequences might follow if I fell into the hands of the Privy Council. I might be put to the question. I might be put on the rack.

Master Revill, you admit that you have been providing information to the French ambassador. You are a spy.

But I didn't know who I was providing it for! I thought it was for you, for the Council I mean.

Ignorance is no defence in law. You must know that.

I didn't pass on anything important . . .

So you're not just a spy but a useless one.

. . . because there was nothing important to pass on, I swear.

Let us be the judge of that. Three pounds a time you were paid – three pounds for nothing? Fetch that rack a further turn, master gaoler.

No! No! Stop. Please. I'll tell you anything you want. What do you want to hear?

What do you want to say, Master Revill?

I heard Giles Cass make comments about the Spaniards in the Mermaid tavern I heard him questioning why we were making peace with them but he speaks Spanish you know I heard Martin Barton comment on the corruption of the court I heard a man called William Inman make a joke about the

*Spanish peace he said it would prove poxy and rotten I heard
Lady Blake –*

Lady Blake?

She was having a conversation with Jonathan Snell. He is –

We know who he is.

They were talking about chairs and falling down.

Chairs and falling down?

Yes, chairs and falling down.

There was a clap of thunder from not far off. If I hadn't
been so absorbed in my thoughts of the rack and the things I
would confess to – that is, to everything – I might have
jumped. Instead, I stopped dead in the street, as the first blobs
of rain started to fall in their idle summer fashion. I was
struggling to recall the exact words which had passed between
Lady Blake and the engine-man during the eavesdropped
conversation. *Then this will come down*, was what she'd said,
pointing at the diagram, and *Oh, it'll come down all right*,
he'd replied. Were they talking about the seat from which Sir
Philip had plunged to his death only a couple of hours before?
What else could they have been referring to?

For the third time that day I passed through the gatehouse
of Somerset House, just as the rain was coming down in
thicker blobs and the thunder beginning to close in. There
was a flash of lightning as I crossed the great courtyard and I
picked up speed. It is surprisingly easy to gain access to these
fine places – much easier than it would be to get inside a
peasant's hovel. There are so many people coming and going
all the time. The gatekeeper wasn't interested and if anyone
else thought to ask your business (which they generally
didn't), they could be fobbed off with any old answer.

The audience chamber where the ill-fated rehearsal had
taken place was still occupied. There were several Spaniards
about. But I was relieved to see that the body had gone. It
was probably laid out in one of the adjacent rooms, or perhaps had already been returned to the Blakes' mansion
further along the Strand. A linen cloth was spread out over

114

the area of the stage where Sir Philip had hit the ground. The chair no longer dangled overhead in space.

Ben Jonson was deep in conversation with Giles Cass. Jonson glanced up as I passed and for a moment didn't recognize me.

"I lost something," I said, gesturing vaguely.

"Oh yes," said Jonson.

"We have all lost something," said Cass. "A great life has been forfeit."

I nodded gravely, as one does at that kind of stuff, and passed on. I slipped around the back of the stage. Things were exactly as they had been a few hours earlier when I'd shinned up the ladder to show Sir Philip where he should go. I glimpsed the barrel-shaped windlass which controlled the ropes. Once more, I grasped the ladder and clambered up. I was no longer much bothered about heights. There were other and more pressing matters to be worried about, like being interrogated by the Privy Council.

Outside, the thunder volleyed around Somerset House.

For some reason I'd expected the platform above the stage to be empty but there were two figures standing on the far side. The Snells, father and son. Like Jonson and Cass down below, they were talking earnestly. To one side of them stood the empty chair, hauled up from below. It was darker than before on the floating platform. I sensed rather than saw the lightning which flickered into the audience room.

The two men looked round when they heard the creaking of the boards.

"Who's that?"

"Nicholas Revill, the player."

"What do you want?" said the father.

"I lost a ring. It's my father's. It might be somewhere around here. I came up earlier with Sir Philip – to show him the way."

"Oh, that was you with him, was it?" said the son in a friendlier tone than his father's.

I pretended to cast around on the floor.

"You won't find much by this light," said Jonathan senior. One of the little oil lamps was flickering by his feet. He picked it up and for an instant I thought he meant to offer it to me, but instead he and his son huddled around the chair from which Sir Philip had plunged to his death. They whispered while the thunder banged about outside. I got down on my hands and knees and felt about for a ring which I would never find since it was safely stored in my room at Thames Street.

"And I tell you it has been," I heard the son saying.

"No. You cannot tell so easily," said the father.

"Show *him*. See what he says," said the son.

"Him? Why?"

"Nick," said young Jonathan over his shoulder. "Take a look at this."

I crossed the platform. With the aid of the oil lamp, father and son were examining not the chair but one of the supporting ropes which had snapped. The son held the end of the rope closer to the light and peered intently through his spectacles. I had the clear impression that the father was unhappy with what the son was doing.

"I don't see exactly what . . . " I said, peering at the rope end.

"It's been cut, Nick."

"But not at *this* point," said the father, seizing hold of the rope with one long-thumbed hand and using the other to jab at some ragged strands of hemp. "It's not been cut here. This is frayed. It's given way."

"It's given way because of the strain, father," said Jonathan, taking back the rope end. There was excitement in his voice. "Look, Nick. Even I can see it. This strand has been severed deliberately – and this strand – and this one too . . . all on the same side. Cut with a knife."

He began to unpick the end of the rough rope, and exhibited one length of fibre after another. I'm no expert but there was a difference between the way in which some strands terminated cleanly while others seemed to have been torn apart. As if he was eager to convince me, the younger Jonathan Snell stood up and craned out over the side of the gallery. His spectacles glinted in the light. Hanging from the main frame by only one hand, he reached for the other dangling rope which had held the chair and snapped. Snell was as nimble as a monkey. Here was someone with a head for heights. He scrabbled for the second torn rope and brought it back into the little circle of light. After a moment's examination he nodded.

"There is the same pattern here. Some strands cut, the rest left to give way under the weight. This has been cleverly done. Too many strands severed and the chair might have fallen straightaway. Too few, and the ropes would have held up without breaking. Sir Philip would have reached the ground in safety."

A clap of thunder resounded overhead, as if whoever had control of such grand effects in the sky was showing his skill in dramatic timing. The Jonathan Snells and I were silent as the implications of the younger one's words sunk in. In his excitement he'd hardly seemed aware of those implications himself, and had talked of the thing being 'cleverly done', almost with admiration.

"Who would do such a wicked act?" I said.

I was genuinely shocked. So, it seemed, was father Snell.

"Be careful, son. You are saying that Sir Philip was unlawfully killed."

"Look at the evidence."

"It is not as easy as that."

"Don't you see, father, that if the rope was cut deliberately then it was not our fault? Yes, it is a terrible thing that Sir Philip has died, terrible, but it is nothing to do with us. We aren't responsible. The evidence here says otherwise."

"You are a fool, Jonathan," said his father. "Who was responsible for this area? You were. Why was Sir Philip not strapped in?"

"Because the belts were not ready, father, you know that. You were up here while he was being helped into the chair, I was over the other side."

"If anyone is to be accused of an . . . unlawful killing . . . then it would be you," said the father, almost fiercely. "The idea is nonsense. You must forget it. Take it as an accident. It is absurd to claim otherwise – dangerous even to think otherwise."

They had almost forgotten that I was there. A horrified bystander, I could see the logic in the argument of each man. The son's was a somewhat cold-blooded argument, maybe – but it's a natural enough response in a disaster to try to shift the blame elsewhere. Except that in this case shifting the blame meant turning an accident into a murder. And the father had a point too. If the death of Sir Philip was what he'd termed an 'unlawful killing' then the first person the authorities would look to would be the person who had charge of the floating platform: Jonathan Snell the younger.

"I do not think that *this* was accidental," said the son, holding up one of the rope ends.

"Who do you point the finger at then, Jonathan?"

"I don't know."

"Then remember that when you point a finger, your other fingers are turned back towards you."

This reasoning, or the finger-picture at any rate, subdued the son. Calmed him down.

"What shall we do?" he said.

I was sorry to see both men so helpless. The son seemed to me an honest, intelligent apprentice while the father was an inventive individual, in love with his pulleys and his windlasses.

"Gentlemen," I said, "I have a suggestion."

Some time later I climbed down from the aerial platform, leaving the Snells still picking over the chair and the ropes. I think I'd convinced them to go along with my plan for the time being. 'Plan' was putting a gloss on it, maybe, but I couldn't think of anything else since a 'time being' was all I had. A very little time being indeed before I must report back to John Ratchett.

Giles Cass and Ben Jonson had gone by now. The thunderstorm too had retreated. I walked across the stage and peered at the spot where Sir Philip Blake had hit the ground headfirst. It was still covered with a pale linen cloth which had turned plum-coloured in the centre. I did not lift it to look underneath. It seemed apparent now that Blake might have met his death through unlawful means. Two of the ropes supporting the throne of Truth had been half severed, there could be almost no doubt about it. Here was a degree of expertise and calculation which pointed to an ingenious murder. Ingenious, because it could have been taken for an accident if it hadn't been for the sharp eyes of the younger Snell.

I left the audience chamber. Nobody queried my presence in Somerset House. In fact, the place was strangely quiet. Earlier I'd wondered whether the body of Sir Philip was still here or whether he had already been transferred to his own house. Now, passing an adjoining room, I saw that he was not yet home. The room wasn't grand, it was barely an antechamber. There was an unidentified shape lying on a table. Unidentified but also easily identifiable, if you know what I mean. Sir Philip had been covered, unceremoniously, with the costume cloak he was wearing when he perished. His head remained hidden, thankfully. The miniature suns signifying Truth, which were sewn on the cloak and made of foil, caught the light of a handful of candles scattered around the room.

Almost without thinking, I entered the little room to pay my respects.

I had exchanged no more than a couple of dozen words with the man, and they'd been more his words than mine, yet he had seemed agreeable enough. Why, he'd asked me if I was connected to the Revills of Norfolk.

I turned into the room, then froze on the threshold. There were two figures, a man and a woman, standing at one end of the makeshift bier. They were clutching at each other. At first I assumed that they must be overcome by grief. There were mild little whimpers and tiny groans coming from them. They hadn't noticed my presence. I stole out of the room again.

As I threaded my way through the corridors and lobbies towards the open air, I wondered what Lady Blake had been doing with her body glued to Bill Inman's.

I remembered when I was young climbing upstairs in the parsonage to get out of the way of the grown-ups after some church occasion – which must, in retrospect, have been a funeral – to discover the new widow all hot and fresh while she was sharing her grief with her late husband's brother. Perhaps there is something in bereavement which makes us cling to life all the tighter. Just as Lady Jane was clinging to the secretary of her husband, and that husband not four hours dead. Could it have been an honest embrace, two people innocently consoling each other? Possibly. But I didn't forget either that dialogue I'd overheard between Lady Blake and Snell senior about a chair 'coming down', and the way they had been sniggering together about it like children. The idea that Lady Blake might welcome her husband's death had already entered my head. Now, close behind it, followed the notion that she might have caused it.

If the sight of her and Bill Inman was an unexpected discovery, the next stage in my researches was intentional. I'd suggested to the Snells, you see, that I might carry out a little unofficial investigation into the circumstances surrounding the death of Sir Philip Blake. This was more or less the task that Ratchett had already imposed on me. It was Jonathan Snell the younger who believed that Blake might have been 'unlawfully killed' while his father had done his best to call it an accident. As long as each man held so firmly to one belief or the other, it could be that a colder eye, a cooler one, might discover something they'd be blind to.

Naturally, I considered the idea that the father himself might have been involved with the death of Sir Philip. That would explain his guilty sniggering with Lady Blake, his eagerness to say that all this was a terrible misfortune. His son had let slip the fact that the father had been in the gallery helping Sir Philip into the fatal chair while he, the son, had apparently been on the other side. True, Snell senior didn't look like a murderer or even a murderer's accomplice, but if every villain wore his villainy on his face like a badge then life would be much simpler and the gaols would be even fuller – and there would be no more mysteries for us to solve.

Almost as an aside, I had asked the son whether he'd observed anybody else up in the gallery. For answer he tapped his spectacles.

"I am good with close work, Nick, but not so certain over a distance, even a short distance. Anybody might have come and gone especially if they didn't want to be seen."

"Or nobody," said the father, butting in.

"When was the chair last used?" I said. "I mean, when it was working properly."

"I rode in it this very morning," said Snell senior.

"And I saw my father lowered in it. There was nothing wrong with the apparatus then."

"There was some give in the ropes, I told you at the time," said the father, still keen to uncover an accident.

I also found out from the son that two or three craftsmen from their workshop had been up on the floating platform in the time immediately before and during the practice for the *Masque of Peace*. Perhaps they would have a clearer idea if there had been any visitors to the gallery. Jonathan consulted with his father who told me, reluctantly it seemed, that at least two of them – whom he referred to only as Ned and Thomas – were usually to be found at some point in the evening at the Line and Compass, an ale-house in Fleet Street favoured by the better sort of artisan.

It was lucky that everything was so close by. I hastened to the Line and Compass, hoping to encounter Ned and Thomas. They weren't there (as I soon discovered) but instead I ran across Martin Barton, the red-haired playwright and satirist. I wondered what he was doing there, out of all the taverns in London, and then recalled that he lived somewhere in the neighbourhood.

He hadn't noticed me. But seeing him in the midst of a little group of working men, I also recalled the odd comment he'd made about there being more honour and honesty in a craftsman's thumb than in whole bodies of the wealthy. Unthinkingly, I'd assumed that his court satire was carried through – like most satires – for form's sake. That is, the satirist is secretly hungering for the very things he condemns. Maybe in Barton's case he really believed what he said, and was therefore consorting with craftsmen as an antidote to knights and queens.

I was on the point of sneaking out of the ale-house when he caught my eye. Too late. He waved me over with a flail of his arm and pulled me down so that I was sitting next to him on the bench. Barton had sunk a few pints by this stage. He was describing the events of the afternoon, the fatal fall of Sir Philip Blake. This was not being done in that respectful tone of voice which most people assume when talking about the death even of someone only slightly known to them. Rather he seemed to enjoy recounting the way in which the ropes had snapped and Blake been tipped forward so as to land on his skull. In fact, Barton more or less implied it was no better than that noble gentleman deserved for the crime of being, well, noble. By the nods and grins from the circle of men – mostly young, I observed, and well-muscled – Martin Barton was finding a receptive audience.

I must have made some involuntary movement on the bench where I was perched. Barton interpreted this as being some objection to his words.

"Well, Nicholas Revill," he said, "you would like it, I suppose? All that wealth and rottenness together. The palace and the high chair."

"If my means matched my wit, I could purchase the world," I said, palming him off with the stale saying. In truth, Martin Barton, drunk, wasn't a person to argue with.

"Well, they don't match, my friend," said Barton. "If you're not born to it and you can't afford to buy it, then the next best thing you can do is go creeping and crawling towards the palace and the high chair. Like Ben Jonson."

"That is unfair," I said, forgetting that I meant to avoid an argument. "Jonson is no one's man."

"I tell you Ben Jonson should have followed his father in being a bricklayer, like young Verney here."

Barton raised his tankard at a brawny fellow opposite who, incongruously, winked back at the playwright.

"No offence to bricklayers," I said, "but if Jonson had joined their ranks, the world would be the loser."

"No, the world would be the gainer because at least we'd have something else to lean against. You can lean against a wall but you can't lean against a pile of paper," said Barton. "There's a wall round these parts somewhere – in Lincoln's Inn, isn't it? – where is it, Verney?"

"At the backside toward Holborn, Martin," said the young bricklayer.

"That's the one, at the backside. Jonson laid that wall, they say," said Barton. "I tell you I'd rather have another wall from Master Ben than a whole folio of new plays."

There were grunts of approval from the drinking circle, and someone made a predictable comment about paper being useful for one thing only, and that wasn't reading or writing. I wondered how Martin Barton got away with keeping this company. In outlook, in education and in just about everything else, he was far closer to Jonson than he was to any of these men, with their limber bodies and broad hands.

"I should not let Jonson hear you say so, Master Barton."

"I am afraid of no man."

"You know he killed a man in a duel once."

"Killing a man is nothing. It's getting away with it that counts."

I thought of the severed ropes in the Somerset House masque. Who knew of them? Only the Snells and myself – and whoever had taken a knife to them in the first place.

"I came here looking for two of the men who were working on the platform from where Sir Philip fell. Ned and Thomas are their names. I was told they often come to the Line and Compass."

"Why?"

"Because they like it, I suppose."

"Why do you want to see them?"

"Because, Master Barton, I mislaid a ring which belonged to my father on the floating platform and I wondered whether one of them had picked it up by chance."

This answer seemed to satisfy Barton.

"Ned Armitage I know," said one of the other young men. "He'll be over at the Snells' workplace."

"Where's that?"

"Halfway down Three Cranes Lane on the left."

"I'll go and look for him now."

"Stay and drink with us, Nicholas Revill," said Barton.

"I'm not thirsty."

"Then give my love to Master Ben when you see him," called Barton to my retreating back. There was a little laughter from his followers.

I was glad to get outside. The late afternoon storm had disappeared and in its place was a clear evening, rinsed of the summer dust. The streets were already drying off. Three Cranes Lane was on the route back to Mrs Buckle's. I would look in and see if either of those fellows was there and willing to talk to me about what, if anything, he'd observed in the gallery above the stage. I would have to go about it carefully.

The story of the dropped ring belonging to my father had worked well enough so far.

While I was walking I thought of what Martin Barton had said about Jonson, about how it would have been better if he'd stuck to bricklaying. Barton came from a more prosperous background than Jonson – he'd even gone to Middle Temple for a time – so it was easy to attribute the remarks to snobbery. But there was jealousy involved too between him and Jonson. Although Barton had scored a hit with his *Melancholy Man*, there was no doubt about who was the more substantial playwright in every sense. Envy and jealousy are the pond in which playwrights – and other writers too, for all I know – swim about, splashing unhappily. For if Martin Barton was jealous of Ben Jonson, then Ben Jonson envied William Shakespeare.

Like the rest of us, Jonson had been present at a genuine tragedy at Somerset House just now but he couldn't write a stage tragedy to save his life. A recent piece called *Sejanus*, which the King's Men had staged, turned out to be worthy of the name of tragedy only on account of the way it was received. 'Disaster' would have been a better word. Convinced of his own correctness, Jonson thought the audience were idiots for not appreciating it properly. Yet, in the middle of his troubles, he had only to look around to see old Bill Shakespeare scribbling comedies and tragedies with equal ease, drawing in public audiences for almost every product of his pen and earning the applause of the royal court as well. It must have been very galling for a man of Jonson's considerable pride and touchiness.

His attitude to his very name showed how touchy he was. Some uncharitable individuals claimed that he was no more than common *Johnson* spelled with an 'h', and that Ben – turning up his nose at being the son of any old John – had decided to drop his aitches in order to stand out from the crowd. Whether this story was true or not, I remembered an occasion when our book-keeper Geoffrey Allison received a very public ticking-off for daring to write *B. Johnson* on the outside of a scroll containing one of Ben's parts – mind you, I think that Allison had done it deliberately.

By this time I'd reached Three Cranes Lane. It runs down towards the river and a set of stairs of the same name adjoining a wharf. There are three stout cranes on the wharf to hoist up the wine barrels for storage in a stone house known as the Vintry. (But I think the wine trade is not what it was in these parts, perhaps as a result of the plague.) There's also a tavern at the top of the lane called the Three Cranes but, in an innkeeper's witty variation on the name, the sign depicts three long-necked birds. The tavern was quiet. Most of its trade would be with wharf-men during the day.

A cool draught of air came funnelling up from the river. About halfway down Three Cranes Lane and on the left-hand side stood a house – more of a little warehouse – with an enclosed yard. I had passed by it a handful of times but never before been aware of the smell of fresh-cut wood which streamed over the wall like the scent of flowers from a garden. Now the wood smell seemed obvious, and I wondered how I could have missed it. There was a gate in the wall which was latched. I opened it.

This must be the right place. There were neatly stacked piles of timber in the yard together with a spoked object under a tarpaulin which had the outline, although smaller, of the windlass that I'd seen backstage in Somerset House. Two carts stood side by side in a corner. The cobbled yard sloped slightly, following the slant of the lane outside. At the top end was a kind of warehouse whose south-facing upper windows had been enlarged to let in more light. Above the windows were projecting beams with hooks which looked like curled, deformed hands. They would be employed in hoisting. I guessed that this place too had once been used for the storage and distribution of wine. The cobbles were stained dark purple in their crevices. Here, over the centuries, the dregs had been scraped out of empty wine barrels. Wine from

France, maybe wine from Bordeaux, like Blanche of the Mitre.

I had a sense of trespassing. For some reason I didn't want to run into the Snells again. As far as I knew, father and son were still at Somerset House poring over the evidence of the 'accident' or the 'murder', call it what you will. Was there anybody in their workshop? I thought of calling out. I had my story ready if challenged, the one about the missing ring. I'd almost come to believe in it myself.

I walked up the yard and peered through the ground-floor windows. The windows were small and some were unglazed. This floor was a single open space and evidently used for storage and general jumble. There was a sort of order among all the disorder, in that similar items were placed together, however pell-mell. I could make out more timber beams and coils of rope and chain, together with half-painted sheets of canvas and a profusion of paint-streaked buckets and tubs, as well as obscure bits of machinery. My heart jolted when I noticed a figure with a drooping head slumped on a mound of tarpaulins. A few seconds were enough to assure me that it wasn't a real person but a counterfeit, presumably used by the Snells for testing their equipment. My heart went racing ahead unchecked, though.

There were double doors in the middle of the building, large enough to admit a cart. One of the doors was ajar. I knocked and cleared my throat. Poked my head inside. No sound. Took my head out again. Stood uncertainly in the yard. Waited for my heart to slow down again. Glanced up. The beams with their grotesque hooks were projected across a cloudless evening sky. To the feeling of trespass was added a growing sense of unease.

I slipped through the open door. Called out more loudly. Called "Ned?" Called "Thomas? Is there anybody there?" I hadn't expected an answer, and there was none.

In front of me was a kind of well which extended as far as the roof. Ropes dangled down from it. Rather as in the

makeshift arrangement in the Somerset House audience
chamber there was a gallery which was reached by a rickety
set of stairs. Next to these was a steep wooden slide whose
surface had been worn smooth by generations of rolling
barrels – or generations of apprentices' arses.

Skirting the various stacks of material on the floor I made
my way to the foot of the stairs. I had the unpleasant sensation of being watched and almost caught the counterfeit
person looking up at me from his mound of tarpaulins, even
though there were no features on his drooping face. He
wasn't very real – something between a scarecrow and a
mannequin – but quite real enough for me in the half-light
and the emptiness of the warehouse.

I climbed the stairs, which creaked under my weight. At
the top there was a kind of trapdoor opening onto the slide,
with a lever mechanism which operated it. Beyond this I
found myself facing a set of small chambers or cells which
opened off from each other like a honeycomb. This impression was enhanced by a sweetish scent that pervaded
them, the smell from glue or paint or soap perhaps. This was
the place where the Jonathan Snells and their workmen put
the finishing touches to the scenery and effects, where they
gave shape to the waves and the clouds, where they gilded
the sun, oiled the cranks, constructed their flying chairs, and
so on. These rooms were as deserted as the lower floor.

Or so I thought until I came to the final one. This was a
little larger than the others. It had a fine view over the roof-
tops and on to the river. It was a view which a merchant
would have paid good money for. Carpenter's implements
were hanging from pegs on the wall, planes and saws and
hammers. A long work-bench faced the window with a set
of sturdy stools tucked underneath. One of the stools was
occupied. A man was sitting on it, slumped forward on the
bench. His back was bowed and his arms flung out in front
of him, as if in propitiation of some unknown power. With
my heart banging in my chest once more, I forced myself to

move forward. The man's head was turned towards me. He had shaggy grey hair. But what I noticed first were the fresh, glistening streaks of red which were scoring a path across the side of his face.

O who hath done this deed?

And what I noticed next was the paintbrush, tipped with red, which the man was gripping in his outstretched right hand. Then my eyes turned towards a medium-sized chest with a curved top which stood in one corner of the room. The paint on the top was still wet. The grey-haired man opened an eye. I don't think he saw me straightaway. When he did he sat up abruptly and nearly fell off his stool. It wasn't just the side of his face which was spattered with red paint, but also the front of his shirt. The shirt was already striped all the colours of the rainbow.

Rapidly I explained who I was and my purpose in coming to the workshop. I was sorry for disturbing him, I said, but was in search of a ring which I'd mislaid that afternoon somewhere in the stage area of Somerset House, maybe in the gallery. A ring which was not valuable to anyone else but valuable to me, since it had belonged to my father. I explained how I'd called out, thought no one was here, climbed upstairs to make sure, and so on.

Ned Armitage – for this was one of the men who'd been present on the floating platform – was a bit embarrassed to have been caught napping, I think. Maybe he believed I would report back on him to father Snell. He was tired, he said, and shaken by the terrible events of the afternoon. The poor man falling to his death. A dreadful mischance. (There was no hint in his words that he thought it was anything but an accident.)

But time and the hour run through the roughest day, Ned went on. There was still work to be done, like this theatre chest or trunk which had to be painted and done with by eight o'clock the next morning. In the middle of the job, he'd gone to pick up some item from the bench and then, overcome by sudden weariness, sat down for a moment. The next thing he knew was that I was standing over him. I apologized again if I'd surprised him and explained that, just for an awful instant, I'd taken him for dead, what with his stillness and those red streaks running down the side of his face.

Well, this has been a day for death, he said, wiping at his cheek with his fingertips, and that's one state he'd happily be mistaken for being in. But, no, he had not found any ring lying in the gallery above the stage and he'd be sworn to it that his mate Tom Turner hadn't picked one up either. I shrugged as if the matter wasn't so important after all, and in truth I felt a bit guilty spinning the same old story to this honest man. However, under the pretence of wishing to exhaust every avenue, I asked him whether he'd noticed anybody else visiting the floating platform before or during the performance, apart from his employers the Snells and Sir Philip Blake.

Yes, plenty of people, he said. They seemed curious as to how the apparatus worked. They wanted to poke about behind the scenes when they didn't have any business being there. The men and women taking part in the masque just assumed they had a right to wander anywhere around or above the area of the stage. They'd climbed the ladder, they'd tugged on the ropes and pulleys, and generally made nuisances of themselves. The trouble was that they were nobles, most of them, they were sirs and lords and ladies, and it was difficult to tell them to piss off.

Had he noticed anyone in particular, out of the lords and ladies and sirs?

Ned Armitage scratched his grey hair. He stroked his cheek and smeared the red paint even more. He thought. Then he proceeded to enumerate the individuals, or some of them, whom he'd observed up in the gallery. He had a keen eye, perhaps an offshoot of his craft. Also a good memory.

Poor Lady Blake, a widow for the last few hours, she had been up there, he said, and another woman who was keeping her company. Then there'd been a couple of gents, one in a red top, and a different gent with red hair. And another one – who must have been playing the part of the Sea or something similar in the masque because he was covered in weeds and shells that clacked together – and yet a fourth man carrying a decorative lantern and wearing a cloak decorated with eyes, painted eyes. And there'd been a foolish woman dressed all in green and a very beautiful one who was foreign and not wearing many clothes. And others besides, all getting in the way and being a danger to themselves and each other, though he could not call them to mind. Maybe one of these individuals had spotted my missing ring.

I thanked Ned Armitage. I felt almost as grateful to him as if I really had lost my father's heirloom and was now on the way to recover it. The light was dimming in this upstairs workshop and he was eager to get on and finish the job of painting the red chest.

I went to shake his hand. He put out his own and then glanced down at his reddened fingertips. There were still streaks of paint on the side of his face as well. He reached into a pocket with his left hand and drew out a piece of neat white cloth. He was about to wipe his hand on it when he paused and looked at the material. He unfolded it and looked more closely.

"What's wrong?" I said.

"I didn't find any ring of yours," he said. "But I did collect something up there and stuff it into my pocket. It must've slipped my mind. This handkerchief."

He held up the cloth. It was a delicate piece of work, spotted with red embroidery. He put it to his nose.

"A lady's from the work – and from the smell. Too good to use for this," he said, splaying his red-tipped right hand.

"Let me take it," I said. "I think I know who it might belong to."

(What did another lie matter, when my whole appearance at the workshop this evening had been founded on a lie?)

Ned handed it over willingly, and I shook him by the hand, ignoring the red paint.

As I was leaving I asked out of curiosity, "That theatre chest you are painting. Who is it for?"

"For a woman to hide in."

"A woman?"

"A boy, I mean."

"Is it for us?"

"You are with the King's Men, are you not? No, this is for Worcester's Men over at the Curtain theatre. I believe that a woman has to hide inside it. Don't ask me why. Who knows why anything happens on the stage? I only make the things."

Thanking Ned Armitage once again, I retraced my steps out of the workshop and through the yard into Three Cranes Lane.

I was reflecting on his words, 'I only make the things.' I'd have wanted to know the name of the play for which the red chest was to be a prop, just as I'd have wanted to know why a woman was hiding inside it. Not that there'd necessarily be much of a reason. Reasons and motivation on stage are often on the thin side. In the playhouse it's the idea that is exciting, the idea of the woman concealed inside a chest. Whether she's trying to get away from a ravisher, or whether she plans to creep out at dead of night and pour poison into the gaping mouth of her unfaithful, sleeping husband – it hardly matters why she's there. There is a woman (or rather a boy actor) inside a red chest, that is what counts with the audience. But, I thought, if Ned Armitage was incurious about the detail of our profession, so was I incurious – or just plain ignorant – about his.

Ned had been very useful, however, and later in my room at Mrs Buckle's I attempted to sort out the information he'd provided.

If Jonathan Snell the younger was correct in his suspicions, then some person had deliberately and skilfully cut part-way through two of the ropes which supported the *deus ex machina* chair, knowing that when the apparatus was actually supporting a human weight the ropes ought to snap and the occupant be thrown to the ground.

It would have the appearance of an accident. If it hadn't been for Jonathan's inquisitiveness, it would still appear to have been an accident. The cutting of the ropes must have been done a short time before the performance started, otherwise there was a risk that anyone examining the chair or the ropes – one of the Snells, say, or Ned Armitage or Tom Turner – would have detected something wrong. Unless, of course, one of those four had tampered with the ropes himself. They, above all, would be in the best position to do so.

The principal question was: if Sir Philip had been murdered, and in such a way that the murder appeared accidental, then who had done it?

And another question which was almost as important: why had he been murdered?

Perhaps the answer to "why?" would give the answer to "who?"

Now I possessed a kind of catalogue of some of the people who'd been up in the gallery during the time before Sir Philip's death. It was easy enough to recall Ned Armitage's words, but slightly harder to invent motives and reasons as to why any of them might want to see this harmless-seeming individual dead. Harder, but by no means impossible.

First, there was Lady Jane Blake. The woman keeping her company was presumably Maria More, acting the part of handmaid to Plenty in the *Masque of Peace*. I didn't know much about Mistress More, except that she had firm views about women not being permitted to play on the public stage. That hardly seemed an adequate motive for murder.

Lady Jane was different, though. William Shakespeare had said that husband and wife did not get on. Was this the common gossip? Did that mean they'd like to see the back of each other? Many wives would like to see the back of their husbands, no doubt, and vice versa. But that doesn't mean they'll go as far as murder. On the other hand, there was the dialogue I'd eavesdropped on at the Blake mansion, the one between Lady Jane and the older Snell. *Then this will come down*, she'd said. *Oh, it'll come down all right*, he'd said. Were they referring to the flying chair from which her husband had fallen to his death? It sounded like it. And if they weren't, then what were they being so giggly and secretive about? And was this the reason why Snell had been so reluctant to listen to his son's suspicions about a murder – because he had been conspiring with her to kill Sir Philip?

Then Ned had referred to two gentlemen in the gallery, one in a red top and another one with red hair. The red-headed one was Martin Barton, I guessed. From my glimpse of the satirist in the Line and Compass ale-house, he hadn't exactly been overcome with grief at Blake's death. In fact, he rather appeared to take pleasure in it, as some people do relish a disaster. Also Barton disliked Ben Jonson. Claimed it would have been better for the world if the playwright had stuck to his bricklaying. Barton disliked – no, he loathed – the court and all its outworks as well. Everything there was foul and decayed. This was a fairly usual position for a satirist to take up, and his snarling hostility towards a large portion of the world had been well on display in *The Melancholy Man*. Barton, with his spindly legs and sharp tongue, preferred the honest thumb of the craftsman. None of this turned him into a murderer, though. What would he have gained out of the killing of Sir Philip? Only that the death disrupted Jonson's masque, to be sure, perhaps put an end to its chances of performance altogether, and that must gratify Barton. I thought of the pond of jealousy which playwrights swim in, splashing unhappily.

The gentleman wearing 'a red top' might have been one of the Spanish grandees, the platter heads. At the practice the

Dons had appeared richly dressed, wearing white and gold together with something purple about their upper halves. But John Ratchett, who had tricked me into becoming a spy, was also wearing a red doublet. I'd seen him shortly after the 'accident' in Somerset House. Had he been there to witness it as well? He'd told me that he knew what had taken place. If he was in the pay of France, then he had the most obvious of motives for trying to stop peace breaking out between England and Spain. An unexplained death could throw doubt on the enterprise and, if not halt it altogether, then impede its smooth progress. But if Ratchett was behind Sir Philip's death, then why had he insisted that I delve into the circumstances surrounding that death? Perhaps to distract attention from his own role in it, or to discover whether anyone else harboured suspicions.

Who else had Ned Armitage remembered as visiting the floating platform?

It was simple enough to identify a couple more of the women. The foolish one dressed all in green was surely Lady Fortune, costumed to play the part of Hope. While the very beautiful one who was foreign and not wearing many clothes was certainly Doña Luisa de Mendoza, playing *La Paz*.

Then there was William Inman, the secretary and right-hand man to Blake, the one taking the part of Oceanus in the masque. Like everyone else he'd been up there in the gallery, covered in weeds and seashells. Maybe he was in pursuit of Doña Luisa, waggling his trident about. Bill Inman appeared bluff and harmless. Yet within barely an hour of his master's death and in the presence of the corpse, I had discovered him and the widow in a hot clinch. Were they united in loss – or in lust? If it was the second, then that must be one of the oldest reasons in the world for doing away with a spouse. Bill Inman and Lady Jane might have conspired together, perhaps with the help of engineer Snell, to get rid of the husband. It would be an unequal match, if it got as far as a wedding. But then unequal matches are made every day. Also I recalled that Lady Blake had come from a comparatively humble background, her father being an apothecary. So she was used to unequal matches, even if the union with Blake had been very much to her advantage.

There was one final figure whom Ned Armitage had identified as being present in the gallery. This one was carrying a decorative lantern and wearing a cloak covered with painted eyes. I recognized the description of the masque figure, Suspicion. The eyes on the cloak are self-explanatory. Suspicion carries a lamp because he is always prying into corners and sniffing out other men's actions. The part of Suspicion had been played by Giles Cass.

I couldn't get to the bottom of Cass. He was someone out of my sphere. I had seen and heard him conversing with the platter-headed Dons in the Spanish tongue. He had made some witty remark when I'd been stuck up in the chair during the earlier practice. Yet he was apparently hostile towards the Spanish settlement, or at any rate wary of it. Hadn't he announced in the Mermaid tavern in front of Jonson and the rest of us that he couldn't see, for the life of him, why we were negotiating with our old enemies? I had not quite believed him at the time and thought he might have been speaking to provoke us. William Shakespeare – who seemed to know everything about everybody – had called him a weathervane. He'd said that Cass had connections with Walter Raleigh before transferring his loyalty to Robert Cecil. No, veering towards Cecil. I doubted that Cass had loyalty to anyone. He turned where the wind blew strongest. But it was Raleigh I was thinking about now.

Sir Walter.

The lion in the Tower.

Raleigh must have seen the spectacle, or at least heard the noise, as the Spanish party paraded up the river the other day. As a privileged prisoner in the Tower, he enjoyed a ringside seat. Except that, far from enjoying this peaceful armada, it would have cut him to the quick.

Raleigh had once been the most hated man in London. It was said – how fairly I do not know – that he had taken his pipe out of his mouth and blown smoke into the face of the Earl of Essex while the latter was on his way to the execution block. Essex had been a great favourite with Londoners (until the time came for them to join him in the perilous business of rebellion), so any enemy of Essex was an enemy of theirs.

But people are fickle. When it came to Sir Walter Raleigh's turn to be accused of treason and of conspiring with Spain, they admired the way he stood up for himself under examination. And, to be frank, I do not think many of us believed that Raleigh would ever conspire *with* Spain, but only against her. He was passionate against the country. Therefore when Raleigh was sentenced to that terrible fate of drawing and quartering – which involved his guts being torn out and his privy parts being cut off and thrown into the fire before his very eyes, prior to his head being severed from his body – there was disquiet among the people. And so the wise King James reprieved Sir Walter from that terrible fate and permitted him to live quietly in the comforts of the Tower, the very place where Essex had met his own death under the warrant of Elizabeth. Maybe this was what the new King had intended all along, to show how *his* justice could be tempered with mercy.

Sir Walter had his supporters, more of them now than ever. The arrival of the Spanish in our town was not the most popular event of the year. The mood of the Londoners on the Thames that recent afternoon had been expectant and curious, but it was not warm or truly welcoming. What if Giles Cass was still dedicated to the Raleigh cause, that is to the anti-Spanish cause? So dedicated that, with or without direction, he had decided to spoil the chances of peace between the two nations? On that interpretation, Cass's ear-whispering closeness to the Dons was a ploy to give the impression he was on their side. While behind everyone's backs he was plotting the death of Blake. A greater effect might have been produced by striking at one of the English principals to the treaty – Robert Cecil himself, perhaps, or the Earl of Nottingham – but that would have been a much more dangerous business than trying for the life of a comparatively lowly courtier. On the other hand, the murder of Blake (if that's what it was) had taken place in Queen Anne's own household, in her absence but right under the noses of the Spaniards. It was a bad omen. Perhaps there was worse to follow . . . ?

So there I had it. The individuals who'd been in the gallery at some point during this fatal afternoon included Lady Blake and Maria More, Lady Fortune and Doña Luisa de Mendoza, William Inman, Giles Cass and John Ratchett (perhaps) or one of the Spaniards (possibly). In addition the Snells, father and son, had been up there, together with Ned Armitage and Tom Turner and perhaps others from the Snell workshop.

There might have been even more people in the gallery whom Ned Armitage hadn't noticed or had forgotten about. I had been up there myself briefly, escorting Sir Philip. In short, if this was a murder, then the list of those who had the opportunity to do it wasn't confined to these named characters. On the other hand, it was . . . interesting . . . that without much straining I could think of a motive why almost any of them might – no more than *might* – have been pleased to see the back of the harmless courtier.

There was no evidence for any of this, apart from the severed ropes. If they had been severed. Deliberately severed. You'd have to be an expert to do that so precisely, wouldn't you? To cut them just enough so that for a few moments they sustained the chair which held Sir Philip, before giving way at a sufficient distance above the ground to ensure his death when he fell. It would surely take an expert hand, like one of the Snells. Would a woman be capable of it? If there was someone to guide her hand, possibly. I suddenly remembered the handkerchief which Ned Armitage had found in the gallery and which I'd taken from him, pretending to know who it belonged to.

I drew it from my pocket. It was made of linen with delicate cutwork and adorned with red spots of embroidery. I held it to my nose. The principal scent was rosewater but underneath there was a darker, muskier odour. A lady's handkerchief. I wondered whether it belonged to Lady Jane or perhaps to Doña Luisa de Mendoza. The very name of the Spaniard sounded like a scent. How should one set about returning a handkerchief to a beautiful Spanish lady? And what would she say in return? *Gracias, señor, muchas gracias?*

These pleasant thoughts were interrupted by a low groan from outside my room. In time I might grow used to Mrs Buckle's sleep-walking. She was drawn out of bed by those visions of her late husband, who appeared to her to be stalking about the house, now seen walking up the stairs, now turning a corner.

I opened the door. My landlady was, as before, standing on the floor below. She held a candle. She was not alone this time. There was no ghost visible, but her daughter Elizabeth was beside her, whispering in her ear, urging her to return to her chamber. The mother seemed reluctant to move and Elizabeth grasped her arm and steered her back towards the bedroom.

I returned to my own room. Something about the scene I'd just witnessed snagged at my memory but I couldn't think what it was.

Here is a letter, found in the pocket

Despite Sir Philip's death, Ben Jonson's *Masque of Peace* was still scheduled to go ahead in two days' time, shortly before the formal oath-taking and signing of the treaty at Whitehall. We learned that Jonson had received a hint from the highest quarters – from Secretary Cecil, in other words – that there was no question of calling off the Somerset House performance. It should be viewed as a tribute to the late courtier. Sir Philip's body lay in the Blake mansion along the Strand. It was due to be transported to the couple's country house for interment in the family vault. (None of these great families is content with one fine house but must have two at least.) Anyway, body or no body, in the matter of the masque, national pride was at stake. It was part of the celebrations surrounding the outbreak of peace. To cancel it would be to cast doubt on the validity of that peace.

Blake's death was officially an accident. As far as I could see, suspicions as to its cause were confined to Jonathan Snell the younger and Nicholas Revill the player. A complication was that John Ratchett was compelling me to report to him on my findings. But what did I owe Ratchett anyway? He was in the pay of the French ambassador (and so was I, indirectly). If I told him – as I intended to – that I had discovered nothing out of place, then he would have to be satisfied with that, wouldn't he? Unless he himself had been responsible for the 'accident'. Even so, by this logic, when I told him that there was nothing amiss and that Sir Philip's fall had been an unlucky chance, the hand of God, and the rest of it, Ratchett ought to be satisfied because he was not suspected. Did this logic work? I didn't know. My poor brain could not contain so much logic.

And suppose it was murder, then was there an obligation on me to try to discover who had done it? No, I decided, there was no obligation, or not straightaway. My first responsibility was to myself, to escape from the mess I was in.

There were several concerned parties to report to on the death in Somerset House. William Shakespeare, for one, had requested that I tell him about anything 'untoward' in our preparations for the masque. You can't get much more untoward than a violent death.

Naturally, WS knew what had happened but he made me tell the story over again, asking questions at various points.

"This *was* an accident, Nick?"

"I suppose so. It certainly had the appearance of one."

"You believe it wasn't?"

"No, but . . . "

"But?"

"Jonathan Snell's son had an idea that the ropes holding the chair might have been cut part of the way through so that Sir Philip was bound to fall to his death. His father says it's all nonsense, though."

"Old Snell knows best, I suppose," said WS.

"I think he's an honest man," I said.

Perhaps there was a hint of a question in the remark. And, in fact, I was interested in Shakespeare's opinion about Snell's honesty. But all the playwright said was, "Honest? I think so too."

"Looked at one way, William," I said, "this was not our fault but to do with the, er, mechanics of the masque. Or it was an act of God."

"An act of God striking at the *deus ex machina*, eh? That's the trouble with these devices, Nick, they let you down when it comes to it."

"Or they don't let you down and you stay stuck up in the air."

"Or they don't. It's much simpler to rely on a handful of foils, some fine costumes and a few choice words. And a bit of blood. Let the audience do the rest of the work inside their heads."

I knew that WS didn't hold with these new-fangled devices employed on stage. Even so, he was shrewd enough to understand that some of the audience liked them and, in a masque at least, they were essential.

"You said once that Sir Philip and Lady Blake were cold with each other," I said, reverting to the subject that was on my mind. "Did you mean . . . what did you mean exactly?"

"Maybe you weren't aware, Nick, that Sir Philip was on the edge of the Essex rebellion? He was lucky not to have been called in and questioned. Cecil must have had his hands full with more important fish."

"I saw the Secretary talking to Sir Philip on the day the Spaniards arrived in town," I said. "He must have forgiven him."

"The Secretary may forgive but he does not forget."

"And what has this got to do with his relations with his wife? Blake's, I mean. Cecil is not after Blake's wife, is he?"

Robert Cecil, for all his forbidding appearance (some would say, his downright ugliness), had a name among women.

"Not at all," said Shakespeare. "Lady Jane was angry with her husband because he had put himself at risk over the Essex business. The kind of anger that comes out of love, perhaps."

"There was no one else involved?"

"Nick, you keep hinting at how much more you know. Tell me."

"I thought that maybe she had a, er, partiality for William Inman."

"Inman? I don't think so. Like Jonathan Snell, he is an honest man as far as I know. Inman was devoted to his late master."

So devoted that he must grope the widow within an hour of the husband's death, I thought but said nothing. I also wondered why, since WS seemed so well informed on the individuals within the Blake household, he had required me to report back on them. That he knew them at all wasn't so unexpected. Through the Earl of Southampton, Shakespeare himself had had connections with the circle surrounding the doomed Earl of Essex. If Sir Philip Blake had been on the edge of that circle, it wasn't surprising that WS was familiar with him and some of his household. A keen observer of men and women, he stored up impressions and characters for later use. At least I assumed he did. It's what I would do if I were a playwright.

We returned to Somerset House for a final practice of the masque. The last one had been abandoned before the end, of course. There was a subdued feeling to the occasion, which was easily explained. The members of Sir Philip's household wore black armbands and none of us felt much like cracking celebratory grins to welcome the outbreak of peace and harmony. Any outsider viewing such a scene would have concluded that the preparations were going badly, very badly. If I hadn't been used to the situation at the Globe playhouse before every performance – the controlled panic, the last-minute decisions – I'd have wondered how we would ever be ready to present our *Peace* within a couple of days. But we would be ready. We always are. It's not merely that the show must go on. Before that can happen, the show must start.

Once again, nobles and commoners filled the audience room in Somerset House. There were *señors* and a sprinkling of *señoras*, as well as a few outsiders who were no doubt drawn by the hope of watching another man plunge to his death or some similar disaster.

Ben Jonson himself took on the dangerous part of Truth.
Perhaps he judged that no one else would be willing to entrust
themselves to the flying chair, even though the Snells were
full of reassurance that the mechanism had been checked and
rechecked. You could never say that Ben was lacking in
courage.

I looked out especially for the widow, Lady Jane. I was
curious, to be honest, about how she carried her mourning.
But when I saw her I felt ashamed for ever having doubted
her. Her face was etched with grief. There were deep shadows
under her eyes. It was all most inappropriate for the part of
Plenty even though, when she was made up, some of the
worst effects were hidden. She seemed determined to go
through with it, however. Her attendant, Maria More, kept
her close company.

At some point during a pause in the action I approached
them, brandishing the handkerchief. They knew me by this
time.

"Forgive me, my ladies, but I found this recently. Does it
belong to one of you?"

"Is that blood?" said Lady Jane, barely glancing at the
handkerchief.

"That? Oh no. That's the pattern. Embroidery, see."

Lady Jane took the handkerchief and examined it. I
suppose that, at a cursory glance, the red spots might have
looked like blood. It was an odd question, nevertheless.

"Why, I think it is yours, Maria."

"I do not think so, my lady."

"It is, because I am sure I gave it you."

Mistress More looked at the handkerchief properly for the
first time.

"Where did you find this, Master Revill?" she said.

"Up in the gallery."

I gestured behind me. We were standing with our backs to
the stage. Maria More looked at the handkerchief once again
then shook her head.

145

"I thought it was one which Lady Blake gave me lately. But it is not, only very like. Here."

She handed the handkerchief back to me. I thought I detected a ripple of distress pass across the older woman's face. Lady Blake turned away at the very moment that William Inman – in his garb as Oceanus – came across to speak to her. They engaged in an earnest, whispered dialogue. I observed them out of the corner of my eye. Whatever Shakespeare had said about Inman being an honest man and one devoted to his late master, it was hard not to believe that there was an 'understanding' between this man and woman.

Perhaps Maria More thought so too for I had the distinct feeling that, in what she said next, she was trying to distract my attention from the whispering couple.

"Have you thought of a reason yet?"

"A reason?"

I don't know why but I thought that she was referring to the death of Sir Philip Blake. Instead, as she quickly made clear, she was talking about the prohibition which kept women from playing on the stage. That old subject. But it was not a real concern with her. She was speaking merely to occupy me.

Then she came closer and spoke like a sister. She was a graceful handmaid to Plenty.

"See here, Nicholas, you have come undone. Let me tie you up again."

I was wearing my dark costume as Ignorance, which had a somewhat rustic feel to it and which was fastened at the side with points. Using her strong and supple fingers, Maria More secured the loose strings. Her hands seemed to linger over the business and I did not object.

"Do you enjoy playing Ignorance?"

"All parts are grist to the player's mill, you know. We take what comes."

"So you are a peasant one day and the next day you're a bishop."

146

"Or a murderer," I said, then added quickly, "or a king."

Was it my imagination, or did she tug a little harder on one of the points when I said 'murderer'?

"It must be diverting to play someone else, to step aside from yourself," she said.

"Oh, we are most of all players when we play ourselves," I said complacently.

She was silent for a moment as she leaned forward to tie the final point in my costume. Plenty's handmaid was herself quite plentiful. I wondered whether she'd been as impressed as I had by my philosophical comment about playing oneself. Evidently not, though.

"That is nonsense, what you just said, Nicholas," she said, standing tall again. "There. You are no longer undone."

"Thank you, Maria. Not for telling me I'm talking nonsense but for doing me up."

I considered making some joke about 'ruin and undoing' – don't raise your eyebrows, enough writers have done it, including WS – but thought it would probably go down badly. Neither jokes nor high-minded musing seemed likely to work with this woman.

She smiled. I smiled back. No hard feelings. Then Maria went to rejoin her mistress, who by this time had finished with Bill Inman.

There was something wrong here, something I couldn't quite put my finger on. It wasn't just to do with the inevitably subdued atmosphere in the audience chamber and the fact that last time we'd rehearsed the masque a man had died. I looked round the room while the break in the action continued – Ben Jonson was in deep discussion with the musicians – and saw most of those whom Ned Armitage had identified as being in the gallery shortly before Blake's death.

There was Martin Barton, the red-haired satirist and spindle-legged playwright, decked out as Poesy and Drama. He had his arm round the shoulder of the young bricklayer whom I recognized from the Line and Compass tavern.

Verney was his name, wasn't it? I wondered what pretext Barton had used to get his friend past the Somerset House gatekeepers but then reflected that it was open house in this palace. I wondered too at Barton's brazenness. Success with *The Melancholy Man* must have gone to his head, so that he enjoyed flaunting his perilous tastes in the Queen's house, thinking himself invulnerable.

In another part of the chamber there was the dazzling Doña Luisa de Mendoza, dressed in not very much, and the rather less dazzling Lady Fortune, dressed in hopeful green. And there was the dapper Giles Cass, garbed as Suspicion. He carried his elaborate lantern for peering into the corners of men's lives and wrapped himself inside the cloak which was painted over with eyes. Like many non-professional players, Cass probably enjoyed dressing up. This one-time supporter of Raleigh was again enjoying a conversation with the two Dons whom John Ratchett had identified from my description. One was a Count, I remembered, and the other a lawyer, the one with a sallow face and hawk-like eyes. Of all the people in the room, it was perhaps Cass of whom I was – not inappropriately – most suspicious.

As I was looking about someone grabbed my arm. I turned round to stare into the glazed eyes of Jonathan Snell the younger.

"Master Revill, Nick, what have you got to say? Have you found the ring that belonged to your father yet?"

No, only a handkerchief, I said, taking out this feminine item and showing it to Snell. Did he know who it belonged to? Snell shook his head. As for the ring, I went on, perhaps it hadn't been mislaid here in the audience chamber after all. Then I started on a lengthy explanation of how, after a visit to their workshop in Three Cranes Lane and through the good offices and memory of Ned Armitage, the names of those who were present in the gallery shortly before Sir Philip's death had come to light. I was on the verge of saying that, if Jonathan was persisting in his theory that the man had been murdered, then it would be possible to attribute motives to most of them. But Snell waved his arms impatiently.

"I've changed my mind, Nick. I was mistaken. It was definitely an accident."

"But the ropes holding up the chair, you were so certain they'd been tampered with."

"My father is surer-sighted than I am, even with these," said Snell, tapping his glasses. "My father is more experienced than I am. My father is right, usually."

He said this in a curiously defeated way and I did not fully believe him. A trace of this must have shown in my face. He was about to say something else when a long-haired, stubbly individual in artisan's clothing tugged him by the sleeve.

"Yer father wants yer."

Jonathan looked slightly alarmed.

"All right, Turner. Tell him I'm coming."

"Wants yer now."

As this hairy individual – whom I presumed to be another member of the workshop gang, Thomas Turner – almost dragged the son off, my feeling of unease deepened. Whereas before I'd been nearly ready to be convinced that Sir Philip Blake's death was indeed an accident, now it appeared to me to be a likely case of murder again. Jonathan's vehement denial somehow suggested the opposite of what he intended.

The rest of the practice passed off uneventfully. Ben Jonson descended in the person of Truth and gave his seal to the perpetual amity which would henceforth exist between England and Spain. He looked comfortable in the flying chair, and you would never have thought from his expression that a man had fallen to his death at this very spot less than forty-eight hours ago. Queen Anne was naturally missing from the rehearsal but otherwise everybody was there, and remembered their lines and moves even if they went through them somewhat mechanically.

The most unsettling aspect of the day so far was what I discovered when I went to the antechamber which had been set aside as a tiring-house. I took off my rustic cloak of Ignorance and put on my day clothes. As I was doing so, I discovered a note stuffed into the pocket of my doublet.

I've grown wary of notes left for me to find. It's happened to me before. They are always tantalizing and generally an invitation to walk into trouble. So was this one, most likely, an invitation to trouble. But it was signed, or at least initialled, by someone I knew.

J.S. Jonathan Snell.

It said: *I cannot say more now. Come to the Three Cranes yard at nine. J.S.*

Would you walk into trouble, if invited? Or would you crumple up the note and throw it to the corner of the room and do your best to forget you'd ever found it?

So how was it that for the second time on an August evening I found myself making my way towards Three Cranes Lane shortly before nine o'clock? Stupidity, perhaps? Foolhardiness? The need to get to the bottom of this strange business?

The second time was very much like the first time. The sky was clear and high and showing more than the first touches of darkness. The tavern with the sign depicting the three long-necked birds stood at the corner of the lane. It was quiet as the grave. A sharp draught still funnelled off the river. And here I was standing at the gate of the Snells' yard.

As before, it was unlocked. As before, the contents of the yard were neatly arranged. Piles of timber, the shrouded windlass, the two carts sitting side by side. I walked up the yard and pulled open one of the double doors. Everything about the ground-floor space looked and smelled the same. Everything except for a red chest or trunk placed slightly to one side of the entrance. I recognized it as the item of stage furniture which Ned Armitage had been painting on my first visit to the Snells'. It was intended for Worcester's Men, he'd said. They were playing at the old Curtain playhouse in Shoreditch. The purpose of the trunk, I recalled, was for a player to hide himself inside. It had probably been painted red so as to draw the eyes of the audience. Red for danger and display.

It was growing dark in the workshop. I called out, not expecting a response, and none came. The place felt un-occupied. I reached out a careful hand towards the trunk, as if the paint might still be wet. It was dry. There was a handle on the lid. The trunk was surely empty, so why did I need to open it? But I did need to open it. I pulled at the handle and levered up the lid. Peered into the interior. Shadows suddenly seemed to swoop down from the gallery above. There was a buzzing in my ears.

Curled up inside the trunk was a body. It was on its side, with its knees drawn up towards the chin and its arms wrapped round the shins, as if clasping itself to itself for a final comfort.

I reeled back. The trunk squatted there in the growing darkness, its lid gaping like a monstrous mouth. I had a choice. I could have walked – or rather run – away from the workshop. Could have pretended that I'd never visited this place. Or I could report the discovery to the headborough and let the authorities take charge. There was no doubt about which would be the responsible course of action.

I was for running away, though.

But first I had to make sure of something.

This was the second time, after all, that I'd encountered a corpse in the Snells' workshop.

I moved towards the trunk once more and nerved myself to make a proper inspection of its contents. It was hard to see much. The head of the body was shrouded in darkness in a corner of the chest. I bent forward and prodded at the curled shape. It was surprisingly springy. The position of the body, with its arms locked round its legs and its head twisted into a corner, would have been impossible for a living person to maintain for long. But this wasn't a living person. It wasn't a dead person either.

The body in the trunk was that figure – half scarecrow, half mannequin – which I had first glimpsed over by the wall of the workshop. A glance showed that it no longer sat on the pile of tarpaulins. Instead someone had placed it in the trunk. The Snells must use it to experiment with the various devices and mechanisms constructed in their workshop. In fact it could take the place of a person in most situations. If you wanted to test the dimensions of a trunk you would fold up your mannequin and stuff him inside it. Unlike a player, he couldn't complain or answer back or demand a pay rise. You could even leave him shut up overnight and he would not reproach you for it in the morning.

I'd been deceived not only by the fading light but by the fact that, when I'd first glimpsed the mannequin against the wall, he wasn't wearing clothes. He was bare, made of coarse linen on the outside and most likely stuffed with rags or horsehair on the inside, probably with internal weights of wood or metal to give him the necessary heft. He lacked the features for a face. Now I could see that he had been dressed in a top and leggings even though the detail of them was invisible to me.

"What have you got to say for yourself, old man?" I said to him. "You gave me quite a fright, thank you."

Then I laughed slightly and coughed as if to cover up my words, and moved away. In truth, I think I was a little frightened that the figure nestling inside the trunk was going to unbend itself and sit up.

I was standing in the centre of the ground floor underneath the well which extended to the roof. I wondered where young Jonathan Snell was. It must have gone nine o'clock by now. As if in answer, a bell rang out from a nearby church to signal that it had only just reached nine. Odd, that much more than a handful of minutes seemed to have passed since I'd entered the workshop. I would give Snell a few moments more to show himself.

Instinct told me to leave now, though. No one was here, no one was going to come here. It was eerie, this darkening work-space. To my right were the steps leading to the upper floor and next to them the steep wooden slide. Ropes and cables dangled overhead.

Instinct told me to leave but I ignored it. I moved forward and stumbled against something. I looked down. At first I took what I saw for a further trick of the eyes or the product of an overworked brain. For there was another figure down here, a different one. It was lying on its back at the foot of the slide. Not a real body, surely. I bent down to examine it. In the first case, what I had taken for a corpse inside the trunk turned out to be false. Couldn't this figure too be an artefact?

But it was real. The dead man's outflung hand was still warm and waxy to the touch. You cannot simulate that. I did not want to feel any further although I held my own hand in the region of his face to detect any wisp of breath. Nothing. There was just enough light remaining to pick out the red doublet. The outline of a solid, plump shape was discernible in the gloom. His head was twisted to one side as if he couldn't bear to look at what had been done to him. This was John Ratchett.

I climbed the stairs until I reached the gallery. The trapdoor which gave access to the slide was hanging open and I skirted it warily. It was larger and more sophisticated than the trap-door in the Globe stage (which you simply pulled up and down by hand). As far as I could see this one was opened by tugging on an upright metal lever set to one side. Doing this must release a catch. In the old days when barrels had been stored on the upper floor they would have been shifted to this point and then rolled down the slide. Now it had happened to a man. If you were standing, unawares, on the trapdoor and someone pulled the lever to release the catch . . . Was that what had happened? It must have been. Ratchett was not long dead but when he'd been in the workshop the light would still have been good. He could hardly have tumbled through the open trap accidentally. I visualized an anonymous hand tugging on the lever and Ratchett dropping through the hole, his head and limbs striking the slide in a tangle, his body hitting the ground with fatal force as Sir Philip Blake's had done.

And then the last light from outside disappeared and I was left by myself in the dark. I groped my way back downstairs. Quiet as a ghost, I skirted the body, retraced my steps out of the workshop and through the yard where I stumbled against an outcrop of cut timber. And so once more back into Three Cranes Lane. I shut the gate quietly behind me.

My way home – that is, back to my lodgings with Mrs Buckle in Thames Street – lay to my right. Instead I turned left down towards the river.

It was a warm night. A few dusty stars were starting to appear. I wanted something clean and fresh, or as clean and fresh as the summer air from the river could provide.

I sat down on the wharf, looking at the fireflies that were watermen. For a long time I gazed at the movement of the lights on the water, my mind a blank. The movement of the boats, which during the daytime appears random, is transformed after nightfall to a kind of dance. This dance was comforting to me at the moment. Over my right shoulder crouched the three cranes which gave this spot its name, together with the stone house known as the Vintry.

It is not always wise to linger about the banks of the Thames after nightfall – and indeed I had recently been attacked on the opposite bank (and been 'rescued' by the late John Ratchett in an incident which I still did not completely understand). But this was the north side of the Thames. It should be less dangerous. In any case, after discovering a body which I had initially taken for real and then another body which I'd at first hoped was false, I felt careless of consequences. If someone wanted to sneak up on me and deprive me of the meagre contents of my purse, then let them do it. My predicament would not be significantly worsened.

But when the cooler air from the river started to clear my head, I understood that I was not thinking straight. Far from getting worse, my predicament was, in one aspect at least, getting better.

John Ratchett was dead. There was no doubt about it. The man who had been in the pay of the French ambassador was dead. The man who had paid me with French gold was dead. The man who had tricked me into supplying him with information was dead.

And so Nicholas Revill was freed of an obligation, wasn't he?

Here my instinctive good sense in slipping away from the scene of the crime like a guilty man became apparent. It was because I might well have been that guilty man in the eyes of the world. No doubt there were plenty of people who'd have an interest in seeing John Ratchett dead or at least out of the way. If he toiled in the twilight world of spies and intelligencers then he must have many enemies. I was one of them. It couldn't be denied that Ratchett's death was convenient for me. I could no longer be 'persuaded' or threatened by him to spy on activities connected with Ben Jonson's masque.

It was possible that he had lied about being in the pay of the ambassador La Boderie, just as he'd allowed me to believe that he was employed by the Privy Council. Maybe he'd worked only for himself. But he was still a dangerous man and – although I owed him a small debt for having come to my aid on the Southwark side of the water – I couldn't be too sorry that he was gone. However, if anyone was searching for a person with a likely motive for wanting Ratchett dead and gone, then I possessed one of the likeliest. So, it was sensible to have left the Snells' workshop without alerting anyone to Ratchett's death.

There were several mysteries here. What had the man with the red doublet been doing in Three Cranes Lane? Sniffing around, presumably, smelling about in corners. Good dog, good intelligencer. Had he been summoned to a meeting in the workshop like me, or had he gone there of his own accord? The biggest question, of course, concerned the identity of the individual who had pulled the lever while Ratchett was standing on the trapdoor. Individual? Perhaps there had been more than one of them.

I got up from where I'd been sitting at the edge of Three Cranes wharf and paced around in the mild August night. From the river came the occasional splashing of oars, the subdued cries of the watermen. Sound travels better at night, especially across water, but the watermen are also less clamorous. I paced around the wharf and thought.

There was an improvised quality to this killing, it seemed to me. Whoever had committed the crime had employed the nearest means to hand, the most convenient method. A trapdoor, a lever. That argued against planning and premeditation. It suggested that Ratchett had turned up at the workshop, sniffing around. That he'd been discovered and got rid of on the spur of the moment. But why had the body been left lying at the foot of the slide? He was not long dead. I couldn't understand why whoever had done it had not also disposed of Ratchett's remains.

The fact that the murder had occurred at the Snells' pointed the finger at someone who worked there. The familiarity with the surroundings, the improvised use of the trapdoor. Unless of course Ratchett's body had been deliberately left in the Snells' so as to throw suspicion on them. But that, in turn, argued premeditation, which I had more or less ruled out.

The only individuals I was acquainted with were the father and son who had charge of the business, and Ned Armitage. Oh, and there was also that lank-haired fellow Tom Turner. There were others employed in the workshop as well, but I did not know their names or their faces.

I instinctively rejected the idea that Jonathan Snell the younger might be a murderer. He had an open, ingenuous quality. He had plainly wanted to tell me something during the practice in the Somerset House audience chamber and, frustrated in this, left the note in my pocket arranging a meeting in the Three Cranes workshop. It wasn't likely he

would have done that if he was planning to carry out a murder
– unless (a little voice whispered) he intended to dispose of
me as well. But I could not square the image of the friendly,
bespectacled young man with that of a cunning killer. And,
if he was not what he seemed but a cunning killer after all,
then why hadn't he waited in the workshop for my arrival?

Another possibility occurred as I paced around on the
cobblestones of the wharf in little circles that echoed the
circles of tangled reasoning in my head. This possibility was
that the note hadn't been written by Jonathan Snell at all but
by his father, who shared the same initials, or by someone
else altogether. In that case, the purpose of the note could
only have been to entice me into a trap. But, also in that case,
the same objection applied. Why hadn't the writer of the note
waited around to deal with me as he had already dealt with
John Ratchett?

I was not so sure about father Snell as I was about the son.
Had the older man been implicated in Sir Philip Blake's
death? There was that conversation I had overheard between
him and Lady Blake, there was his insistence that the
husband's death had been an accident. It seemed evident that
the two deaths, that of Blake and Ratchett, must be
connected. The second victim had tricked me into
investigating the death of the first. And there was a queer
similarity between the way both men had died, falling fatally
through space.

All this time I had been absorbed in my speculations as I
walked restlessly about the wharf. Now some sound or sight
brought me back to myself. The watermen's lights, fewer in
number now, were still hovering out on the river. The three
cranes were hunched by the waterside near the solid block
which was the Vintry house. I thought I detected a flickering
motion by the corner of the house. I stood very still and
looked to one side of the place for several minutes, since it's
easier at night to pick up movement on the edge of one's
vision than full-face. Eventually a dog crept out of the

shadows and disappeared on the other side of the lane. If it was more than a year old, the animal was lucky to have escaped the attentions of the catchers, who had been especially active during the plague and its aftermath. There were far fewer dogs about since the authorities had ordered their strict control. Dog-catchers had been living in clover recently. So had murderers, it seemed.

The dog's good fortune in having survived made me consider my own. If John Ratchett's murderer had unaccountably left the scene that didn't mean that he might not choose to return. It was a foolish idea to linger scarcely a hundred yards from a murdered man.

Briskly I walked up Three Cranes Lane. As I passed the gate which led into the Snells' yard I didn't even turn my head.

Where should I lose that handkerchief?

I must have been more affected by my discovery than I knew because when I returned to my lodgings in Thames Street it was Mrs Buckle's turn to be concerned.

"Are you all right, Nicholas? You look as though you've seen a . . . "

"No, I haven't seen one of those. It's been a tiring day, though."

All I'd seen was a couple of bodies, one real, one fake. For an instant it crossed my mind to confide in Ursula Buckle. Here at least was someone who could have no connection with the goings-on in Somerset House or Three Cranes Lane. But caution prevailed. If I had found a dead man, a murdered man, then it should be reported to the authorities. Why hadn't I done this? For whatever reason I had not done it, and there was no need to involve anyone else in my actions (or inactions).

Instead I gratefully accepted Mrs Buckle's offer of wine and gingerbread. The runny-nosed serving girl had long since retired for the night as had Elizabeth. We were alone in the kitchen of the house, a single wax candle on the table between us. It was a warm night and I was sweaty after my rapid walk from the river. Mrs Buckle was in her day things. She wore black of course, still in mourning for her husband. But black became her, as it does many widows. There was no lack of black in London during these years. Dog-catchers and tailors and coffin-makers, those that had survived, were all doing nicely.

I was conscious of Mrs Buckle's soft presence across the table.

"I am afraid that Lizzie and I will have to move after all, Nicholas."

"Oh no. Where will you go?"

I almost said, where shall *we* go? But she did not answer the question anyway.

"You know that Hugh's cousin has been demanding more rent. Now I have discovered that Elizabeth has been borrowing money from Mrs Morris next door in order to pay him. She has been paying him direct. I would have been too proud to borrow from Mrs Morris, Lizzie said . . . "

"Would you?" I said.

"I don't know. Yes, probably I would have been. But I cannot allow my daughter to do what I am unwilling to do. So we must move somewhere smaller, out of town perhaps. Cut our coat according to our cloth."

The candle flickered and the light, feeble though it was, seemed to pick out the delicate groove of flesh which ran between Mrs Buckle's nose and upper lip. The widow sounded calm and resolved. I thought of the few pounds which I had received from the late John Ratchett. Some of those pounds had already been spent on the French girl in the Mitre. Shamefully spent, some people would say (but I only thought of this because I was in the presence of the respectable Mrs Buckle). In atonement Mrs Buckle could have the little that remained of the Ratchett money but, at best, it would only delay the inevitable. It sounded as though her late husband's cousin was determined to get her out of the Thames Street house. But what was I supposed to do? I could hardly accompany them if they moved out of town, even if they wished me to. I had to stay within walking distance of the Globe playhouse.

"Do not look so troubled, Nicholas," she said.

It is surprising how much expression you can read by the glow of a single candle on a summer's night.

"If I do it's because I am troubled on your behalf, Mrs Buckle."

"Thank you."

She smiled. For no reason, or as if in mockery of the widow's warm smile and all the life that was in her, the image of John Ratchett flashed across my mind's eye. That unfortunate wretch lying on the ground, his outstretched hand still warm and waxy, his head turned away. I felt sweat break out across my forehead and begin to run down into my eyes. I reached into my pocket for something to wipe it away, thinking to find the handkerchief which I'd attempted to return to Lady Blake or Maria More. The handkerchief wasn't there. I dug deeper into the pocket, felt about in other places. No, it was gone. Well, it hardly mattered. That delicate handkerchief was no one's property, apparently.

"You've lost something, Nicholas?"

"Yes."

"What is it?"

"It's not important."

"I mean, what is the matter? Something is wrong. You don't look well."

I saw a dead man recently, I wanted to say to her. Just as you are accustomed to glimpse a dead man stalking about this house, so I too have seen one this last hour.

But I said nothing. Instead, and hardly aware of what I was doing, I got up and moved around the table. I took Mrs Buckle by the shoulder and bent down and kissed her cheek. She stiffened slightly and I was about to shift away, my own cheek hot and red from a combination of the night, the wine and embarrassment, when she turned her face towards mine and we kissed, kissed properly.

She broke away and again I was prepared to retreat, feeling I had somehow overstepped the mark. But Mrs Buckle was

161

not finished. She half rose from her seat and, awkwardly, we wrapped our arms about each other and kissed once again – this time improperly, you might say. She was warm and soft and her widow's weeds stuck to my clammy shirt while my hands did their best to slide over her back.

After a while we stood unmoving, holding on to each other. The candle was swaying in the draught from our bodies. It gave enough light for our purposes.

"Do you know, Nicholas, it is exactly a year and a day since my husband died?"

"You have never told me the date before, Mrs Buckle."

"I do not want to see him again, not tonight. He appears in my dreams."

"Then you must stay awake."

"He means no harm, you know. He was a good man although he was a stern one."

"I know."

All this time we spoke in whispers.

I raised a hand and, with my forefinger traced out the groove above her lip, feeling I was taking a fearful liberty. The groove was slightly damp. Then I let my hand slip down to her breast. She sighed and fell against me, somehow into me.

"We must find somewhere for you to stay awake," I said.

"There is my chamber."

"Then we should go there."

We separated. I picked up the candle from the table but she gripped my wrist with one hand. She had a surprisingly firm grip. She leaned across me and snuffed the candle-flame with the fingers of the other hand. The air was full of the smell of the smoking wick.

"Darkness is best," she said.

"Yes."

I replaced the candle on the table.

Still holding me by the wrist, she led the way towards the stairs. We were quiet as guilty children. We climbed the stairs, crossed the creaking space in front of her chamber, eased open the door, shut it fast behind us, crossed the boards to her marital bed and fell upon it as thankfully as sailors making a landfall.

I left Mrs Buckle's bed almost as soon as it began to grow light. She was at least half asleep, but I think she was conscious of my departure and made no move to stop me. I gathered up my tumbled clothing and inched open the door. I climbed the steeper stairs to my own bedroom and dropped on to the narrow bed. I must have fallen asleep – properly asleep for the first time that night – for the next thing I knew the sun was well up in the sky and the sound of cartwheels and plodding hooves was rising from Thames Street, together with the cries and whistles of day.

I lay there for a while, reflecting on the events of the prevous evening and night. While I did so I began to regret that I had not stayed snug next to Mrs Buckle in her bed, or that she was not squeezed up beside me in the rather more cramped conditions of my own bed. Yes, I could do with her now. But something prevented me from getting up and going in search of the widow. For one thing, I knew that she normally rose early. For another, the other two occupants of the house – Elizabeth and the clumsy, runny-nosed serving girl (whose name, incongruously, was Grace) – were also likely to be up and about. I did not imagine that Mrs Buckle would want either of them to know what business the landlady and her tenant were engaged in. I wasn't sure I wanted them to know, either. *Darkness is best*, she'd said, blowing out the candle before we crept upstairs like mice, like bad children. Maybe she was shielding her own blushes and mine, but she was also safeguarding us from discovery. I wondered what I was going to say to her this fine morning. I wondered what she was going to say to me. Oddly, these speculations were a cause of faint apprehension.

Odd too that I still thought of her as 'Mrs Buckle', even more after the event than before. To address her as 'Ursula' seemed an almost greater intimacy than any she had so far granted, although she had unthinkingly called me 'Nicholas' and from time to time during the course of last night 'Oh Nicholas'.

My mind drifted along on these generally pleasant currents until it was suddenly snagged by the image of John Ratchett, the spy, the intelligencer. The body on its back, that warm hand as if there was still life in it. From there I moved on to the image of Sir Philip Blake and the surprise on his face just before he fell out of his flying chair. For sure, these two deaths were connected. One was murder intended to look like an accident, while the other was murder plain and simple.

I may have fallen asleep again for by the time I came to from a confused mixture of dreamlike sights and sounds – which included three wharf cranes crouching by the water, a wandering dog and a body curled up in a red chest – the sun had risen a couple more notches in the sky.

Now I did get up from my comfortable little bed. I put on my clothes. As I was doing so, I remembered the handkerchief which I had been searching for so as to wipe my sweaty forehead the previous evening. The one with the delicate cutwork and the embroidered dots which Lady Blake had mistaken for drops of blood. Well, since it had belonged neither to her nor to Mistress More, what did it matter if it was lost?

But it did matter. And the realization that it did hit hard. For I must have mislaid the handkerchief at some point between leaving Somerset House and returning to Mrs Buckle's. The most probable spot was in the Three Cranes workshop where I had stumbled over corpses both real and sham. Even then the dropping of the handkerchief wouldn't have mattered much, since it had originally been given to me by Ned Armitage in that very workshop – or rather, I had taken it from him under the pretence of knowing who it belonged to.

The problem was that at least three people had been shown the handkerchief yesterday during the rehearsal for the *Masque of Peace*. They were Lady Blake, Maria More and

Jonathan Snell the younger. They knew it was in my possession. It was unlikely that the first two would go on a visit to the Three Cranes yard but it was Snell's place of work. Most likely the son was already there on this fine August morning. If he came across the spotted handkerchief then he would know that I too had visited the yard last night. And if – no, not if, but *when* – that was combined with the discovery of a dead body, suspicion would inevitably point its scabby finger in my direction. True, Snell himself had called me to a secret meeting last night but then he had failed to turn up. He must have assumed that I too would not appear or would not even read the note, perhaps. Nobody ought to know of my presence in the yard. Until that nobody picked up a carelessly dropped handkerchief.

Scarcely bothering to finish dressing, I shot off down the stairs and out of the house. On the way, I encountered my lover of last night.

"Why, Nicholas – " she began.

"Oh, there is no time, Mrs Buckle. Later."

Was I deceived but did I, even in my rush, detect a slight expression of relief on Mrs Buckle's features?

Once more I walked towards Three Cranes Lane. Thames Street was crowded and I had to thread my way between carts and horses and traders and shoppers, meandering in the sun. By the time I was nearing the corner of the lane I had calmed down slightly. Wasn't it just as likely that the handkerchief had been lost somewhere else? And, even if I had dropped it in the yard or in the workshop, then that did not necessarily connect me to the death of John Ratchett. His body must have been discovered by now. It would be safer to let others handle this dangerous moment.

Turn back, Revill. Don't poke your hand into a hornets' nest. If you aren't already under suspicion, then appearing at the very instant when a body is being picked up from the ground will certainly bring you to notice. I didn't even have an excuse for being at the yard.

Turn back. Return to Thames Street and see what mood Mrs Buckle is in. Perhaps we could . . .

Too late. For the younger Snell, coming from the opposite direction, rounded the corner of Three Cranes Lane at the same moment that I did. We almost collided. I'm not sure he would have recognized me if we hadn't encountered each other so close. His spectacles glittered in the morning light.

"Why, Nick, what are you doing down here?"

What was I doing? Looking for the spotted handkerchief? No, I couldn't mention that without the whole business coming out. The missing ring? No, that was a stale story. These ideas flashed through my head inside a second. I was groping about for a pretext – out for a morning stroll? going to hail a ferry from the wharf steps? – when I observed a change come over Snell's face. He looked confused. Abruptly, he clapped a hand to his mouth.

"My God, you have come to meet me."

Now it was my turn to be confused.

"Meet you, Jonathan?"

"I left a note stuffed in your doublet pocket telling you to meet me at Three Cranes . . . "

"You did?"

Ignorance seemed the best policy.

" . . . at nine in the morning."

At that instant, on cue, a nearby bell rang out the time. It was indeed nine o'clock. The chimes were muffled by the sounds of day but it was the same bell from the same church which I'd heard just twelve hours ago, shortly before I discovered the body of John Ratchett lying on the workshop floor. A look of alarm appeared on Jonathan's face.

"My God, you did not come at nine last night, did you?"

"No," I said. "Why? Should I have done?"

"No, you shouldn't. Shouldn't have come at any time. I am sorry for misleading you, Nick."

"What did you want to say?" I asked Jonathan Snell, thinking that if he was prepared to adopt this apologetic tone as well as owning up to the note then he could not have had a hand in the murder of Ratchett.

"Nothing, it was all a mistake. I never had anything to say. I shouldn't have left the note. And since, from your reaction just now, you never found the note, it doesn't matter. You never found the note?"

"I never found the note," I repeated after him.

If I was lying, which I was, then I was pretty certain that he was lying too. He did have something to say. But he was not going to say it now.

All this time we had been pacing together down Three Cranes Lane. No need to ask what Jonathan Snell was doing. He was on his way to work. And now we had reached the gate in the wall which led to the Snells' yard.

My heart was beating fast. I should walk off now towards the wharf, hail a ferry, be rowed across the water, get out on the opposite bank and go to my own place of work. Simple, no? There was a dead man lying in the workshop. They must have found him by now, surely. Whether they had or not, it was none of my business. Unless they'd also discovered a spotted handkerchief discarded near the body. Then it would be my business.

I hovered undecided by the gate. Jonathan Snell looked preoccupied. He had not repeated his question about what I was doing in Three Cranes Lane, but asked a different one instead.

"You've been here before?"

"What? Oh, yes. I was here a couple of days ago. I spoke to your man Ned Armitage."

"A good workman, Ned."

"Yes."

Jonathan had his hand on the latch of the gate. Perhaps he was the first to arrive at the yard this morning. But no, he wasn't, because I could hear the sounds of sawing and someone whistling inside. I waited for cries of alarm to come flying over the wall. Yells for "Help!", shouts of "Murder!" None came. Was it possible that no one had yet noticed Ratchett's corpse, lying sprawled and broken at the foot of the slide?

Snell lifted the latch and pushed the door open. Over his shoulder I saw the well-ordered yard and a couple of men at work inside. Calmly at work.

Ask to accompany him, or walk on?

Curiosity was drawing me in. There was also the matter of the handkerchief. But fear whispered that I should get away now, before the cries of alarm rang out.

"Can I come in?" I said.

This was the test. If Snell was involved in anything criminal, then he must surely refuse me. If he didn't, then it was proof of his innocence. Half a proof, anyway.

"Why do you want to come in?" he said.

"I – I think I may have mislaid something here – when I came to see Ned Armitage."

"Not your father's ring again?"

Was it my imagination, or was there a mocking glint to his bespectacled eyes? After his earlier moment of alarm, he was back in control.

"That was elsewhere," I said, pulling a face. "I am careless with my belongings, I regret to say, and can ill afford to be."

Jonathan Snell paused, his body blocking the entrance to the yard. His face was pale and, with his expression creased against the sunlight, he looked more like his father. Eventually he shrugged.

"If you like."

He didn't ask me what I was searching for. Each of us was holding out against the other.

Snell walked over to one of the workmen, who was loading up a cart with short lengths of timber. A horse was tethered nearby. I recognized the workman as Tom Turner, the lank-haired fellow. He was whistling while he worked, apparently a happy man. He stopped as Snell approached him and the two fell into conversation. Snell seemed to have lost interest in me and the reason why I wanted to look inside his father's workshop. That was fine with me.

I wandered up the sloping ground and towards the double doors which stood in the middle of the frontage. This time the doors were flung wide open. I stopped a few yards off. My visits to the Snells' yard were becoming a repeated experience, like a play practice. On previous visits I had found bodies indoors, both real and sham bodies. The sunlight was too strong for me to see the interior clearly from this distance.

I glanced over my shoulder. Jonathan Snell was still talking to Turner. A second workman was bending over a saw-horse. The air was full of the scent of fresh-cut wood. I glanced down, then looked more closely at the ground, which was a compound of earth and sawdust and wood shavings and fragments of nutshell. In among the darker shades there was something light. Well, I had found one thing I had come for. The cutwork handkerchief lay crumpled near a pile of timber. I half remembered stumbling and falling in the yard the night before. It must have dropped out of my pocket then. Quickly I stooped and retrieved the handkerchief, which had by now assumed a quite mysterious importance in my mind.

Then I moved towards the entrance to the workshop. In front of me was the familiar array of items, including the red trunk. The lid of the trunk was wide open. (Had I shut it the previous night after finding the curled-up figure? I couldn't remember.) I was pleased to see the mannequin figure, still in his clothes, sitting once more on top of the pile of tarpaulins. I almost waved to him. He was back where he should be. I had already glanced towards the area at the bottom of the stairs and the slide. The floor was empty. There was no body. Ratchett had gone.

Your suspicion is not without wit

With a final burst of trumpets, Truth came down to earth with hardly a bump. Considering his bulk, Truth dismounted gracefully enough from his flying throne and looked around at those awaiting his judgement. Truth had a question to answer. Hope and Resolution had summoned from on high this mighty figure, who knows all things in the past, present and future. Hope and Resolution accordingly stood in postures of expectation while the less reputable of us – such as Suspicion, Ignorance, Rumour and the rest – cowered at the corners of the stage, shielding our faces from the glare of Truth. Don't ask me how they'd done it, but the Snells had contrived an effect which seemed to turn the area where Truth (or rather Ben Jonson) was standing into a blaze of light. From out of this blaze loomed Jonson's red visage, like the sun in winter.

The question which Truth had to answer was whether the new-found peace and concord between England and Spain would endure down the ages. Now, common opinion on the street might have been that the new-found peace would be lucky to endure until Christmas. But this was the *Masque of Peace*. So the answer to the question, 'Will this last?' was, yes, it would last. It had to be the answer. It was written. Ben Jonson himself had written it, and he was about to deliver his own lines. The necessity for eternal peace was also written down in a treaty which would be sworn to and signed the next day in the chapel at Whitehall.

Truth opened his mouth:

O speak aloud, you denizens of earth.
Give reason why you call across the firth
To those far distant, and unequall'd skies,
That squared circle of celestial bodies,
And bring down from heaven's synod
This Truth who sometime is a god,

intoned Jonson.

There's a funny thing about masques. The characters in them are always announcing who they are, although their costumes usually signal this clearly enough. And they are always calling on others to explain why they (the others, that is) have done something, even though it's bloody obvious most of the time.

We'd reached the closing stages of Ben's celebratory piece. The audience chamber of Somerset House was packed with the great and the greater. The greatest of all – King James himself (the first of that name to rule England but the sixth of Scotland) – was absent, but we had his consort Queen Anne on stage beside us, playing the English Peace. I don't think anyone had really believed the King would turn up. He did not have his predecessor Elizabeth's appetite for plays. In fact there was some question as to whether he really liked them. We'd put on WS's *As You Like It* for him at Wilton House during the plague time and Abel Glaze swore that he'd caught the royal gob in mid-yawn during the performance and had overheard him saying at the end in his Scots lilt, "Oh weel, oh weel" like a man emerging from a tedious sermon.

But if we didn't enjoy the King's company we had his Queen's. I could see her clearly at this moment, little more than a dozen feet away. Fortunately I'd been permitted to abandon the gauzy mask which was part of my Ignorance outfit. Jonson said I looked as though I was taking part in a children's game of blindman's-buff. Instead of wearing the mask he told me merely to look stupid and mulish, and (to his credit) made no comment about the lack of acting skills which would be required. So I was able to see the Queen. I'd seen her before of course, since she'd attended a couple of our performances as King's Men but she had been a spectator rather than a participant.

What can I say about Anne, as witnessed in action and from close quarters? She could not have held a candle to our late Queen, nor do I think she would have attempted to. She was a bony, beaky-nosed creature with a sallow face, not obviously attractive. Inevitably, I thought of the rumours which were swirling around her and the King. About how she was no longer welcome in his bed but kept up her separate establishment here in Somerset House. About how the King's affections were currently directed towards the Pembroke brothers, whose family owned Wilton House, while his wife consoled herself with her three children and her devotion to music and dance.

In Ben Jonson's piece she moved elegantly and spoke her few lines clearly with only the trace of an accent. Maybe it's not my place to compliment a queen, but I'd say that her performance was especially creditable since she had not attended a single rehearsal. I wondered whether she had gone through her words and moves in private with her ladies-in-waiting. But, take away her titles and the deference which surrounded her, and there was nothing very regal about Anne of Denmark. I'd met our Elizabeth once, you see, and stammered my way through our conversation, scarcely daring to look her in the face. But in my humble view the Virgin Queen laid down a standard for royalty which will not easily be matched, let alone outdone.

The audience for the *Masque of Peace* was more attentive than I'd expected. For one thing they didn't have the King to distract them. If James had been present then most eyes would have been on him, most of the time. He was known to dislike this sort of attention, and maybe that was one of the reasons why he'd decided to stay away. But for a noble audience there were other diversions apart from watching the monarch or the play, diversions usually to do with the after-effects of food and drink. I'd made knowing comments to WS about them being pissed or asleep but there was little sign of that. Instead there was polite applause for the music, only a little chattering while we were declaiming our lines (though none at all while the Queen spoke hers), and even the occasional gasp at the staging.

The arrival of the Spanish Peace in particular provoked gasps of delight from the women – and groans of desire from the men – and much clapping. This was mostly to do with the beauty of Doña Luisa de Mendoza, and her scanty costume. I'm afraid Anne couldn't compete in this area, even though she too was showing a fair bit of bosom. The shell-clad William Inman ushered *La Paz* across the Ocean, delivering lines about how his waves curtseyed and his billows bowed down low at the sight of this beautiful voyager. Meantime, in the background, Sir Fabian Scaridge – one-time barber, now full-time knight – puffed and panted as a Favouring Wind.

When Truth came down to earth there was, apart from the tootling trumpets, absolute silence in the audience chamber. This was not just because the spectacle of Ben Jonson descending was impressive enough – and he did look more god-like than the unfortunate Sir Philip – but because everybody must have been aware that a man had fallen to his death at this very point in the action a few days earlier. But this version of Truth, decked out in the very robe that Sir Philip had worn during his fatal plunge, landed safely and began to speak. And went on speaking.

And still Jonson was rambling on:
For Truth will shortly put men's foes to flight
And bestow on all an universal light
with plenty more in the same vein. I was sure he'd added a

few extra lines once he'd taken over Blake's part. Even more than most actors, Jonson liked being centre stage. I caught the eye of Giles Cass who, in the role of Suspicion, was half kneeling on the opposite side, right hand held up to shield himself from Truth's dazzling glare. Like the other negative qualities, Suspicion would shortly be banished from the stage. Cass winked at me. I felt uncomfortable. It suggested that we were somehow in collusion.

Cass had spoken to me before the performance while we were backstage, in among the scaffolding that supported the backdrop and curtains and the whole apparatus of the gallery. I was peering between a gap in the curtains, watching the audience take their seats. I noticed that the two groups, English and Spanish, were tending to sit in different parts of the hall. They were easily distinguished anyway. The Spanish were even more elaborately dressed than the members of the English court. The women were darker and more attractive. The men looked prouder than their English counterparts. Their ruffs were wider – when some of them looked down, their bodies would surely have been hidden from their eyes – and their hats higher. Two tides of language met from opposing sides of the audience chamber. Whether they mingled it was hard to say. Perhaps they mingled at the edges.

I sensed someone standing by my shoulder and, turning, was surprised to see Giles Cass. He was costumed as Suspicion, wearing the cloak covered with its painted eyes and carrying his elaborate lantern. He placed the lantern on the floor and peeked through the gap in the curtain. He seemed as interested in the gathering audience as a true player would have been.

"All eyes, Master Cass?" I said.

"That is Charles Blount, Earl of Devonshire," he said, putting his mouth to my ear and extending a finger through the gap. He was indicating a chubby-faced, clean-shaven individual who was seating himself near the front. "He has been talking to the Spaniards about the treaty. Did you know that he is living in open adultery with my Lady Penelope Rich?"

"And there is Charles Howard," I said, determined not to be outdone in the courtier-spotting stakes. Howard was the Earl of Nottingham, the Lord High Admiral, the white-bearded but vigorous gentleman whose example had prompted Ben Jonson to go in search of an afternoon brothel.

"Dear old Charles Howard!" said Cass, standing back and dabbing at his lips. "His new bride was heard singing on their wedding night but nobody knew whether it was to keep the old man awake or to get him to go to sleep."

"Perhaps it was from joy," I said.

"And, look, there is our great Secretary."

Sir Robert Cecil was being carried in a chair to the principal place at the front of the audience, the one that the King would have occupied had he been present. It was a mark of Cecil's standing – although 'standing' was not the appropriate word for him – that he should take this central position. The little hunchbacked figure was helped from his chair and fussed over by several attendants while he took his seat. I felt uneasy at seeing Cecil, even though I was mostly concealed behind the thick curtains.

"You know the King calls him his beagle, he is so service-able," whispered Cass in my ear. I was almost disappointed that Cass could only refer to Cecil's new nickname and had nothing to say about the great man's bedchamber habits, since this seemed to be what interested him.

"No, I didn't know he was the King's beagle," I said. "How should I know that? Look, I am all Ignorance."

I tried to make light of it but grew still more uncomfortable. I did not want to be the recipient even of gossip from Cass. I wonded why he'd fastened on me. His fastidiously wiped lips still carried the scent of liquor. I would have moved away but he put a hand on my shoulder.

"I hear you have been asking questions about the death of Sir Philip Blake," he said.

I went cold.

"I haven't – well, one or two questions maybe. The seniors in my Company were concerned about the effect of – of what happened – on the reputation of the King's Men. One of them asked me whether there was anything strange about it. I meant no harm."

"If you ask me," said Cass, "Sir Philip was lucky."

Curiosity overcome unease for a moment.

"*Lucky*? To have fallen to his death?"

"Our Secretary, Sir Robert Beagle, was pursuing him. He thought that Blake was plotting against the Spanish peace. Now, isn't that ridiculous!"

I shrugged, trying to dislodge the man's hand from my shoulder. I'd rather have been doing anything else at that instant, even flying in a chair twenty feet above the ground.

"I once heard Cecil say," said Cass, "that he would welcome Blake's death. And now he is dead. And so I say it's a good thing – for Sir Philip Blake and for Sir Robert Beagle. A convenient death."

"I know nothing of this," I said.

"Keep it that way," said Giles Cass. "Ignorance is best."

I turned and looked him in the face. The dapper man winked at me.

And now here was Cass, at the end of the *masque* performance, once again winking in my direction. This did not make for a quiet mind. Who was he with? Was he a secret Raleigh supporter, as his Mermaid tavern comments had suggested? Or was he really with Cecil, who was no friend to Raleigh? As to Cass's remarks about Sir Philip Blake and his supposed plotting against Spain, they made little sense either.

At last Ben Jonson reached his peroration as Truth. It was official. Peace between England and Spain was here to stay. It would endure longer than the mountains, it would outlast the oceans, it was a monument to the far-sightedness and magnanimity of the Spanish King Philip and the English King

James. With this dollop of flattery and with an obeisance in the direction of Queen Anne, Truth at last shut his gob.

We concluded with some music and dancing, and then the *Masque of Peace* was finally done, with much clapping and cheering. Straightaway the non-professionals in the cast jumped from the stage and paraded around to receive the congratulations of their friends. All at once there was refreshment everywhere. It seemed to rain wine while delicate sweetmeats were scattered about the room like manna. Lord and Lady Fortune, Sir Fabian Scaridge with his good wife Agnes, Lady Blake and Maria More, Bill Inman and the rest were surrounded with back-slappers and cheek-kissers. Even the Queen's whitened complexion was showing red. Our noble actors glowed with the gratification of a good job well done. And why shouldn't they? There is almost nothing better in this world than being part of a company at the end of a successful performance, quitting the stage in the knowledge that you have pleased others for two hours of our shared earthly existence.

Of course, one advantage for the nobs was that they didn't have to bother about the prompt return of the scrolls to the book-man or of their costumes and little props to the tire-man. In fact, some of them seemed distinctly reluctant to change out of their gear. Most people like dressing up, provided they don't have to do it for a living. We lesser characters, however, must go off to the little antechamber and account to Bartholomew Ridd for the state of our outfits. I was on my way there, in the wake of Abel Glaze and Laurence Savage and the others, when I passed Doña Luisa de Mendoza, *La Paz*. She was being closely attended by the two Spaniards whom Ratchett had identified, the gentlemen with the great ruffs.

As I walked by she looked up and smiled at me. What a pang went through my heart! I had not spoken a word to her during our two or three rehearsals, and now I wondered what response I would have got if I had dared to approach her. Perhaps I should produce the spotted handkerchief, which I still possessed, and ask whether it belonged to her. This delicate item, it is yours, my lady? *Gracias, señor, muchas gracias*.

But these agreeable dreams were broken by Giles Cass, who moved into step beside me. For some reason he was fastening on me like a leech. He was about to open his mouth, probably to pass on another titbit of gossip, when one of the ruffs – the hawk-eyed lawyer, I think – made a complicated bow in our direction. Cass halted and returned the bow. I did the same, happy enough to stay in the neighbourhood of Doña Luisa.

"*Señores, beso los manos,*" said the other grandee, touching his fingertips to his lips to show what he meant.

This led to an even greater outburst of bowing, as if each side was competing with the other in courtesy. I thought I caught Doña Luisa smiling, as though at men's foolishness. When we eventually broke away, Giles Cass whispered in my ear, "Very good but I would wish that they had stooped a little lower and kissed our *anos* rather than our *manos*."

As crude wit went this was satisfactory, but I wondered at a man who was so friendly with the Spaniards in their presence showing them so little respect out of earshot. I changed into my day-gear. I noticed that Cass did not, preferring to continue in his part as Suspicion as long as the party lasted.

The rest of the evening dissolved into a blur of candlelight and wine and music and dancing and the rest. There were three distinct groups in the audience chamber. At the top were the nobles who'd been among the players and the spectators, both English and Spanish. I noticed that the Queen and Cecil slipped away early. They had a country to run, or at least Cecil did. Then came the professional players. And somewhere to one side were the musicians and the mechanicals, that is, Snell's men. Both Jonathans were present too, together with their principal craftsmen Armitage and Turner.

In between the nobles and the mechanicals were figures with a foot in neither camp, such as Giles Cass or Ben Jonson. Or Martin Barton, that scourge of corruption, who was quite happy to load himself down with courtly dainties. I noticed him in conversation with a handsome Spanish youth with finely slashed sleeves to his doublet. Without a language to share between them, they were gesturing a lot. They might not have a common language but they understood each other well enough. And I also noticed how Lady Blake, the recent widow, seemed to be content to drown her sorrows in drinking and dancing. And her husband barely cold in his grave.

If I sound a bit jaded, then it's probably because I did not drink as much as everybody else in the room. My head isn't that hard. Also it was preoccupied with other things. I was bothered by Giles Cass's words. *Keep it that way. Ignorance is best.* If he was referring to the death of Sir Philip Blake, then I was happy to fall into line. I would ask no more questions. The same applied to the shadowy demise of John Ratchett. It was almost as if I had dreamed of his presence in the Snell workshop, lying outstretched on the ground. For sure, Ratchett had gone when I returned the next day. But I knew that he had been there at nine o'clock in the evening just as certainly as that he had disappeared by the same hour in the morning.

Still, what was there to worry about? No one could connect me to this agent of the French ambassador (if that's what he really was). We had met twice in the Pure Waterman tavern in Southwark, a borough where men do not willingly tell tales, and we had endured one conversation in the Strand. It would be very bad luck if anyone knew both of us and remembered seeing us together. Ratchett was no longer around to make me comply with his demands for 'information'. Whoever had disposed of him had also done me a favour. That was how I should look at it.

I was mulling over these things in an obscure corner on the far side of the audience chamber when I became aware of a great stir running through the room, like the breeze through the summer trees. Groups of talkers and drinkers and dancers were swirling tighter and faster, then breaking apart and coming together again, gaining and losing numbers as they went. Abel Glaze weaved towards me, brandishing a glass which probably cost the equivalent of a month's wages and slopping most of its contents on the floor.

"Why so long-faced, Nick? Wassamatter?"

"Am I? Sorry."

"Get pissed like me."

"What's happening?"

"C'm on, less go see."

"Where?"

He said something which sounded like Terence, and with his free hand almost dragged me across the great chamber. After a time it became evident that we were headed not for Terence but for the *terrace*, where a great many other people were also heading. After a little more time, and from snippets of excited talk interrupted by shrieks and giggles, I understood that two individuals – a man and a woman – a noble man and a noble woman – had been caught out on the terrace. Caught at it on the terrace. Caught at *it*. Charles Blount and Lady Penelope Rich, were they? Or the Earl of Rutland and Lady Rochester, were they? No one knew. No one cared. We would soon find out anyway, all of us streaming out through the doors and floor-length windows into the summer's night.

The air was soft and moist, with the promise of rain off-stage. The flagstones underfoot were dry. Overlaid with cloaks and cushions they would provide a soft bed for urgent lovers. Good luck to them, I thought, although being as eager as everyone else to witness this disgraceful scene, this disgraceful and amusing scene, of a couple of bare-arsed nobles. Though presumably by now they'd have had time to pull up their hose and pull down their skirts. Purses and jewels go missing during performances, to say nothing of handkerchiefs and rings. What is reputation by comparison? I even had the time (or maybe just the sobriety) to feel faintly sorry for Ben Jonson since what everyone would remember from this evening would not be the glories of the *Masque of Peace* but the antics of the audience. And what would the Spaniards think of us? In a different way, of course, our reputation as English might even be enhanced. Look, we can be hot-blooded too.

About half of the masque audience was now milling about on the wide terrace of Somerset House. The night view up and down the river felt spacious even if it was mostly invisible. The watermen's fireflies bloomed in the darkness. The crowd was starting to mass down towards one end, where the action apparently was.

Abel pulled me in that direction.

"C'm on."

We found ourselves on the fringes of a group. The terrace of Somerset House had a grand set of stairs in the centre leading down to the river, while more modest sets (to allow for the arrival of players and other riff-raff) had been constructed at either end. The crowd was drawing towards the eastern steps, that is, those closest to London Bridge. A couple of cresset lights were burning in brackets beside the steps.

I'd been wrong when I thought that what the audience would remember from this evening was not Ben's masque but the couple caught *in flagrante*. Whoever the naughty couple were, they were no longer of much interest. Death trumps sex, just about. What the audience would remember was the body which at this very moment was being borne up the eastern stairs by a group of retainers and then laid carefully on the flagstones at the top. Instinctively, the crowd drew back.

Abel's hand fell away from my sleeve. The cheerful shrieks and giggles faded out. I barged my way near to the front. Water was flowing in streams from the body and, more particularly, from his clothes. They were heavy garments and had soaked up plenty of water. I guessed the body had been spotted just before the weight of his garments dragged him out and down for good. Otherwise he might have sunk to the bottom before he reached the Bridge. If the current had taken him as far as that, then most likely his corpse would have been battered beyond recognition by the mighty piers.

But he was recognizable now. Not his face, which was angled away from me and half in shadow, but his weighty cloak. The cloak was made of some dark fabric, darkened further by the water, and it was covered with painted eyes. Well, I thought, Giles Cass has gossiped his last.

The set phrase of peace

T he next day, which was the 19th of August in the year of 1604, we were present at a great and historic event. It was the signing of the treaty between Spain and England in the King's palace at Whitehall.

Of course the King's Men were not significant players in all of this but merely there to swell the crowd. As Grooms of the Outer Chamber, we had to dress up in our doublet-and-breeches livery, made out of those four and a half yards of red cloth, and stand tucked away at the side looking suitably impassive while the King and his entourage processed into the Chapel Royal. The Chapel was already crowded with Grooms more senior than us, individuals such as Grooms of the Privy Chamber or Grooms of the Wardrobe. There were also courtiers, diplomats and the rest in attendance.

We waited a long time for the King to appear but no one seemed to mind too much. You can't mind it when a king is late. Certainly I didn't. It gave me the chance to think. Gazing around, I saw our seniors. As you can when you've spent a lot of time in the company of the same group of people, I was able to recognize them all by the backs of their heads, by the corner of their shoulders, by their dress, their postures. There was John Heminge, there were the Burbage brothers, Richard and Cuthbert, and Augustine Phillips. Will Shakespeare was present of course, as well as Thomas Pope, who had lately quit the King's Men because of sickness but who had been determined to attend this ceremony in the Whitehall Chapel. I noticed my friends Laurence Savage and Abel Glaze wearing the same impassive, mask-like expression which was probably fastened to my own face.

While we were waiting I cast my mind back over the events of the previous night at Somerset House. The successful performance of Ben Jonson's *Masque of Peace*, the high spirits which followed it, the rumour about the noble couple who were *at it* on the terrace (I never did discover who they were, or even whether they existed in the first place). Then, as a final act in this drama, the recovery of Giles Cass's body from the river, its slow dripping progress up the steps, the way it had been deposited, almost delicately, on the terrace flagstones, the water that pooled about the body where it lay.

I must have been one of the last people to speak to Giles Cass, or rather to hear him speak. He had made that rude crack about the Spaniards kissing our *anos* instead of our *manos*, and before that he'd intimated that Sir Philip Blake was lucky to have perished when he did. The Spanish joke wasn't to be taken seriously unlike the remark about Blake's lucky death, I assumed. And then only a couple of hours later Cass had turned up dead himself.

A coincidence, it seemed. An accident, probably. For it appeared that Cass had slipped and struck his head when he was standing near the bottom of the same set of stairs up which his body had been carried. There was blood on the edge of a stair just above the high-water mark. Two or three individuals thought they'd observed him going down the steps about half an hour earlier. This I heard from Ben Jonson, who was among the crowd on the terrace watching the body being retrieved.

There was nothing odd about these last sightings of Cass except for the fact that he was apparently alone on an evening when company was the rule. But then I'd been alone myself, brooding in an obscure corner of the performance room. So Cass must have descended the stairs – to wait for someone down there? to look at the night-view across the river? to hail a ferry? – until he arrived at the position where he lost his footing. It was easy enough to do. The lower stairs, which are regularly covered by the tide, are coated in weed and slime. There is a wooden railing for the benefit of foot-passengers but the steps are wide and anyone standing in the middle of them would have no handhold. Supposing Cass had suddenly turned, his attention caught by a movement on the river. Or that he'd twisted round, hearing a sound behind him. He'd been drinking, like almost everybody else. Distracted, unsteady with drink, his foot slithers on the slime and weed. He falls backward or he falls sideways, he strikes his head on the stone step.

And then – or so I imagined it – Cass had lain there, bleeding and perhaps senseless until the tide rose sufficiently to ease him off his perch and into its watery clasp. Or, in another version, Cass had lost his balance and hit the stone step hard enough to leave traces of his fall but not enough to knock himself out. Then, groggy, unsure of his whereabouts, he had staggered upright and lurched forward into the water. But, however it had happened, the outcome was the same. Giles Cass drowned after striking himself on the head.

I couldn't feel much sorrow at Cass's death but it was still a troubling event which had brought the Somerset House celebrations to a sombre conclusion. As his body had been lifted up from the terrace so that it might be decently stowed indoors, his head fell backwards and his mouth gaped open. River water dribbled from his mouth. I thought of that frequent gesture of his, the way he dabbed at his lips as if some grease were smeared on them. I thought of my last sight of Sir Philip Blake with his gaping mouth, of John Ratchett with his still warm hand. The place on the terrace where Cass had been lying was dark with water but there were yet darker stains in the region of his head.

An accident perhaps – nobody seemed to think any differ-ently – but I went to look for myself. Once the body, still cloaked in its garb of Suspicion, had been carried inside and the crowd had dispersed, I lifted one of the cresset torches from its bracket. I walked down the steps, clutching at the wooden railing and taking particular care when the going became slippery underfoot. In front of me stretched the river. It felt as wide as the ocean. Water slurped at the stairs.

I swept the torch around in the region of my feet. It gave off more smoke than light. Any traces below the waterline would have been washed away, but I was lucky – if finding evidence of a death counts as lucky – for almost immediately I discovered some bloody marks. Standing in the dark, which was made deeper by the torch's moody flare, I envisaged the ways in which Master Cass might have met his end. Diverted by a light out on the river, distracted by a noise over his shoulder. I looked around. I was a little below the topmost step. In other words, out of sight of any people on the terrace unless they came to the very edge of the flight of steps and looked down. No one to see him fall, no one to hear the dull thunk of a head hitting stone, especially not over the sounds of celebration from inside the audience chamber. True, the gossip had it that there'd been those noble individuals out on the terrace – Charles Blount and Lady Rich, or Rutland and Lady Rochester – but, if they were ever there, they'd had their hands full at the time and would not have been aware of a dying man.

There was a different noise coming from the Somerset House audience chamber now. The music had stopped. The party was over. A dead man had brought it to a close. Less harmonious bangs and thuds were audible and for an instant I wondered what was causing them. Then remembered that the Snells and their workmen would most likely be working late into the night to take down the scaffolding and stage.

I lowered the torch once more and inspected the stains at the edge of the step. If there'd been any doubt about what they were, it was dispelled by what I found as I peered closer. Human hair, two or three little hanks of it, was embedded in the dried clots of blood. Cass's hair was dark, about the same shade as mine, but straight and short. Here were hairs that showed up straight and dark in the torch's flare – plain evidence of how and where he'd met his end. There was something forlorn about these little traces of the dead man.

I stood up and returned to the top of the steps, almost losing my footing as I went. I replaced the torch in its iron bracket and went to lean against the stone parapet, facing the river. The stone was warm from the day's sun. As far as I was aware, I was the only person on the river-front terrace.

Three men dead.

Firstly, Sir Philip Blake, courtier. Cause of death: falling from a height during a masque rehearsal. An apparent accident, although a possible murder. Anyway, he was dead and gone, his body carted off to the family's country house in Loamshire or somewhere just as remote and rustic.

Secondly, John Ratchett, agent to the French ambassador, Monsewer La Boderie. Cause of death: also falling from a height, as the result of standing on a trapdoor and having it open under his feet. Not an accident surely, although it might have been a suicide. (This thought had not occurred to me before. Could a person standing on the trapdoor in the workshop reach the lever? Not a plausible way to go, surely. Not an obvious method of self-slaughter.) Anyway, Ratchett was dead and gone like Sir Philip. Certainly gone, for his body had disappeared. I was the only person to have seen it apart from the individual who had engineered his death in the first place and the one – the same one? – who had taken him away from the Snells' workshop.

Thirdly, Giles Cass, go-between, diplomatic smoother. Cause of death: drowning after a blow to the head. An apparent accident.

At this moment I felt something wet and warm slide down my cheek and was surprised because I hadn't known that the death of any single one of these men meant so much to me. Then a second blob tapped me on the forehead and, in an instant, there came the soft drumming of summer rain across the royal terrace. A soothing sound to wash away the bitter remains of the day. The torches started to sizzle and gave off yet more smoke. Then the rain started to come down in earnest. Whatever traces there'd been of Master Cass on the river-stairs – a little of his blood, a few of his hairs – would soon be washed away and he would be no more.

I turned to hurry indoors. One of the ground-level windows giving on to the terrace was still open. In the few seconds between leaving the riverside parapet and entering the audience chamber I was overcome by a strange conviction. Strange, because it arrived from nowhere. And a conviction because I was as sure as anyone could be without any evidence or logic to support the idea (that is, very sure indeed) that the deaths of Blake and Ratchett and Cass were all linked. That each man had been murdered, probably by the same individual or individuals. And lastly that it was the responsibility of Nicholas Revill, who had recently distinguished himself by playing the part of Ignorance, to disentangle the truth from out of this peculiar jumble of events. To pull out all the threads. And it was my responsibility because I was the only person to hold all those threads in my hands. No one – apart from the murderer or murderers – knew as much as I did.

Inside the audience chamber the sounds of enjoyment had given place to the occasional shouts and whistles of labourers as they dismantled the scaffolding and stage. The gallery from which Blake had made his fatal descent was already stripped of its curtains and screens. In one corner of the great room were piled the stage effects: the sun and the clouds, the scalloped waves through which *La Paz* had made her elegant progress. There was sufficient light for the workmen to see what they were doing but none of the concentrated blaze of a performance. Even the central spot where the King would have been enthroned had he attended the masque looked dim and uncared for. There is almost no place on God's earth so forlorn as the playhouse which almost everyone – players and audience – has quit. You wonder whether anyone will ever come back, even while the reasoning part of your head says that the very next day there'll be the usual bustle of lights and laughter, of groans and applause.

There were perhaps a dozen men in the audience chamber. Judging by their livery, some of them were Somerset House attendants working to clear this space so that it might be ready for the Queen once more after the Spaniards' departure (which was imminent). I recognized Ned Armitage and Tom Turner from the Three Cranes yard. Up in the gallery, which looked oddly naked without its curtaining, stood the figure of Jonathan Snell near the unprotected edge. His spectacles glinted. I wondered that he wasn't afraid of walking off the edge, with his poor sight.

I looked around for father Snell and after a moment glimpsed him in what had been the backstage area but was now an open space. He was bending over the windlass, the one that had taken six men to put into position. He must have heard me coming or seen me out of the corner of his eye since he glanced up when I was still yards away. His sight was keener than his son's for he said, "Nicholas Revill, isn't it? What are you doing here? Your fellows have gone home."

"I've been looking at the river."

He did not query this but said, "Now you're here you can lend a hand."

"Willingly."

"Then take that chair and put it with the other stuff over in the corner. I'll get someone to help you."

He pointed at the 'throne' on which the figure of Truth had descended at the conclusion of the *Masque of Peace*. It was still sitting in the centre of the stage at the place where Ben Jonson had landed.

I didn't move. If I was going to say anything it had to be

said now. I put my hand on the older man's arm. He'd been about to summon one of his workmen.

"Wait, Master Snell."

He looked curiously at me. There must have been something in my voice, a tension, a discomfort.

"Yes?"

"I have a question."

The question really was, did I think this individual with his expert hands and ingenious mind was a murderer? No, he was probably not a murderer. But in any case this is not a question you can ask straight out. My tongue turned to stone.

"Master Revill, are you well?" said Snell, his tone somewhere between concern and impatience.

Now I had to speak. So, for want of anything better, I poured out an account of how I'd heard – no, overheard – the conversation between him and Lady Jane during the rehearsal at the Blake mansion. That conversation about *Then this will come down*, and *Oh, it'll come down all right.*

Snell looked baffled. I felt my face turning red.

"You overheard this conversation, Master Revill?"

"Yes. I didn't mean to. I was on the way back from . . . I had been relieving myself."

"Relieving yourself."

I grew redder yet and could think of nothing further to say. Would I had said nothing at all.

"You eavesdropped on us."

"I was behind an arras."

"And why do you think my talk with Lady Jane about *things coming down* and so on, why was this significant?"

When your cheeks are as hot as a forge, can they get any hotter? Yes, they can.

"Forgive me, Master Snell, I have been stupid and presumptuous."

"I would not disagree with you there."

"It's just that there have been three deaths connected to Ben's *Masque of Peace* – "

"Three deaths?"

"Two, I mean. Sir Philip Blake and now Giles Cass."

"So you suspect some mischief, exactly as my son did?"

Strangely enough I was pleased that Snell mentioned this, since it made me feel less isolated, less absurd in my viewpoint. Even so I noted that he'd used the past tense in talking about his son's belief.

"It's possible," I said.

"Possible that I might have been conspiring with Lady Blake to do away with her husband? Yes?"

"Forgive me, Master Snell."

A wave of expressions had crossed his face while we were talking. When I'd mentioned the 'three deaths' (by mistake including that of John Ratchett), Snell had looked uneasy, it seemed to me. This was followed by indignation, even anger. Now, however, a glint of humour came into his eyes.

"All right, Nicholas Revill, for the *relief* of your curiosity I shall tell you what Lady Blake and I were talking about while you were cowering behind an arras."

"I don't mean to pry."

"Of course you mean to pry."

"All right, I do."

I waited, half embarrassed, half curious. Whatever he was about to say was not going to be a confession of murder.

"Tell me, you know what I am referring to by a 'seat house'?"

"It's a kind of jakes, isn't it?"

"A jakes, a privy, a necessary room, call it what you will," said Snell, warming to his theme. "There is a man called Harington, Sir John Harington. He was a favourite of our late Queen Elizabeth on account of his good looks and for having translated some poem from the Italian."

I nodded away as if I'd heard of this Harington fellow but really without the slightest idea of who or what Snell was on about. It didn't matter. The engine-man was caught up in his own words. There was the same kind of animation in his face as when he'd talked about the windlass and its intricacies.

"In my eyes, Sir John is truly distinguished for one thing, whatever else he has done. He has given much thought to our bodily needs. He has – I won't say perfected – but he has brought to a high pitch a device for ensuring that human waste is swept from eyes and nose by a combination of cisterns and valves."

I must have looked disbelieving or perhaps merely baffled for Jonathan Snell swept on in prophetic vein, "The day may come, Nicholas, when chamber pots and jordans and night-soil men will no longer be needed, at least in grand houses like this one. When you require to attend to your bodily necessities you will shut yourself away in a private room, a closet with a standing supply of water. And, at the end of a process, you will simply pull a lever or a cord to release a cascade of water and so flush away the unsightly traces of our animal nature. This is the jakes of the future."

"Where will it go to, the waste?" I said, slightly repelled (that someone should have wasted – ha! – so much time and thought on such matters) but also interested despite myself.

Jonathan Snell waved his long-thumbed hand in the direction of the Somerset House windows and said, "The river is wide. The river is deep. Plenty of room out there. Now, is your curiosity *relieved*? I use the term advisedly. This is what I was discussing with Lady Jane Blake, the installation of one of these devices in her house on the Strand. There is your plot, there is your conspiracy. Lady Jane is in the forefront of progress and improvement. She is an apothecary's daughter, you know, not one of your nose-in-the-air noblewomen. I am proud to call her my patron."

"I see. Thank you for explaining so much, Master Snell. I'm truly sorry for having – for having misunderstood you both."

"Have you spoken to her?" he said, quickly.

"Of course not. Now I'm covered in confusion. I should not have been listening to your talk with Lady Blake. I should not have jumped to conclusions."

"Oh, that's all right, Nicholas."

He had not called me by my first name before, and it was pleasing to be forgiven – or at least to be excused – even at the cost of appearing a bit of a fool. Snell beckoned to one of his craftsmen. It was Tom Turner, the lank-haired fellow.

"Now, if you two will put your hands to it, that chair is to be shifted from there – to there."

Together Turner and I manhandled the throne of Truth from the stage to the side of the audience chamber, where all the other portable effects were stacked. The ornamentation had been stripped from the chair and it was quite plain and compact although too large for one man to carry. I had entrusted my weight to this device, as had Sir Philip Blake and Ben Jonson.

We placed the chair next to a full moon which, without the benefit of candlelight, looked tired and wan. I said to Turner, "You'll use this again?"

"What's that?"

"This chair. You'll use it again?"

The question, which had been casual, seemed to be un-usually difficult for Turner to answer. He scraped his hand across his stubbly chin. "S'pose so," he said eventually from behind his curtain of hair. Unlike his mate Ned Armitage, Turner was a man of few words. But why shouldn't he be? He was a craftsman, expressing himself through his hands.

I helped to shift a few more objects. After that the Snell workmen turned their attention to the laborious task of dismantling the wooden scaffolding, something which would surely occupy them for several hours of the night. I slipped out of the audience chamber, though not before encountering father Snell once more. He gave me a broad grin to which I replied with a sheepish smirk. I made my way through the passages and antechambers of Somerset House, a familiar route by now. I passed knots of Spaniards, still jangling in that strange tongue which sounds both sweet and sharp. They kept later hours than we English did. The same mixture of cooking odours which I'd noticed on my first visit, oily and blossomy odours, hung about the dining areas. After the departure of the old enemy, his smell would linger on for a little.

I had a fantasy of meeting Doña Luisa de Mendoza once more in the corridors but I did not. Perhaps she had already slipped between the rose-scented, silken sheets of her bed. The thought of her slipping between the sheets was as sweet and sharp as the incomprehensible Spanish language – and I hadn't even met Doña Luisa! I hastened through the great court and past the gatehouse and so out into the damp night.

By the time I returned to the house in Thames Street, Mrs Buckle was in bed. Not surprising since it was gone midnight. If I'd known my landlady better, I might have disturbed her. As it was, the only person I disturbed was her daughter Lizzie who was downstairs but skittered away when she saw me, muttering some words about not being able to sleep.

That made two of us for when I at last got my head down on my top-floor bolster, I found it hard to drift off. The events of the day swirled around in my head. A lot had happened. The successful performance of the *Masque of Peace*; the presence of Queen Anne (that angular lady from Denmark but one unexpectedly skilful in dancing); the death of Giles Cass; and the embarrassing closet-dialogue with father Snell.

I believed what he'd said about the new cisterns and valves and the rest of it. It was too far-fetched a tale not to be true. I'd thought that he and Lady Jane Blake were plotting the death of a husband when all the time they were conspiring to build a better jakes. No wonder they'd been a bit secretive. No wonder they'd been acting a little like giggly school-children conversing on adult matters. My respect for Jonathan Snell increased. He was not merely a creator of descending chairs and scalloped waves but a potential master of the privy. My respect for him increased – but I'd look at him with different eyes in future.

It may seem odd but the fact that a man had died by drowning during the course of this Somerset House evening impinged on me less than the conversation with Snell. I wasn't sure that Cass's death was going to impinge much on anyone. Ben Jonson, who'd spoken to me on the terrace as we gazed at the body lying on its back, had not sounded like a man who was either shocked by what had happened or touched by grief. Presumably Sir Robert Cecil might regret it from a practical point of view, but Cecil had many men in his employment, both directly and indirectly.

After Master Snell's account of the 'privy' conversation I was no longer so sure that the deaths of Cass and Ratchett and Blake were linked. Wasn't so sure that they'd been murdered. This was the second time I'd changed my mind in the course of an evening. Perhaps there was an 'innocent' explanation for everything after all. The first and third deaths were accidental while the middle one was a suicide. Perhaps Ratchett had stood on the trapdoor and pulled the lever himself.

And then again, perhaps not.

A fanfare of trumpets from an overhead gallery broke into my thoughts. We were back in the Chapel Royal at Whitehall Palace, the day after the masque performance at Somerset House. A historic day, this 19th of August, the day of the signing of the peace treaty between England and Spain. We were still awaiting the arrival of King James, although the fanfare was to signal his imminent appearance. There's a form to these royal displays but I had the sense that James had kept everyone hanging about for a little longer than was considered proper, especially considering the presence of our Spanish guests. The King was known to have a distaste for large groups of people, even the ordered crowds at court. He preferred being out in the open, hunting in the field. Not to like presenting yourself in front of your own countrymen is a strange failing in a monarch, and one that is hard for a player to understand.

195

None of the King's Men had a clear sight of our patron as he processed into the Chapel in full ceremonial fig. We were bowing too low, of course. But I'm afraid that there wouldn't have been that much curiosity among us about James in any case. We'd already played before him on two or three occasions, and so we were familiar with his features. Unlike our last monarch, King James did not provoke much curiosity, let alone excitement. He was said to be intelligent and, aside from his passion for hunting and for the company of young men, to love nothing more than a learned dispute. He had penned poetry in his youth and, more recently, written some book or other on the business of kingship. Yet who would not have substituted all of that for half an hour in the presence of Queen Elizabeth? James was not physically striking either. His eyes were deep-set, as though they were hiding in their sockets, and he displayed a queer, shambling gait as he made his way up the aisle.

When he reached the east end James seated himself on a kind of throne, which was less grand than a throne in an audience chamber because this was, after all, the House of God. The rest of us remained standing, bareheaded and silent. Only one other person was seated and that was Sir Robert Cecil, who was presumably allowed to keep his chair on account of his rank (and his hunchback condition). I was able to see almost nothing of the Secretary but recognized his voice as he read a preamble to the treaty. Cecil announced the formal outbreak of peace between England and Spain but it was a document so larded with fine, circumlocutory phrases that it seemed to cover things up rather than to make them plain.

Then King James got to his feet and swore an oath in Latin to honour the treaty, with God's good help. There was a Scots twang to his Latin that was quite pleasant to listen to, whether you understood the words or not. After that a Spanish gentleman whom I assumed to be the Constable of Castile, since he was the leader of their party, also undertook in Latin to

honour the treaty. Then the King and the Constable fastened
their signatures and seals to a little pile of documents – not
that we could witness much of the procedure from our obscure position – and all this while we stood quiet and patient.
Then the King walked jerkily out of the Chapel, with the
audience or congregation bowing low once more. The effect
to an observer would have been of a summer breeze wafting
over a field of corn, especially since (though everyone's hats
were off) there were many feathers in evidence. We
straightened up in time to see the Constable of Castile stalk
by, his haughty demeanour a contrast to our monarch's
uncertain gait, followed by Cecil being carried in his chair,
and then the rest of the two parties in descending order of
precedence.

And that was that, more or less. There was to be a feast at
the Banqueting Hall, to which we weren't invited. I heard
later that the two sides tried to drink each other under the
table, and that the King was particularly eager for toast after
toast to be drunk since the Constable of Castile presented
him with a fine gold and crystal cup when the first health
was pledged.

The public – that is to say, people like us – was allowed to
watch the animal fights in the palace courtyard. It was the
King's bears against greyhounds, followed by mastiffs baiting
a tethered bull. But I've never had that much of an appetite
for the bear-pit so I slipped off. I tried to tell myself that I'd
been present at a piece of history-making (something to tell
the grandchildren, although before you can have grandchildren you have to have children) but it didn't convince.
Treaty or no treaty, England and Spain might be at war again
in a year or two. It was all a matter of show.

I had a privileged glimpse behind the scenes on my way
out of Whitehall Palace. Getting lost in the building, I was
passing, for at least the second time, a great pair of double
doors. They'd previously been shut but were now open.
Glancing in, I saw the English and the Spanish on opposite

sides of a brocade-covered table. Among them I recognized the white-whiskered visage of Charles Howard, the Lord High Admiral, as well as Charles Blount, the chubby-faced Earl whom Cass had pointed out to me in Somerset House. At the near end of the table sat Secretary Cecil, with a pen, ink-well and single sheet of paper in front of him. On the other side of the long table, like so many knights ranged for combat, sat an equivalent number of Spanish grandees. I recognized the Count and the hawk-eyed lawyer whom Ratchett had identified, together with the Constable who had lately sworn the oath in the Chapel Royal. In fact I recognized so many of these men that I felt we'd already been introduced.

I was still staring into the room when Cecil's great domed head swung towards me, like a lumbering but dangerous beast. Then most of the table turned their heads in my direction. Yet they weren't really looking at me, a poor player, a nobody. Rather it was as if they were sitting for a collective portrait so that this instant could be commemorated down the ages. History sat heavy on their shoulders. Then the double doors were slammed shut by unseen retainers and once more I resumed the business of getting lost in Whitehall Palace.

A couple of days later, after more feasting and toasting and pledging, the Spaniards left town. Somerset House was restored to its rightful owner. It was said that Queen Anne lost no time in decamping from Whitehall and returning home. Home for her was evidently any place where her husband was not.

It was a somewhat longer journey home for the Spanish. They withdrew downriver with little of the pomp and ceremony which had attended their arrival. Londoners, always quickly jaded, showed no curiosity about the departure of the old enemy, the insolent foe. Before the Spanish arrived in London, there'd been relief that they were not bringing their own fleet upriver as far as the city. (This was the reason they had initially disembarked at Dover since the Privy Council could not permit them to accomplish in peace what they'd never achieved in war.) But now I don't suppose anyone would have cared if they'd come and gone with a whole fleet of ships. They might have been a touch cocky in their demeanour, they might have spoken a strange language, but they didn't wear horns and some of their women were beautiful.

I wondered what Sir Walter Raleigh thought to see them go. I wondered too about the legal niceties of the case against him. Since he'd been accused of conspiring with Spain – and ignoring the fact that this was an absurd charge in the first place – could he any longer be considered guilty of treason? For our old enemy was our new friend. We were all conspirators with Spain now, or at least the King and Secretary Cecil and the rest of the pack were. So where did that leave Sir Walter? An interesting problem for our legal friends in Middle Temple and Lincoln's Inn there. Whatever was to happen to him, at least Raleigh had been spared the traitor's ultimate and dreadful fate: to have the hangman cut him open and thrust bloody hands into his warm entrails even as he hung alive on the scaffold, and to witness this man draw the guts before his face, and then to have his private parts cut away and cast into the fire before his eyes . . . it was too horrible to think about, yet it was somehow impossible not to think about it if your mind drifted in that direction. My mind had been drifting in that direction quite a lot recently. I suppose these horrid pictures were prompted by Giles Cass's remarks to me about Sir Philip Blake. About how he was lucky to have died when he did since Secretary Cecil, James's beagle, was on his trail. Certainly he had perished quickly compared to what his time on the scaffold would have been. If Cass was telling the truth, of course . . .

But back to our Spanish guests. They disembarked somewhere beyond Greenwich and travelled overland to

Dover where they boarded their own vessels and sailed away, to drop off the edge of the world for all I knew.

I enjoyed Mrs Buckle's company for one further night. Or rather I would have done had her late husband not come between us.

Relations were a little awkward, maybe more awkward than they would have been if we'd never shared a bed. I was not certain whether she wanted to resume our connection, to put it coyly. But three or four days after the performance of the *Masque of Peace*, we again found ourselves sitting up late, sharing some wine and chatting. I had been telling her of the Spaniards, since I had seen them at close quarters, and of the Queen's skill in dancing. I found myself gazing at the pronounced groove above her upper lip. I knew it now, a little, but I would not object to knowing it again, it and other things. To round off our chat, like the final item in a feast, I mentioned the drowned man who'd been fished from the river outside Somerset House.

"Who was he?"

"The drowned man? Someone called Cass, Giles Cass."

"A great man?"

"No. Or, if so, only in his own estimation."

"Did he have a wife?"

"I don't know. Does it matter?"

"It would to her."

But the question of whether Cass had a wife was of little interest to me. Of no interest at all in fact. Although unlike Martin Barton in other respects, he too had seemed not the marrying kind. Cass's loss was not much regretted. Even Ben Jonson, when I referred to the subject a day or two later, had shrugged his shoulders and said something in Latin about death being common to all men. As for the way Cass had perished, nothing could have been more ordinary. Men, women and children fall into the river every day. It is London's great receptacle.

Back to the living . . .

Mrs Buckle and I retired to her chamber. I only knew she wanted this by her instruction to me to follow her in five minutes. She must have been fearful of our footsteps being heard in unison, and alerting Lizzie the daughter or Grace the servant-girl. I crept along, by instinct, although I knew that if I were innocently going up to my own chamber I would have walked carelessly enough.

We lay down on her marital bed in an oddly decorous fashion. The single illumination came through the casement window from a nearly full moon. I thought of those husband-and-wife figures who stretch out beside each other for their eternal rest on the top of a church tomb. These weren't very warm or encouraging thoughts. I put my arm across so that it rested on Mrs Buckle's breasts. Except in one part, I felt as stiff as one of those pieces of tomb statuary. Mrs Buckle was still wearing her day clothes, her widow's weeds. They showed up inkily in this light. Suddenly she too stiffened, in apprehension.

"See where he comes!"

She grasped my hand tightly where it clutched her left breast. By this time I was lying half across her. I turned my head. There was nothing to see, just the moonlight picking out the few bits of furniture in the bedchamber: a padded stool, a large chest, a small cupboard.

Mrs Buckle sat up abruptly. I sensed rather than saw her staring in the direction of the window. I thought she'd forgotten my presence but when she next spoke it was to me, not to whatever she'd glimpsed across the room.

"You see him? Oh, you must see him."

"There is nothing – "

But I never finished the sentence for a weird alteration in the moonlight occurred. It was if a sheet of thick glass, full of flaws, was moving between the window and the bed where we were lying. The moon's whiteness was splintered into fragments as it poured into the room. I felt the place go cold.

It had been a warm summer's night, now it turned as chill as spring. Goosebumps broke out on my arms.

"In his habit as he lived," said Mrs Buckle in a whisper. "He is leaving now."

The disturbance in the moonlight passed and the room was filled once more with the planet's steady, unhuman glow.

I'd never seen a ghost before and wasn't sure that I'd seen one now. Perhaps it was no more than a trick of the light, a tattered cloud moving in front of the moon or a momentary blurring in my vision. But the hair on my head told a different tale. And whatever I'd glimpsed, imperfectly, Mrs Buckle had seen in full. Her late husband, the Reverend Hugh Buckle, would not leave her in peace.

The widow did not have to ask me to leave her. To be honest, after this latest visitation (if that's what it was), I wasn't in the mood for it. Nor was she. We made our half apologies – "I think I'd better . . . " and "Perhaps it would be best if . . . " – and I slunk upstairs to my own room, although not before ensuring that Mrs Buckle was content to be by herself for the rest of the night. She might have shifted rooms, although that would hardly deter a ghost. Perhaps her enforced move from Thames Street was a good thing after all.

I was shaken by the apparition. Baffled, too. What did the late Reverend Buckle require? To frighten his wife into propriety? To scare off an interloper in his bed? If so, he'd succeeded. But are ghosts so petty-minded? Oh yes, I thought, they must be. Why should they be any different from the rest of us? And then I wondered whether the ghost was walking for another reason altogether, and not out of jealousy. If so, it was a mystery. And, as it turned out, a solution to this mystery was to be found, like so much else, in the works of Master William Shakespeare.

He that was Othello

The first play we were scheduled to put on at the restored Globe was WS's tragedy of the Moor called Othello. The theatre looked much better for its new coats of paint and general sprucing-up. It was over four years now since the Globe had been erected on this spot, and for a quarter of that time the place had been left empty during the plague. Indeed, the fabric of the building was considerably older than those four years since the timbers had been the ones originally used for the theatre in Shoreditch, dismantled and transported across the frozen Thames during the course of a bitter winter.

A good, meaty tragedy was required to open proceedings and there was a double advantage in staging *Othello* at this point in late August. Its popularity had already been proved by a short run in the spring of the year, and Dick Burbage had added to his fame by his interpretation of the title part. The seniors knew that word of mouth would bring in new audiences as well as those who'd be happy to see it for a second time. The other reason was that, as WS had indicated to me, we were due to perform *Othello* in front of the court at Whitehall in the near future. So the opportunity to refine the play – not in its verses, of course, but in the details of its action – was welcome. You might have thought that King James would prefer fresh plays, never exhibited before the public. In fact, insofar as he had any taste for plays at all, it was for old favourites. The very first play we'd performed for our powerful patron, *As You Like It*, dated from Elizabeth's reign.

I'd resigned myself to a couple of minor parts (the soldier, the senator) in the revived *Othello* but I was lucky in the misfortune of one of my friends. Laurence Savage had taken the part of the dupe Roderigo in the spring production and had been assigned the same role this time. Laurence made a good dupe, he could assume an air that was at once doltish and calculating. He had that cowlick over his forehead which seemed to speak volumes. But by bad luck on the day before the rehearsal he ate too many oysters in the Mermaid tavern, keeping company with Ben Jonson, and the same night he was puking his guts up and the next day he was feeling exceedingly sorry for himself. Laurence dutifully turned up for the *Othello* rehearsal but the only part he would have been suitable for was playing a revenant from the grave. Dick Burbage sent him back to be sick in his lodgings and drafted me in his place.

"I'm sorry, Laurence," I said, clapping my friend lightly on the back as he passed me at a rush, heading for one of the waste buckets stationed about the Globe playhouse for the convenience of our patrons.

I wasn't really that sorry, but at least I tried to keep my pleasure at being given a larger part within bounds. Even if Laurence returned fit and well for the actual performance, I would be allowed to keep the role of Roderigo provided I made a decent go of it during rehearsal. I collected my lines from Geoffrey Allison, the book-keeper. The scroll was a comforting size. Allison told me to take care of it. He tells everyone to look after their parts, even the seniors. Losing the scroll containing your lines is a hanging offence with him, just as damaging your costume is with Bartholomew Ridd. I retreated to a quiet corner of the playhouse and started to study my lines.

Formerly I'd been of the opinion that nobody mattered very much in *Othello* except the Moor himself, his wife

Desdemona and his scheming soldier-companion Iago. It's funny, though, how being given a slightly larger character than you expect causes you to revise your notions of that character. Roderigo *is* an interesting figure after all, I discovered, more interesting than the somewhat bone-headed Cassio. I much preferred being Roderigo to, Cassio. There was a greater scope in the part. Roderigo is Iago's dupe, his tool. He believes himself to be in love with Desdemona, and this is the first lever that Iago uses to topple him and everybody else from their perches. I would even get to wear a disguise since Iago instructs Roderigo to put on a beard when, in his lovelorn fashion, he follows Desdemona and Othello to Cyprus. Eventually Roderigo will die on that island, stabbed in the dark by his 'friend' Iago. There was a bit of meat to this role and I settled down to a more careful study of the scroll with the relish of a dog who's just been thrown an especially tasty bone by his master.

However, as I scanned the lines, other thoughts intruded. I kept hearing echoes of the recent events at Somerset House and elsewhere. When Iago repeatedly instructs Roderigo to 'put money in his purse', I couldn't help hearing those very same words used by John Ratchett when he'd persuaded me – in effect, tricked and bribed me – into writing reports for the 'Council'. Surely Ratchett must have seen the spring performance of our play and, whether he was aware of it or not, was putting himself in the shoes of the machiavellian villain. And when Roderigo talks of rushing off to drown himself in the canals of Venice, I remembered the death of Giles Cass in the Thames. (The coroner had sat on the case and pronounced Cass's death an accident, so that was that.) Above all, I saw in the character of Roderigo and the way he'd been duped by Iago a slightly uncomfortable reflection of the way I'd been drawn by Ratchett into the whole affair surrounding the *Masque of Peace* and the Blakes.

I'd been made a fool of, no doubt. But there was a nagging feeling in me that we'd all been made fools of in a larger sense, just as Iago makes fools of everyone from the senators of Venice to the garrison on Cyprus. Maybe this was the effect, or the fault, of Shakespeare's *Othello*. Of reading his lines and then seeing the skeleton of the play once again clothed in flesh and blood during our practice. The tragedy of the Moor is controlled by a master-manipulator, a shadowy figure who stands behind or above all the mayhem and murder which he delights in producing. And all the time he is the bluffest, plainest, most downright person you could imagine, is Iago!

Behind the real-life tragedy of the death of Sir Philip Blake, and the less lamented departure of Giles Cass, and the almost unknown demise of John Ratchett (but still known to me and to at least one other), I wondered whether there was a similar machiavellian figure in the shadows, an Iago, manipulating events for his – or her – benefit. It must have been the heated atmosphere of this play, seething with plot and counter-plot, which provoked these suspicions in me once more. At the end of *Othello*, the truth comes out, although it's too late for everyone by that stage. I did not know whether the truth concerning the death of Blake, the man who'd played Truth, would ever emerge.

Since I was uncertain what could – or should – be done, I settled for doing nothing. But no sooner had I decided this than a couple of conversations started to put matters in a different light.

The first conversation was with Abel Glaze. During a pause in the practice he congratulated me on securing the part of Roderigo.

"From Ignorance to a dupe isn't such a big step," I said, referring to my role in Ben's *Masque of Peace*.

"Oh, come on, Nick, you know you have to be smart to play stupid. Speaking for myself, I'd rather play the zany than the hero."

They say that inside every clown there's a serious man, a tragedian, struggling to get out but I'm not sure that this was the case with Abel.

"Can I ask you to play the judge now, Nick?" he said.

"Play the judge?"

"It's not the right word. But I'm in a bit of a difficulty. You see this?"

Glancing round as if to ensure that no one was watching, Abel produced a metal flask from his pocket. He shook it. There was liquid inside. The flask, made of finely chased silver, looked vaguely familiar.

"This belonged to Sir Philip Blake."

I recognized it now. I'd seen Blake take a swig from it on the day of the fatal practice at Somerset House, before he climbed up the ladder to the gallery. Dutch courage, I'd thought at the time.

"Where did you get it, Abel?"

"I picked it up from the stage floor after he fell. Remember?"

All I remembered was Abel heading towards the body. And before that, the crack of Sir Philip's head striking the ground like a nut being split open. And after that, the blood pooling out from beneath his cloak.

"I wasn't looking too closely."

"I don't know what came over me exactly," said Abel, "but I saw this lying on the stage and while everyone else was attending to the body, I pocketed it."

"Finders keepers," I said.

"I don't want to keep it now. But who should I give it back to? I wouldn't want anyone to think I'd stolen a dead man's flask."

It struck me that this was precisely what Abel had done, so maybe my reply to him was a bit curt.

"Don't return it then."

"Well . . . "

He almost writhed in discomfort. There must be something else troubling him. Abel had made his living through dubious means on the road for many years before he joined the King's Men. If he hadn't exactly stolen cash or goods, he had certainly parted the foolish (and the not so foolish) from their money with profitable regularity. Some of the magpie habits of the road had obviously stuck with him and he'd snatched up a dead man's property almost without thought. Finders keepers. Considering all of this, why was he getting into a tizz over a mere flask, even if it was made of silver?

Once more Abel glanced around. If he was worried about being watched, he needn't have been. Dick Burbage, who was playing the Moor, was deep in conversation with Henry Condell who was playing Iago. Shakespeare was standing slightly to one side, as if he was mediating between them. Other members of the company were taking their ease, glad of a pause in the practice. Some were lying down in shady spots. It was muggy during these dog days towards the end of August. Reassured that he was not observed, Abel unscrewed the cap and held the flask out to me.

"Smell."

I smelled something fumy and fiery.

"It's aqua vitae, isn't it? I expect Sir Philip needed a drop or two to, ah, fortify himself with during the rehearsal. It wasn't altogether comfortable in that flying chair, you know."

"No, there's something else there, something bitter. An underscent. Smell it again."

I raised the flask to my nose for a second time and sniffed. Abel might have been right, but I couldn't really detect anything. Well, maybe just a fugitive wisp of another smell in among the fiery fumes. I returned the flask to Abel.

"What are you getting at?"

"Did you see Sir Philip just before he fell? I mean, immediately before."

I nodded.

"What did he look like?" said my friend.

"What did he look like? What would you look like if you were about to fall more than twenty feet to the ground? He looked terrified. White in the face. His mouth was gaping open."

"But no sound came out. He wasn't shouting, he wasn't cursing, or exclaiming, or screaming?"

"I – I don't know. There was music being played in the background. It might have covered up any sounds he made."

"It had stopped by then, the music."

"If you say so. Yes, you're probaby right, the music stopped. When people saw that he was in trouble, everything halted. So Blake didn't curse or scream. What of it?"

Abel gulped. He looked even more uncomfortable than when he'd confessed to taking the flask.

"I'm new to this kind of speculation, Nick."

"What kind of speculation?"

"Your kind of speculation."

I said nothing. I wasn't sure where this conversation was going but I had an inkling, and was half eager, half wary.

"What if the contents of this flask had been adulterated?"

"You mean drugged?"

"Drugged."

Abel looked at me, as if glad that this possibility was out in the open. I saw no reason to conceal my own suspicions about Blake now.

"So you think there was something strange about Sir Philip's death too," I said.

My friend grabbed at my arm. His face lit up.

"Who else thinks so? Do you think so?"

"I did, for a time," I said cautiously. "And Jonathan Snell, the younger one, he had suspicions that the cables supporting the flying chair had been tampered with."

"There you are then!"

"No, wait. Snell retracted his story later after his father had had a word with him. There was absolutely no proof of anything."

No proof but plenty of suspicion and unease. I had not yet said anything to Abel of my doubts concerning the deaths of John Ratchett (whom he had never met as far as I was aware) or Giles Cass. I wondered whether now was the moment to come clean with him.

"Have you tried it?" I said instead, indicating the flask which he was still clutching.

"Do you think I'm a complete fool, Nick? What if it contains poison?"

"That doesn't make sense though. If anyone was going to poison Sir Philip then they wouldn't need to arrange for an accident to happen to him in the flying chair. Poison is much quieter, less dramatic."

Abel was unwilling to let go of his theory and now said, "Perhaps whoever drugged this flask did not intend to poison him outright but only to subdue him. This could have contained a sleeping draught so it would be easier to put him in the chair and send him on his way. Don't you see?"

"Maybe."

Had it happened like that? I visualized a couple of figures in the gloom of the gallery hoisting Sir Philip, drugged and pliant, into the throne of Truth and then shoving him into space, with the ropes half severed. In that case the Snells (one of them at least) would have to be involved or, if not them, then Ned Armitage or Tom Turner.

"You're convinced of this, Abel?"

"I was able to see Sir Philip's expression just before he fell, Nick. White-faced and terrified, as you said. But also strangely . . . I don't know . . . it was like watching someone having a nightmare which you can't wake them from. Beyond help. That would be explained by a drugged flask."

This seemed a lot to have observed in the instant before the man fell to his death but then Abel was sharp-eyed and shrewd. His theory that Blake had been drugged was plausible. It may be unfair, but drugs and poisons make you think of women. Specifically, they make you think of wives. I recalled that Lady Jane Blake was the daughter of an apothecary. But that wasn't too significant. Women require little instruction in knowing what herbs to dry and combine to make potions and poisons, all they need is mother wit.

"What do you think? You've solved mysteries before, Nick."

"I've been wrong more often than I've been right."

"An injustice has been done here," he said.

"I think so too," I said, surprising myself with the words.

"What are we going to do about it?"

"*We* are going to think on it."

"Oh," said Abel. "Are you so busy with your widow and her daughter that you can't attend to a crime? I think you must be busy with your landlady's daughter for I see a little colour rising in your face."

"It is hot here," I said.

We were standing at the edge of the shade cast by the canopy over the Globe stage. Above us was the freshly painted zodiac and the sun and moon. The real sun had crept round during our talk and was beating down hard. Some words about the widow seemed called for. But all I could come up with was, "Mrs Buckle is well, thank you."

"*Mrs* Buckle . . . how proper, Nicholas. But I'm glad she's well. And her daughter now?"

"I never see her. And for your information, Abel Glaze, I shall shortly have to move out of the Thames Street lodging because *their* landlord seems intent on pricing them out of house and home."

At that moment, and fortunately, Dick Burbage clapped his hands for the rehearsal to continue. Abel said quickly, "There is still space in my lodgings in Kentish Street."

"Thank you, Abel."

I was touched by my friend's concern. All the little irritations between us faded away. As the rehearsal went forward, and during the periods when I wasn't required, I considered what Abel had said about Blake being drugged by the contents of the flask. Maybe he was right. And naturally, caught in the middle of this plot-ridden play by

William Shakespeare, my suspicions started to swing back towards Lady Jane Blake and Jonathan Snell the elder.

Towards the end of the practice I went round to the front of the stage to the groundlings' area, to occupy a small part of which our customers pay a penny each to stand for the duration of the play. I wanted to see Dick Burbage's final tragic turn as Othello, after the Moor has confronted Desdemona over her supposed infidelity and then smothered her on the marital bed. I was already dead, in the person of Roderigo. I'd been killed treacherously in the course of laying an ambush for Cassio. The ambush itself was treacherous, of course, but my death was doubly treacherous, the result of being stabbed by Iago under the cover of night and confusion. (Iago, that shadowy figure in the background, pulling strings, arranging outcomes.)

Dick Burbage's turn as Othello was already the talk of the town, and had been since the first performances in the spring. His voice, naturally resonant, sank a notch or two lower to play the Moor. Although this was only a rehearsal he had blacked up his face and hands. Through some trick he contrived to make the whites of his eyes stand out so that he looked like an angry, cornered beast. He was grand yet barbaric, even as he smothered his wife and then grieved over her body. His anger with Iago, when the truth had been revealed, was terrible to see; his anger with himself was even worse.

When Othello had finished and stabbed himself and the order had been given for Iago to be escorted away and tortured – he vows never to say another word under torture, and I believed him, he never would – there was an outbreak of spontaneous applause from the dozen or so of us scattered in the groundlings' area. To think that you could have this, standing here, for just a penny! It was like purchasing a whole world, a pearl beyond price. It was only a practice, however, and being a practice, there was no final song or jig from us players. I turned to go back to the tire-room since I was still in my Roderigo outfit.

I almost stumbled over Martin Barton who was sitting at the bottom of the steps which led to one of the tiers of seating (twopence or threepence – still cheap at the price). Barton too had evidently been watching the closing moments of *Othello*.

"Ridiculous, isn't it?" he said.

"What is?"

He waved a languid arm towards the stage where Burbage, Condell and the rest were trooping off.

"The whole thing."

I said nothing and made to move on. But it wasn't so easy to get away from Barton.

"That business with the handkerchief, for example. Just picking it up like that! How convenient. How absurd."

In the middle of the play Iago finds a handkerchief dropped by Desdemona and uses it to further ensnare the Moor, telling him that she has given it to her supposed lover Cassio. Barton's words called to mind the handkerchief dropped in the Somerset House gallery, the one which apparently did not belong either to Lady Blake or to Maria More.

"I don't see why it's absurd, Master Barton," I said. I didn't much care for the satirist and knew that he was merely being provoking. Even so, I rose to his bait.

"So much hinges on a silly bit of linen," he said. Barton stretched out his legs and yawned. I saw down his gullet. A dainty blue hat sat askew on his red hair. I willed it to fall off. "Couldn't our friend Shakespeare have come up with something more substantial than a silly bit of linen?"

"Probably he wanted to show how great outcomes sometimes depend on small accidents," I said, quite pleased with the insight.

"Oh, how profound," said Barton.

"Besides, Martin, I seem to remember you made great play over a little codpiece in your *Melancholy Man*. Great outcomes, little things, you know."

"That was in fun. A small codpiece does not make a

tragedy. On second thoughts though it may do . . . Anyway, getting back to Master Shakespeare, all this fuss over cuckolding, it's hardly realistic."

"Oh, I don't know. What would you do if your wife was unfaithful, Martin?"

"That is a mischievous question."

"As if yours aren't," I said, falling into his mode. "Answer me anyway."

"I am not married and not likely to be married, as you are well aware, Nicholas. But, if you mean, would I run my wife through if she'd been run through by another man in a different sense? Would I cover her face with a pillow – as we've just seen Master Dick smother that nice boy-player Peter Pearce – because she had been covered by another man in a different sense? If you mean any of that, then no, I don't think so. What about you, Nicholas? Would you do anything so *savage*, so *animal*?"

"Like you, I am not married – "

"You are not like me, but never mind."

I ignored him and said, "I don't think I would kill out of jealousy but who can say what he would do if driven to extremity."

(The previous night in Mrs Buckle's chamber flashed before my inward eye. The shimmerings and distortions in the moonlight. Her husband's ghost, had it been? Jealous, was he?)

"If I speak as a playwright now, and a not unsuccessful one," said Martin Barton, undeterred, "it is to tell you that cuckolding and horning and infidelity are fit for one thing only. And you know what that thing is? It is laughter. I used them for laughter in my *Melancholy Man*. Remember?"

"I had a part in that, Martin. I played Lussorio the murderer."

"They are about to revive my *Melancholy Man*. It will be interesting to have it put on straight after this piece of Master Shakespeare's. We shall see which the audience really approves of."

"Yes, we shall," I said.

For some moments Martin Barton's eyes had been tracking someone over my shoulder. Now he said, "Ah, here he is."

I looked round. Peter Pearce was parading past us. Peter had taken the part of Desdemona in *Othello*. He had wiped the white paint from his cheeks and the red paint from his lips and was dressed in his everyday clothes. He was chatting to Andrew Larch, another boy-player, who had played Emilia, the wife to Iago and confidante to Desdemona. They were talking as closely together as they had talked in character on stage.

I noticed Martin Barton's gaze show real animation for the first time. He almost bothered to sit up from his lounging position at the bottom of the steps. It was evident that, of the two boys, he was interested in Desdemona. He had already referred to *that nice boy-player Peter Pearce* (and, besides, Andrew Larch was comparatively plain).

"Look at that elegant foot," said the satirist when Peter was still within earshot. "And that wandering eye. And then, Nicholas, think of a region somewhere between the two."

I had a bit of a soft spot for Peter Pearce, in an innocent sense. He had played Cressida to my Troilus in Middle Temple almost two years ago. He'd enjoyed an exceptionally long career as a boy-player and at any moment his voice must start to go, irretrievably. There were already signs of it. Desdemona might be his swan-song and he could hardly go out on a more plangent note. Then he'd graduate to young-man roles. I was pleased to see how he and Andrew Larch paraded past Barton and me without paying either of us any attention. Peter's 'parading' wasn't provocative either, I think, but merely the result of his having played female roles for so long.

"I'm sorry," said Martin Barton. "Have I offended you? Shocked you, Nicholas?"

"What in?"

"My comments about young Pearce."

"It's the satirist's business to offend, isn't it? But no, Martin, you haven't offended me. Plenty of people would no doubt agree with you about Peter Pearce."

Barton appeared almost disappointed. Whether it was because I wasn't 'shocked' or whether he didn't like the idea of other men fancying Pearce, he now said, "Then let me tell you something really offensive."

"A joke?"

"It might as well be. A joke on marriage. I have heard that Lady Jane Blake – she who played Plenty in Ben's absurd masque – is to get married again."

"What! But her husband has not been dead for more than a few days!"

"I know," said Barton gleefully. "Could you invent a better joke on the notion of fidelity and marital bliss?"

"Who's she marrying? Not Bill Inman?"

"Inman?"

"He played Ocean in the *Masque of Peace*."

"Oh, that one. Covered in shells. No, she's not marrying him but some obscure country cousin. So they say."

"Who says? You know this for a fact?"

"I have it on good authority, on the best authority in fact. That snooty woman who accompanies Lady Jane told me so."

"Maria More."

"Yes, her. Anyway, does it matter who her mistress is marrying? She'll observe the formalities, naturally. She'll let a decent period of mourning go by – let's say, half an hour or half a day if pushed – and then she'll be leaping into bed with her new man. Obviously she is a lady of large appetites as well as large everything else. All that flesh! Ugh. Fancy being swallowed whole by her."

He shuddered with a horror which probably wasn't altogether pretended.

Despite myself I was – if not shocked – then surprised. This was a pointless response for whatever Lady Jane Blake did or didn't do was no particular concern of mine. Martin Barton got up on his spindly legs and stretched. He was pleased to have squeezed some reaction out of me at last.

"This is why I say our great Shakespeare is unrealistic, Nicholas. Why he is almost unworldly. In the real world, a man dies and his widow remarries within days. So much for marriage vows and eternal memory. But in the stage-play world, men are prepared to kill on mere suspicion."

Barton wasn't making a serious point but having a dig at WS. Nevertheless, his revelation about Lady Jane made me think. If it was true – and presumably it must be true if Barton had heard it directly from Maria More – then it tended to darken the cloud of suspicion which had already started to hang once more over the widow.

Like everyone, I've heard stories about hasty remarriages. The stories of grieving spouses getting yoked again in double-quick time as if they cannot bear to be alone and free. There was that woman from Bermondsey who wed the tailor who'd come to measure her up for her mourning gear. She buried her first husband on the Tuesday and married her second on the Wednesday. I wondered whether he'd charged her for the mourning suit. And I remembered that moment from my childhood when I'd discovered a new widow sharing her grief exclusively with her late husband's brother, in an upstairs chamber. Even Shakespeare, whatever silly claims Barton had made about his being 'unworldly', had provided an example of a rapid rematch in the shape of Hamlet's mother, Gertrude.

Gertrude was a murderess, of course.

Or, if she did not actually have a hand in her first husband's murder, she connived at it.

Or, if she did not connive at it, she was happy to accept the result: a fresh man in her bed.

I wondered about the obscure country cousin Lady Jane was marrying. Had she too connived at Sir Philip's death to secure a fresh man in her bed?

My sweet Bianca?

There is a whore in *Othello* who goes by the name of Bianca. She is in love with that bone-headed lieutenant, Cassio. The wicked Iago says somewhere in the play that it is the strumpet's curse to beguile many while being beguiled by one. And he was right too, if my experience with my friend Nell was anything to go by. For Nell had loved me, and me alone, as I believed . . .

But enough of that.

Iago's claim about strumpets did not apply, however, in the case of my newish whore Blanche, the girl from Bordeaux. She was not beguiled by me, despite the similarity of her name to WS's Bianca.

Blanche . . . Bianca . . . both names are to do with whiteness, with purity, and so are highly inappropriate for a whore. For an instant, a little bit more than an instant, I wondered whether Shakespeare had also been a patron of the Mitre brothel in Southwark and had there encountered a French girl whom he had transformed into an Italian one.

Pleasure with Blanche was a pleasure but it was still business. A candle on a table near her bed illuminated a sandglass which regulated her time – and her customers' time – more strictly than a preacher's. In this everyday object I saw a disconcerting reminder of my father the parson, who would often position a sand-glass on the edge of the pulpit when he started to sermonize. His was a simple object created from two bulbs of glass joined with tallow. After the first half-hour was up he would turn it with a flourish. Blanche's device of measuring time was smarter than my father's but she kept as strict a watch on her sand-glass as my father's parishioners kept on *his*.

On my next visit to the Mitre I found myself following the events in *Othello*. It was as if Shakespeare was writing my behaviour. Just as the play was guiding my suspicions about a hidden manipulator of events, an off-stage Iago, so too it was guiding me in more minor decisions. In the same way that Cassio makes a gift of a handkerchief to Bianca, so I made a gift of a handkerchief to Blanche. Cassio's handkerchief comes, indirectly, from Desdemona. Mine came from – who knew where it came from? It was the one that I'd obtained from Ned Armitage at the Three Cranes yard, under the pretence that I knew its owner.

It was a gift made on impulse. I fished it out of my pocket while I was dressing at the end of a visit to the Mitre.

"I have a present for you, Blanche."

"*Pour moi*? But wot izzit? Show me."

"You must close your eyes."

She did, though it was so dim in her little room that there wasn't much difference between keeping one's eyes open or keeping them shut. It had been the same in Nell's crib at Holland's Leaguer. Whether it is to preserve the strumpet's blushes (unlikely) or to enhance her charms (more probable) or to save the client from a knowledge of his shame (but this depends on the client), Blanche was one of those who liked to keep things dark.

Blanche took the handkerchief which I placed in her hand. She brought it close to the single candle and examined the fine cutwork and the embroidery of dainty red spots. The feel of the material alone would have indicated quality. Blanche sniffed at the handkerchief.

"Zis – it belong to a lady?"

"It does now."

She giggled, as if she understood this somewhat oily compliment. Probably she did. I felt that she understood more than she let on.

"Do men give you many things, Blanche?"

"Now and zen."

She glanced instinctively towards the wall. There was an array of objects hanging from hooks and nails. I'd noticed them before. They reminded me of trophies, items won in combat. Now I took the candle from the bedside and passed it over the items. Some of them might have seemed out of place in a brothel – a crucifix, for example, and a little psalter such as a well-born lady might carry – although I have learned that no one can be as pious as a whore in her holy moods. Other items, like a pomander and a silver necklace, were more predictable. She was obviously the recipient of quite a few gifts, rather more often than *now and zen*.

At some of them I paused and said, "This was a present?" and "This one too?"

Blanche squinted at the object, nodded and mixed her yeses and her *ouis* until she said, with a touch of irritation, "Why you ask?"

"I don't know. Just curiosity. I am glad you are so – popular."

"And you – you zink I am worth – 'ow you say – worth ze candle, Nicholaas?"

"Oh yes," I said, replacing the candle by her bedside as if to demonstrate the literal truth of the saying. The light flickered across her breasts. There was a mole on the upper part of her right breast, which I had not noticed before (the mole, I mean). I also noticed that, according to the sand-glass, my time had run out. For once Blanche hadn't mentioned this, and I was secretly pleased. I settled up with her and left the Mitre.

Instead of going back over the Bridge straightaway, I hung around a couple of my old haunts hoping to find some company, preferably of the playhouse variety. But I saw nobody in the Knight of the Carpet and the only people I recognized in the Goat & Monkey ale-house were that disreputable couple, Tony and Charity Thoroughgood, who had attempted to rob the Buckles outside the Globe playhouse. They pretended not to know me, but I caught Tony casting sidelong glances in my direction and then nudging his wife and whispering in her ear. He was most likely saying something about the impudent player who'd deprived them of a nice little haul during one fine evening back in the spring. I wouldn't have lingered in the old Goat but I was damned if I was going to shift because *they* were there, nudging and whispering, so I ordered a pint from Master Bly, the landlord, and sat somewhat morosely in a corner, watching the Thoroughgoods.

As I did so, it occurred to me that they might be the ones responsible for that attack on the river bank, the one from which John Ratchett had rescued me. There'd been a woman shouting "Kick 'im! Kick 'im!" and that could have been Charity Thoroughgood in an unrefined, bloodthirsty mood. I'd been assuming that the attack was somehow linked to Ratchett's machinations but perhaps it was coincidental, and he had genuinely preserved me from a worse kicking. If I'd felt in a more bloodthirsty mood myself I'd have confronted the Thoroughgoods there and then but instead I glowered at them from my corner before forcing my thoughts elsewhere.

I thought of the snug chamber in the Mitre brothel. All those trophies on the wall. Blanche had certainly done well. Many men must appreciate her talents. I wondered why men give gifts to whores, over and above the necessary payment. Is it because they – because we – wish to turn a cold transaction into an exchange which is warmer, more human?

I didn't know the answer to this question but it joined a jumble of others inside my head. To begin with, there was something about the scene in Blanche's crib which niggled at me, although it hadn't crossed my mind until I was sitting down in the corner of the Goat & Monkey. What was it? It hovered at the edge of my mind but I couldn't drag or tease it out into the open. I felt it was connected in some fashion with the business surrounding the death of Sir Philip Blake, but that made no sense at all. What linked a nobleman in the Strand and a whore in the Mitre? There was an obvious answer to this – indeed, it was barely a question – but it wasn't at all the answer I was groping for. I concluded that the link was no more than that handkerchief, as tenuous as that. The handkerchief that had belonged to one kind of lady and now belonged to another kind.

And why on earth had I questioned Blanche so closely about the presents she'd received from her customers? *This was a present?* and *This one too?* Such an inquisition was a sign of jealousy, to be sure. Pray God I wasn't falling for a whore once more. I remembered what it was like to lose my heart, or a portion of it, to such a woman. It doesn't make for peace of mind, because it's impossible to forget what she does for a living. Also, there's not much future in it, either for them or for us. For the most part whores get raddled and then proceed to fall apart with the pox. A few grow into madams, like Bess Barton in Holland's Leaguer, and a few more marry and turn respectable. One or two may even marry up. But they rarely escape their past. If a customer weds a woman from the stews, then he is well advised to move with her to another town so as to avoid people's wagging tongues.

No, if I was thinking of marrying it could be no whore. A widow, a young and beautiful widow, such as Blanche had recently supposed I was lodging with, would do me fine. Mrs Buckle could not be described as either young or beautiful. But neither was she old and crabbed, not by a very long way. And, with her, the other reason for marrying a widow (in other words, money) would be quite absent since she had next to none. But I could not marry her – even assuming I really wanted to, even assuming she would be willing – since she was still haunted by her husband. Her jealous husband.

Jealousy is the green-eyed monster, says Iago. Once jealousy possesses you it turns your life into a torment. Better to sleep in ignorance and believe that your bed has never been disturbed. Otherwise, a lifelong torment. And a torment beyond life perhaps. Can jealousy be felt after death? Mrs Buckle's husband was troubling her from the security of the grave. Had Sir Philip Blake, another dead husband, been the jealous type during his lifetime? Would he be returning from the grave to haunt his ample wife once she'd married her country cousin?

This imminent remarriage, the indecent haste of it, made me think once again of Gertrude in WS's *Hamlet*.

Then my mind went spinning off in new directions, sparked by that play.

Two more questions.

What are the reasons why a ghost comes back to earth?

And how can you best expose a murderer?

When it came to exposing a murderer I couldn't do it by myself, that much was obvious. Since Abel Glaze had broached the idea that there was something odd about Blake's death without any prompting from me, I took up the subject with him again.

He listened. His first reaction was to doubt what I was saying and I grew a bit tetchy.

"But you were the one who claimed that an injustice had been done, Abel. You asked what we were going to do about it. What *we* were going to do."

"And your answer was that *we* should think on it. Are you the only one who's allowed to change his mind, Nick? Maybe it was an accident after all."

"All right. I'll do this alone."

"No, you won't," said Abel. "Or at least not until you've told me exactly what it is you're planning to do."

"Better than tell you, I'll show you."

Once again Abel and I had been talking in the Globe. This

time it was at the end of an actual performance of *Othello*, which had gone off very well. There'd been tears for Desdemona, gasps and hisses for Iago, and absolute silence for Othello. Henry Condell said something complimentary about my Roderigo, which was pleasing since I'd been playing at close quarters with him. Now we had changed out of our stage-gear and were tired, sweaty and cheerful. Abel congratulated me too, in his ironic style, on my portrayal of a dupe. In this expansive mood I took him to one side and unfolded my rediscovered suspicions about the Blakes, based in particular on the news that Lady Jane was shortly to remarry. As I said, he was sceptical at first, but agreed to follow me.

We didn't have far to go, only to the roof of the playhouse.

There were galleries and private boxes at the upper level, favoured by the better-off customers as well as those who valued their privacy, usually the same people. The boxes were provided with curtains, ostensibly to protect the occupants against the rain or the sun but really to safeguard their secrets from prying eyes. But above and behind the stage could be discovered different secrets, ones relating directly to our stage-play world. Up here, for example, was the 'thunder-run', a descending trough of wood down which an object like a bowling ball was sent when the noise of thunder was required on stage. There was a pole up here from which our flag was flown during performances and, by tradition, it was from a position at the foot of this pole that a musician blew a trumpet each afternoon to announce the imminent performance.

The most important feature of this upper world was a hut or cabin which housed the equipment used to lower objects or people to the stage floor, and occasionally to raise them up. In essence this was similar to the machinery employed by the Snells during the Somerset House masque, that is a hoist and a windlass-type device to control the hoist as well as a permanent chair for the *deus ex machina*. There were whole webs of rope and cabling inside the hut, and set into the floor was a hinged trapdoor which opened on to the painted canopy or 'heavens' above the stage.

I'd always thought of the hut as being small – which it was in comparison to the grand scale of the playhouse – but it was large enough to accommodate half a dozen people, even if in cramped conditions, as well as all the lifting-and-lowering equipment. If the hut had been able to take off and fly away and settle down on a farmstead somewhere it would have made a very ample home for a peasant family or two. It had an entrance which faced the door leading from the passage in the upper gallery. It had a thatched roof and several little windows, and on top of the thatched roof was the statue of Hercules symbolizing our company of players. Hercules was up here because this roof-peak was the highest point of the entire theatre. One thing held up another, beginning with the theatre itself. The Globe contained the stage that was roofed by the canopy which carried the hut which wore the little thatched roof that sustained Hercules who bore the weight of the world on his shoulders.

I'd been up here before but never ridden down in the chair. Nor did I intend to now. All I intended was that this spot on the top of the Globe – on top of the world, one might say – should be the place where a murderer was unmasked.

Around the hut there was a wide wooden walkway, covered with rushes to prevent too much echoing from footsteps. Beyond this the canopy roof turned to thatch and sloped slightly. If you laid yourself out flat and started to roll as a child rolls down a hill, there was nothing to stop you falling out and down into the groundlings' area before the stage. It was a disconcerting thought but one that only occurred to me when I was up here, dozens of feet above the ground.

Abel and I stood on the walkway at the front of the hut looking at the view over London. In winter this is often obscured by smoke and dirty air but at the end of a fine summer's day there is usually nothing more than a heat haze which, rather than impeding the view, softens it. The distant towers and spires on the far bank assume a golden strangeness which you know does not properly belong to them. To our right was London Bridge. If I'd squinted I could have made out the blobs – the traitors' heads – displayed on the southern end. Distance did not lend them any enchantment.

"What are we doing up here, Nick?"

"This is where I plan to bring him."

"Him?"

"Bring him. Bring her. The person who was responsible for the death of Sir Philip Blake."

"Because whoever it is is afraid of heights?"

"I don't like heights much," I said. "But the person who killed Blake wasn't afraid of heights, I think, because they must have been fiddling around with ropes and so on in the gallery at Somerset House. No, it's more that I hope to startle this person into giving himself away. Or herself away."

"Like a guilty thing upon a fearful summons," said Abel.

This was a line from *Hamlet*. Abel had recently been told he might be given the part of Horatio in a forthcoming revival, so it was on his mind. Even so it was funny how that play kept cropping up. The line he'd quoted describes how the ghost is startled by the crowing of a cock. Funny how ghosts kept cropping up.

"Yes, it's what Hamlet the Dane does," I said. "Tries to scare a show of guilt out of a murderer. Shows his uncle Claudius a murder in a play, like the murder he committed, hoping he'll give himself away by his reaction."

"That's an old device," said Abel.

"Maybe, but sometimes the old ones are the best ones. Anyway, we're not going to stage a play so much as a – a situation."

"How? What situation?"

"I'll tell you."

I told him.

He said it was a madcap scheme. Did that mean he didn't want to take part, I asked. No, he said, he'd still take part. Nonetheless it was a madcap scheme. He was probably right.

The first thing we had to do was to obtain the costume which Blake had been wearing when he plunged to his death. The last time I'd seen the 'robe of Truth' it was shrouding his corpse in an antechamber in Somerset House. No, that would have been the second to last time, since Ben Jonson had worn it for the actual performance. Therefore Bartholomew Ridd must have recovered it and had it cleaned in time for the masque. The fact that a man had died in the cloak, and that it was spattered with blood and gore, was immaterial.

We needed to borrow the costume but an outright request was impossible. Even to ask about costumes was risky unless it was to do with a forthcoming performance, since Ridd would grow suspicious and want to know why we were asking. Abel and I went to visit Bartholomew in his quarters, one of a couple of small rooms which led off the tire-house. We chose a quiet moment. Ridd was sitting on a stool, examining a doublet.

"Bartholomew – " I said but got no further. The tire-man held up the doublet as if it was contaminated.

"Look at this! Just look at it."

I looked and saw a dark stain down the front of the doublet.

"Do you know who was wearing this?" said Ridd.

"I wasn't," I said.

"It wasn't me," said Abel.

"The question was rhetorical, purely rhetorical," said Ridd. "This item of Globe clothing was worn by – well, never mind who it was worn by – but I can tell you that the wearer was someone who should have known better."

"One of the seniors?" said Abel hopefully.

"Someone who should have known better," repeated Bartholomew, divided between indignation and loyalty.

227

Abel tried again to mollify the tire-man by saying that the stain on the doublet looked like sheep's blood. Even Ridd couldn't object to the use of sheep's blood (which simulated the human variety) since he knew as well as anyone that without frequent blood-lettings on stage our Globe audiences would dwindle away fast. But Abel's suggestion was scornfully rejected by the costume man.

"*This* is not sheep's blood, Master Glaze," he said. "Smell it. Go on, smell it."

He thrust the offending portion of the costume under my friend's long tapering nose. Abel sniffed and shrugged.

"I'm not sure," he said.

"Well, I am sure," said Ridd. "It's drink is what it is. This piece of Globe property stinks of the ale-house. Which means that Master – never mind who – means that he has broken the rules and taken his costume to an ale-house. Probably the Goat & Monkey, full of low people. Or the Knight of the Carpet, full of even lower people. How can one expect younger players like yourselves to observe the rules if the seniors and shareholders ignore them?"

We tutted together and then Abel shook his head while I nodded mine. All that Ridd required was that we went through the motions of sharing his outrage. I wondered about the identity of the naughty senior who'd worn a tire-house doublet to go to the tavern. I wondered whether Ridd would berate him about it. Probably he would. Whatever else you might say about Bartholomew, he was no great respecter of persons.

Abel and I had been standing in this little chamber for five minutes or more and still hadn't touched on the reason we'd come, or rather on the pretext. Nevertheless, the stained doublet was a providential way into the conversation.

"Bartholomew ," I began again, "Abel and I have been in dispute about the best way to remove blood from a garment."

"The best way is to avoid fights and disputes altogether. That way you will have no blood to remove."

"This was no fight but a nose-bleed on a fine silk shirt," said Abel. Like most players he was an accomplished liar. "How do I get rid of it? Nick says buck and lye while I say good old soap and water."

(I didn't have much idea about 'buck and lye', by the way. But I'd heard my mother talking about it.)

"You are both wrong," said Bartholomew with an expert's pleasure. "Buck and lye is too fierce for bloodstains. And soap and water are not precise enough."

"What would you use?" I said.

"What would I use? I am not a laundrywoman, Nicholas Revill. Although of course I take an interest in these things. The most efficacious way to remove blood is with milk or with salt and water, if the stain is old. If the stain is new, on the other hand . . . "

"Yes, yes?"

We were both almost interested despite ourselves.

" . . . then you can spit on it. Spit works well."

I was about to work round to the subject of the 'robe of Truth' from the masque but Bartholomew Ridd spared me the trouble by raising it himself.

"I told the laundrywoman to use milk and then salt and water on the costume worn by the man who died lately – the one who fell from that silly chair – what was his name?"

"Sir Philip Blake."

"Whoever it was."

"Did it work, the milk or the salt and water?" I said.

"No, none of it worked, which is why I told her to rub salt directly in the marks. Anyway it is as good as new now. It had to be for when Master Jonson wore it. See for yourself. It's in there."

He nodded towards the other little chamber and then bent his head once more over the stained doublet, sucking in his breath noisily between his lips. Abel and I went next door and pretended to examine the cloak, which was draped over a table. Ridd was right, it did look as good as new. You'd never have known that a man had died wearing it. There was no trace of blood or gore on it. The miniature suns which decorated it and which indicated the dazzling power of Truth were newly burnished. This had all been easier than I'd expected. We'd located the cloak. But of course we couldn't remove it from the tire-room, at least not yet.

"Satisfied?" said Ridd, as we were leaving. "Have you picked up some tips on shirt-cleaning?"

"Thank you, Master Ridd," said Abel.

"What works for ale-house stains?" I said, indicating the guilty doublet.

"Oh, soap and water," said Ridd with resignation. "They will wash out with time. Time is another great cleanser, along with milk and salt and the rest. With this dirty doublet, though, it is not the offence so much as the principle of the thing."

"Tell Dick Burbage about it," said Abel.

"Who do you think was wearing this?" sighed Bartholomew Ridd.

Later, Abel and I discussed who should be involved in the little scene we were planning to play out.

"Each one of them," I said. "There are not very many. There is Lady Jane herself and her maid-companion Maria More. There is William Inman . . . "

"Who you saw in a clinch with the widow."

"Yes, he must be invited. And Jonathan Snell, the father."

"I thought that you heard them discussing the most innocent subject, Nick. Pipes and cisterns and privies. Innocent but unseemly."

I'd told Abel just about everything in the attempt to persuade him to go along with what he'd termed a madcap scheme. This included the eavesdropped discussion in the Blake mansion, which Snell had already explained to me as what you might call a *privy* talk. I believed him about that particular conversation but still thought there might have been some understanding between the wife and the engine-man to dispose of the husband. The way he'd tried to mini-mize the son's discovery of the severed ropes, for example. The fact that I had discovered the body of John Ratchett on the floor of his workshop. This tended to point the finger of suspicion at the father – but not at the son, who had first drawn my attention to the ropes and whose later denial that anything was wrong might be attributed to the influence of Jonathan senior.

"Yes, we should definitely add Master Snell to the list," I said. "And I have been wondering about Martin Barton."

"But he's a poet, he's a playwright," said Abel Glaze, who still retained a perhaps exaggerated respect for these pro-fessions despite a couple of years spent in the playhouse.

"So is Ben Jonson. Yet he has killed a man, even if it was in a duel."

"Why would Barton want to see Sir Philip dead?"

"He envies Ben Jonson, he would be glad of anything that disrupted one of Ben's productions."

"Death is an extreme form of disruption," said Abel. "And killing one man because you don't like another man's work seems a – a roundabout way of doing things."

"Well, since you put it like that . . . " I conceded. "But I did hear Barton talking in the Line and Compass tavern about Sir Philip's death, almost as if the poor man deserved to die. And we all know how Barton despises court life . . . "

"It's a pose," said Abel. "Barton is better born than any of us. His disdain of Jonson is because Jonson was once a bricklayer."

Abel had accounted for Barton's attitude so exactly that I could not think of any objection, although I still recalled Barton's words in the ale-house, *Killing a man is nothing. It's getting away with it that counts.*

"Very well," I said. "Leaving aside Barton, there are just four of them. That is: Lady Blake and Maria More, Bill Inman and Jonathan Snell. Each of them might have had a reason for wanting Sir Philip dead, or at least for helping another of the group who did. Lady Jane because she's after another husband or because the last one found her out in some infidelity. Maria More because she is devoted to her mistress. Bill Inman because he too seems to be devoted to Lady Jane."

"Or because he wants her for himself."

"She seems much desired," I said.

"And Jonathan Snell? What's his motive?"

"I don't know. Money? The challenge of killing a man and making it look like an accident?"

Abel looked dubious.

"I still think this is a madcap scheme, Nick."

"Why are you going along with it then?"

"Friendship. And because I believe nothing is going to happen."

"If nothing happens I'll drop the whole business," I said. "Lady Blake can marry her country cousin in peace."

"That's good of you," said Abel.

Your mystery, your mystery

I crouched in the gathering dark on the roof of the Globe playhouse thinking; Abel was right. This is a madcap scheme. Abel himself was sitting only a couple of yards away from me. We were in the shadows of the hut on top of the playhouse canopy. My friend said nothing out loud but inwardly he was probably cursing himself for agreeing to help. His only consolation could be that, when nothing happened and we both of us went home, he wouldn't be the one who looked a complete fool. I stood upright and started to pace up and down the rush-strewn wooden walkway.

The scheme, the madcap scheme, had not started altogether well. It had been a simple enough matter to get into the playhouse after hours since I'd deliberately left a window unlatched in a passageway overlooking the alley known as Brend's Rents. I'd gone in first (this was my idea after all, and this would be my fault when it all went wrong) while Abel gave me a leg-up and kept watch outside. There was still more than an hour of daylight left. Once I was inside, I latched the window and waited in the behind-stage passage, listening for sounds. There were none. The place seemed empty. It should be empty by the middle of the evening, all the life and activity of the Globe being concentrated within the periods of practice and playing. There was always the chance, however, that someone – one of the seniors, say, or Bartholomew Ridd or Geoffrey Allison the book-keeper – might be working late.

Standing in the gloomy passage which I'd walked up and down countless times in the last four years, I felt like a trespasser. This was a foolish feeling, I told myself. You cannot trespass in your own workplace. But it was my actions, not my instincts, which were truly foolish. And it was trespassing since I had no business being here, no business at all. If found and challenged, I planned to say that I'd returned to pick up my part for next day's play (which was not WS's *Othello* but Barton's *Melancholy Man*). This at least was 'true' since I had hidden my scroll in an obscure corner of the tire-room. I almost hoped to be found and challenged. That way I could pick up my 'lost' lines and return to my lodgings, no damage done.

But there was no one to find me and put me back on the right path. I walked along the passageway, my footsteps echoing unnaturally loud inside my head if nowhere else, and made an entrance on to the bare stage. I'd be out here tomorrow afternoon, once again playing Lussorio in *The Melancholy Man*. Lussorio was a murderer but I doubt if he felt much guiltier than I did at this moment. I opened my mouth to say a few lines from my part in the play but no sounds emerged. I couldn't recall a single thing which Lussorio said or did. My mind was blank. It happens to players sometimes. You can only hope that it does not happen when you're actually standing on the stage in front of a paying audience. Maybe I did need to retrieve that lost part from the tire-room after all.

I cleared my throat and tried again. Some words came out but they weren't from *The Melancholy Man*. Instead they were Roderigo's from *Othello*:

I have no great devotion to the deed,
And yet he has given me satisfying reasons:
'Tis but a man gone: forth my sword: he dies.

My voice resonated around the vacant galleries. The sun

dropped below the roof and the exposed interior of the playhouse turned as deep and shadowy as a valley on a summer's evening, although the sky overhead was still a pale blue. I had the eerie sensation that I was being watched from the empty tiers of seating. Oddly, this feeling was much stronger than when one actually was being watched by a houseful of spectators. And why had I chosen those particular lines from *Othello* or rather why had they slipped, unbidden, into my head? It must be that Roderigo is waiting in ambush as he utters them, waiting to kill Cassio. Just as Abel and I were waiting in ambush, not to kill but to find a killer . . .

I'd almost forgotten about Abel Glaze and hastened to the little office where Sam, the principal doorkeeper and money-gatherer, kept his keys. Sam was a little limping man who went round securing the exits, both public and players', after everyone had left the theatre. His last act was to lock himself out and take himself home (he lived somewhere by the Southwark Bear Garden, I think) with his bunch of keys. The one door he was unable to secure, ironically, was that to his own office since the wood had swollen and it would not shut properly. "I've told Master Burbage about it," he'd said to me that very morning when I was checking to make sure that the door hadn't yet been repaired. "It's not safe. Some bugger'll take advantage and get in here one of these days." I had nodded, reflecting all the while that that bugger would be me, and feeling dishonest in every atom of my body. "They spend all that money on tarting up the place out front, tarting it up to buggery," Sam continued, "all that money on the stage and the rest of it and then they don't bother to see to a simple job like this door. It's all show. I've told Master Burbage."

Now I eased open the swollen door to Sam's office and ran my eyes over the range of keys hanging from pegs on the wall inside. Conveniently, they were labelled, 'west door', 'tire-room' and so on. I slipped those two particular keys off their pegs and went round to the west door. Abel was waiting.

"What took you so long?"

"Sorry."

Once Abel was inside, I shut the outer door but did not lock it. Abel looked as uneasy as I felt. We made our way across to the tire-room, using Sam's key to get in. There was not much light down here but quite enough to see that the 'robe of Truth' as worn by Sir Philip Blake and then by Ben Jonson in the masque had gone from the little chamber adjacent to the tire-room. We might have searched for it but, given the poor light and the sheer number of costumes stacked or hung up in these rooms or folded away in chests elsewhere, the chances of finding it were small.

I went to rummage in a corner of the main tire-room.

"It's gone, that costume," said Abel.

"I know. We won't lay our hands on it now. There's no time."

"So what are you doing, Nick?"

"Looking for my part in tomorrow's play. Here it is."

I unearthed the *Melancholy Man* scroll from the place where I'd hidden it earlier. Abel didn't bother to ask me about this little rigmarole. Perhaps he'd already given up hope. I would have given up hope in his place. I would have been questioning my friend's sanity. Nevertheless, he followed me without speaking to the top storey of the theatre and from there we emerged on to the open roof with its hut and walkways.

So, without the costume, the first part of my scheme had foundered. And now, on the roof of the Globe, I had the feeling in my guts that the whole plan was doomed, as it deserved to be. For I'd been intending to snaffle the 'robe of Truth' from the tire-room and then to confront . . . someone . . . and to surprise him (or her) into a confession or at least into a guilty response. Perhaps the drama of the setting and the idea of the costume had warped my brain. My self-appointed role was as the finder-out of truth. A 'truth' which would be delivered from this elevated position on top of the world, the point from which the god descends to put right the affairs of mortals and lay down the law. But now, in the fading light of a late summer's evening, my plan seemed both arrogant and foolish. Who did I think I was? A *deus ex machina* equipped with superhuman powers? No, a poor player who was grotesquely out of his depth.

I looked up at the wide sky. The evening star twinkled in the east. The moon hovered on the other side, as if delaying to make an entrance until the night should begin in earnest and he could make a better show. I knew some players who were like that. I hoped night would fall soon. Then I would declare the madcap scheme a failure, and Abel and I could slink off to bed. Something kept me here until then: the fear of appearing a fool (but I was that already) or the hope that 'someone' might come (and a stronger, conflicting hope that they would not). And since I was here so was my faithful friend, Abel Glaze, who was now sitting with his legs extended and his back propped against the cabin containing the lifting gear. I wondered whether he'd fallen asleep. Whatever happened next, it was not his fault. The blame lay exclusively at the feet of N. Revill.

I'd written letters, you see, to the four individuals Abel and I had discussed: Lady Jane Blake, Maria More, William Inman and Jonathan Snell. Four epistles to four different recipients but with identical contents. Each letter made an unsubstantiated accusation, claiming that Lady Blake – or Maria More – or Bill Inman – or Jonathan Snell – had had a hand in the killing of Sir Philip Blake during the practice for the *Masque of Peace* at Somerset House. I gave no specifics, reckoning that when it came to slanderous accusations the best policy was vagueness. Each letter was unsigned, showing what a courageous correspondent I was. Each letter indicated that the recipient's guilty secret would be safe with me (the anonymous writer) provided that he or she turned up at a certain place at a certain time to discuss 'arrangements'. I hinted at money, I hinted at sealed lips.

The plan was simple. If any of the four responded to the letter it was a fairly sure sign that he or she was guilty. For, if you were innocent, there was a natural reaction to receiving such an anonymous accusation. The natural reaction would be to read the letter with horror, with disbelief, with incomprehension. To dismiss it as the work of a person who was mad or malicious or both. To tear it into small pieces and cast them down the privy and flush them away, perhaps in one of those new devices which Lady Blake and Jonathan Snell had been conspiring over. In short, to try to forget about the letter's existence. That would be the normal, natural response in the circumstances. It's how you or I would react, isn't it?

The one individual who wouldn't behave like that would be Sir Philip's murderer. The murderer might be horrified to be accused, especially anonymously, but he or she would be much less likely to tear up the letter, to forget about it et cetera. Instead the guilty person would – or should, if all went according to plan – follow instructions to turn up at such-and-such a place, at such-and-such a time, in order to silence me either with money . . . or with a more binding method. This second possibility was one reason why I'd wanted Abel's company, since I was conscious that, if my belief about Blake's death was right, I was dealing with an individual who was both ruthless and cunning. An individual who was possibly responsible for the deaths of John Ratchett and Giles Cass as well.

When I was penning those unsigned notes in my lodgings I experienced a schoolboyish thrill. Now, by the chill light of evening, my actions appeared dangerously stupid. I had accused four upright citizens of complicity in a murder. If a single one of them was guilty, this might be justified. But not a single one of them *was* guilty. I grew increasingly convinced of this, and of my foolishness, as the moon inched up the sky and the air grew colder.

I had sealed up the letters and handed them to a lad I'd found lounging in Chancery Lane. I didn't know him and didn't ask his name. Anonymity all round. Three of the letters were destined for the same place, the Blake mansion in the Strand not far off. I told the boy to hand them personally to the gatekeeper, promising there'd be another penny when he came back and described the gatekeeper to me. He asked no questions but ran off. I hung about on the corner of Chancery Lane, half enjoying the secrecy and the contrivance, and thinking that I might be cut out for a spy after all.

Then the boy came back to tell me about the large hairy wart on the gatekeeper's cheek. Since this was the only feature of note which the Blake gatekeeper possessed, I knew that he'd delivered the letters. I imagined the letters being passed from the gatekeeper to a household servant, one of those yellow-liveried fellows who glided about the place like a fish, and then eventually finding their way up to the individual recipients, Lady Blake, Maria More, William Inman. I imagined each person tearing at the seal, unfolding the paper – cheap paper, for this anonymous writer was no better than a cheap extortioner – and reading the slanderous words. It was at this point in my imaginings that doubts started to creep in.

Too late to go back now. You can't recall a letter once sent. The boy was still hanging about at my elbow, hoping for more errands, so I gave him the final letter and another penny, telling him to take it to the Snells' workshop in Three Cranes Lane, making sure it went to the older Snell, the father. I instructed him to bring back some news about the colour of the gate. He scuttled off in the opposite direction. I waited some more, the doubts growing stronger with every passing minute. This errand took longer than the first one, or so it appeared to me as I paced about or leaned against a wall. I remembered that Ben Jonson was supposed to have had a hand in building a wall in Chancery Lane, or was it in Lincoln's Inn? Eventually the lad returned to inform me that the workshop gate was painted green (it might have been green – I couldn't remember) and that he had entrusted the letter to a long-haired man who'd promised to pass it to

Master Snell. Mission accomplished. I gave the messenger his final penny.

The die was cast. Four honest citizens had received letters which more or less accused them of murder. It was up to them whether they reacted to this outrageous slander or whether they simply threw the accusations away. A third possibility was that any one of the four might alert a local magistrate and come in search of the anonymous slanderer. Somehow, though, this seemed the least likely course of action. It would be too much . . . trouble. Alerting a magistrate would mean showing the letter to him. It would risk opening up an investigation into Sir Philip's death which, even if not murder, had some shadowy aspects to it.

I had set the time of assignation for eight o'clock this evening and the place as the roof of the Globe stage. I had hoped to to startle the murderer into an avowal of his, or her guilt, by rising up in the robe of Truth and pointing the finger of blame at whoever emerged on to the roof from the upper gallery *like a guilty thing upon a fearful summons*. It may sound far-fetched, this dressing-up and finger-pointing, but all I can say is that it worked for Shakespeare. That was in a play, of course, and he was perhaps a little more subtle.

To arrange a meeting at this dramatic location, and to give directions on climbing to the roof of the playhouse, would inevitably suggest that the anonymous accuser had some connection with the Globe. But many people had connections to the Globe, not just players but costumers and doormen and painters and the like. There was no particular reason for the anonymous letters to be traced back to N. Revill. I had even made an attempt to disguise my handwriting but this had produced such a blotchy, ragged scrawl that it looked like a child's efforts, so I reverted to my normal hand.

There was still some light in the sky. Abel had his eyes closed. I settled down with my back against the cabin wall. Thinking I might as well make some use of this blank time before somebody came, before nobody came, I reached into my pocket and fetched out the scroll which contained my part for the next day's play, that is, Martin Barton's *Melancholy Man*. Earlier on the bare stage I'd been unable to remember a single word or action belonging to the murderous character of Lussorio, but when I peered at the lines in the half-light it came back to me.

Barton had made comments about William Shakespeare being 'unrealistic' for using a device like a handkerchief in *Othello*, as well as for taking seriously subjects such as cuckolding and infidelity when they were only fit for laughter. Well, when it came to a lack of realism his play took the prize. I'd never read or seen or acted in such an absurd hotchpotch as this thing of Barton's. Blood, satire, laughter, they were all mixed up together until everything was as clear as mud. But the audiences, in their new post-plague mood, liked it, which was the reason why it was being given a revival.

I won't weary you with the detailed plot of *The Melancholy Man*. Suffice it to say that the story concerns a Duke – Italian, naturally – who escapes an assassination attempt arranged by his wife's lover. As Lussorio, I was one of the murderers who failed to do him in. The Duke comes back in a hermit's disguise to flit around the outskirts of his court, passing bitter, satirical commentary on the parade of grotesques who populate it. No one guesses that this shag-haired hermit is actually the Duke until he whips off his disguise at the end of Act Five and puts the world to rights. Just as I'd planned to put the world to rights from the rooftop of the Globe.

Absurd, to think that a Duke could pass himself off as a shaggy hermit in the play. But not as absurd as believing that I was capable of acting as a *deus ex machina* in reality. In Barton's case the hermit disguise was a pretext, of course, since dirty old hermits are well known to be moral philosophers. It was a pretext for the playwright to vent his bile about courtly pretensions. Everyone was a parcel of seething rottenness, everyone was food for worms. (Everyone except well-muscled craftsmen and boy-players, no doubt. Not that

Barton actually said this.) In my case, I had no excuse for my *deus ex machina* act. At least Martin Barton was earning an honest living. I was likely to lose mine altogether if anyone discovered what I'd done, what I was doing now.

It was getting too dark to read and I put the scroll back in my pocket. Even if anyone did arrive for the 'meeting' I probably wouldn't be able to see them properly. I leaned my head back against the roughcast wall of the cabin and closed my eyes.

Various shapes crossed my mind's eye. Or rather they weren't shapes so much as a queer mixture of pictures and ideas which had taken on some pictorial form.

One was the signing of the peace treaty between Spain and England which we'd attended a few days previously as Grooms of the Outer Chamber. It wasn't the ceremony which preoccupied me, the King shambling up the aisle of the Chapel Royal and so on. It was the thought that had come to me afterwards, that *It was all a matter of show.* The same thing had applied to that glimpse of Cecil and Howard and the rest sitting opposite the Spanish Constable and his *señors* in the chamber at Whitehall Palace, as if they were waiting to have their portraits done. *A matter of show.*

Another reflection must have been prompted by the fact that I'd just looked at Barton's *The Melancholy Man*, or rather at my particular lines as Lussorio. I and others had failed to kill the Duke, who then reappeared to indulge himself as a shag-haired hermit dispensing his bitter wit on all sides. The Duke still lived on but not in the person of the Duke . . .

Then I had an image not from a play but from real life. It was of the craftsman-painter Ned Armitage as I'd first encountered him in the Three Cranes workshop with the marks of red paint on his face. He'd been painting a chest for a stage presentation by Worcester's Men out at the Curtain playhouse. What – or who – was meant to be hidden in the chest? I'd found a body in the same chest in the workshop on my second visit but that body was a mannequin. There was a real body further in, though, that of John Ratchett sprawled on the floor. By the next morning he'd disappeared as if he'd never existed.

On the subject of chests: Mrs Buckle had a chest in her room. Was it red? I didn't know, never having seen her bedroom by daylight, never having been that interested in her furniture. What did Mrs Buckle's chest have to do with all this? Nothing. Leave her chest behind. But I would have liked to return to Mrs Buckle's chest, in another sense. My friend Blanche – no, my whore Blanche – she had a mole on her right breast. Perhaps Mrs Buckle had a mole too. That would be amusing, the wife of a parson and a French whore sharing moles. But I wouldn't know what Mrs Buckle had on her chest. I had not seen her in full daylight, not in that way. *Darkness is best.*

Then I thought of Master Bartholomew Ridd and what he'd said about the best way to remove bloodstains. Avoid fighting first of all. But if you do spill blood you should use milk, or salt and water to clean it up. If it's fresh, then you should spit on the stain. Spit works well. What had the laundrywoman used on the 'cloak of Truth' as worn by Sir Philip Blake and Ben Jonson? She'd tried milk, but that hadn't worked. Nor had salt and water.

When I was little I had a toy which was made of some shiny wood. It was carved in the shape of an apple and was ingeniously constructed so that it came apart segment by segment. It was a simple matter for my childish fingers to pull the apple apart but much harder for those same fingers to put it back together again. Yet it would go together. I had watched my father reassemble the apple times without number, when I'd gone to him with teary eyes or a cross face. He was a patient man, with me at least. "There," he'd say, placing it in my open palm, "there's nothing to it." And it was true, there was nothing to it when he was the one who was doing it. But as soon as I'd taken the apple apart once more, I could not for the life of me recall how it all slotted together. Then one day I managed to take the apple apart *and* put it back together, so I squirrelled it away in a chest and never got it out again.

The items that were floating about in my head were like the pieces of that apple. They should fit together, should fit perfectly, but somehow I could not quite do it.

I recalled Giles Cass's words about Sir Philip Blake. That he'd been lucky to die when he did, considering that the beagle, Secretary Cecil, was on his tail for plotting against the Spanish peace, therefore for being on Raleigh's side. Sir Walter Raleigh . . . who'd narrowly avoided that dreadful fate of hanging, drawing and quartering . . . hanging, and while still alive – though barely – having bloody hands thrust into his entrails . . .

I thought too of Lady Jane Blake's hasty remarriage to a country cousin. A lucky man perhaps. To be marrying into all that wealth, a country house far away and a mansion close at hand on the Strand. To be marrying a woman who was an apothecary's daughter and who'd recently played Plenty in a royal masque. She'd come up in the world, had Lady Blake. All that flesh, a nice prospect for someone. I wondered whether the country cousin would be brought up to town to see London, for the first time perhaps. Or maybe he'd already seen the city . . .

Some pieces of the mystery – some pieces of the apple – seemed to come together inside my head and for a moment I thought I had it. Then it slipped from my grasp.

I wasn't really asleep all this time while I was sitting on top of the Globe for I suddenly heard a noise within the depths of the building. Abel heard it too, a kind of thud. He tensed and sat up. In the fading light we waited for another sound but none came.

After a moment Abel said, "I have been wondering, Nick."

I braced myself for a bitter comment or at least a critical one. How I was all wrong, how this was a waste of effort.

"Do you think they'll ever build another spire on Paul's?"

Abel gestured across the river. The great church was almost opposite us, a little to our left. Its outline bulked larger and grander than any other building on the far side. Once, years ago at the start of Elizabeth's reign, St Paul's possessed the tallest spire of all the London churches. But it was struck by lightning and burned down. It had never been replaced although there was talk of it from time to time.

"I don't know," I said.

"It would be a fine thing," said Abel.

"A fine thing," I repeated.

And that seemed to bring this futile evening to a close. There was no point in lingering up here on the roof of the Globe any longer. The air was turning chilly with more than a hint of autumn in it. No one was going to come now. My scheme wasn't so much madcap as just plain foolish. Time to get out of the playhouse, and return here in the proper form for tomorrow morning's rehearsal of Barton's *Melancholy Man*. To return not as trespassers but players. Not as arrogant finders-out of truth but as humble honest craftsmen.

Abel stood up and stretched. I moved away from the cabin and along the walkway towards the door into the upper gallery. Then we heard it.

'A strange truth'

There was no doubt about it this time. There were footsteps coming up the gallery stairs. More than one set of footsteps. My first thought was that they must belong to a couple of the seniors. They'd found out about my plans and were coming to deal with me. It was no more than I deserved. I'd trespassed on my own workplace, I'd stolen keys (and would have stolen a tire-room costume if I could have laid my hands on it), I'd written slanderous letters, I'd inveigled an innocent player into participating in a foolish scheme. I had brought the King's Men into disrepute. I would be asked to leave the Company straightaway. No more than I deserved.

All this passed through my mind in a flash. The footsteps drew nearer. In a moment the door which led from the topmost gallery on to the roof would be opened. Abel grabbed my arm and pulled me back. Without saying a word, we slipped around to the far side of the hut, the side that faced towards the river, and crouched against the wall. We'd be out of sight of anyone making a cursory inspection from the doorway. Maybe we could get away with it.

We heard the gallery door opening and the tread of feet as people – only two of them by the sound of it – emerged into the open. It was more than half-dark by now. There was the glimmer of lamplight from round the corner of our hiding place. This suggested that whoever was up here on the roof felt little need to conceal themselves. Unlike us, they were entitled to be here. The tables were turned. We'd been intending to trap a murderer. Now it was Abel and I who were trapped and trying to hide, most likely from our seniors. I waited for a shout, a summons. But nobody spoke, nobody said a thing, not even in a whisper.

This was strange, that nobody was speaking at all. After an age had gone by, I motioned to Abel to stay where he was and crept forward very slowly on all fours until I reached the corner of the roughcast wall of the hut. Like a wary tortoise I peered round the edge. There were two men standing at the other end of the walkway. They had a lantern with them but it was placed on the rush-strewn ground so that I glimpsed only their feet. They had their backs to me and were looking towards the door which gave on to the gallery passage. The door was still open.

I retreated behind the shelter of the wall and signed to Abel that there were a couple of them. He cupped his hand and whispered in my ear, "Burbage? Shakespeare?" I shook my head. Like me, he'd assumed that anyone on the roof must be here legitimately, and at this time of night that was most likely to be the shareholders. But the outlines I'd seen had not been those of Dick Burbage or WS or of anyone else that I recognized from the King's Men. Even so, I had an idea who the two were.

Then we heard more steps coming up the gallery stairs. Not one or two sets of steps but several. These were no shareholders come to rebuke us, and to throw me out of the Company. This was much more serious than the mere loss of my job. My heart was beating hard and a sweat broke out on me, despite the growing chill of the evening. I suddenly understood that my madcap scheme, far from failing, was about to become a great success. I understood some other things too. The pieces of the apple, which I'd been struggling to fit together, slotted into place without effort while I was paying attention to something quite different. *There's nothing to it.* I saw how the trick had been done, more or less.

I also understood that Abel's life and mine were in great danger. Our best, our only, chance of survival was to keep absolutely silent and still, and pray that our visitors would be satisfied with a glance around the roof. (I didn't think that they would be though. They'd been invited up here. Invited by an idiot.)

Now more people emerged from the gallery on to the wooden walkway. There was the shuffle and clump of feet, several pairs of feet, some light, some heavy. The oddest aspect of all this was that no word had yet been uttered. Abel grasped at my arm once more. I sensed his bewilderment and fear. I was fearful myself, but not bewildered, not really. It was small compensation but I could have told him what was happening – or at least could have told him why this little group was assembling on the roof of the Globe playhouse – except that to talk would be to reveal our presence.

But, although we hadn't been seen, our presence was already known. Or mine was at least.

"Master Revill," came a voice. It was Jonathan Snell, the father, the engine-man.

"Nick, are you there?"

Now I recognized the sound of the son.

"It was wrong to cast you as Ignorance in that masque, you are much more ingenious, Nicholas," said a woman. That was Maria More.

"You wrote a letter," said the bluff tones of Bill Inman.

"Please come and talk to us, Master Revill," said another man whose voice I also recognized.

Hiding was pointless. In a moment they would inspect the walkway which ran round the hut and they would discover Abel and me, crouching in fear of our lives. If I showed myself to them before that and caused a distraction, Abel might make his escape.

Again signalling to my friend that he should remain where he was, I stood up and walked round the corner.

"Here I am," I said. "You want to talk?"

There was a cluster of individuals standing on the area of the roof between the upper gallery door and the entrance to the hut. They had at least three lamps between them which cast a good glow across the group and enabled me to identify them. I knew who I'd find up here anyway. I knew it all now, more or less.

There were both Jonathan Snells, the father and the son, the latter wearing his spectacles. They were the ones who'd arrived first on the playhouse roof. There was Lady Jane Blake, wrapped up well against the night-chill. Next to her was the elegant Maria More, still more the mistress than the mistress. There was honest, bluff Bill Inman. And standing next to him was that equally honest craftsman Ned Armitage and the lank-haired fellow from the Three Cranes yard, Tom Turner. Seven individuals altogether.

I'd been looking for one, at the most two. There were seven of them!

"Well," said Jonathan Snell the older, "you have found us out."

"I have now," I said. I gazed up at the sky. The moon was at the edge of my vision.

Someone shivered with an intake of breath, Maria More I think.

"Let's go inside here," I said, gesturing behind me. "It is more . . . private."

Like a host ushering guests into his house, I showed the company inside the hut. It was not built for comfort, but it got us out of the night air. There were a couple of stools in here, as well as the *deus ex machina* chair. The lifting gear loomed in the shadows thrown by the light of the lanterns. The seven disposed themselves around the little room. There wasn't much space. I stood in the doorway, unsure whether this was to prevent any of them leaving or to give me the opportunity of escaping on my own account. I could be through the gallery door and halfway down the stairs before they set off in pursuit. I had the advantage of knowing the Globe's entrances and exits. But I owed it to Abel to let him leave first. Besides, I did not feel in imminent danger. Rather, it was these seven individuals who seemed to be expecting me to act.

"What do you want?" said Bill Inman. "Do you want money?"

"No," I said. "That was just a device to get you here in the first place, the belief that I was after money."

"You're alone?" said the older Snell.

"Quite alone," I said, a little louder than necessary and for Abel's benefit.

"You have no magistrate concealed up here?" said Lady Jane.

"No magistrate, no authority, on my life," I said.

"What *do* you want then?" said Snell, echoing Inman but with more emphasis.

"The truth," I said.

There was no immediate answer to this ambitious demand. Then the younger Snell said, "I think that Nick deserves that at least. We can only lay the truth before him."

To my surprise Maria More nodded assent at this and Tom Turner said simply, "Yes."

"But you are already in possession of the truth," said father Snell. "Or you think you are."

"Oh, I am," I said with more confidence than I felt. "The fact that you're all here shows that I am."

I did not say that the truth had come to me only moments earlier. Instead I said, "But let me try it for size. You can put me right if I go wrong in the details."

Nobody spoke. I drew breath and began my story.

"Everything seemed to stem from the death of Sir Philip Blake, although this strange business began before that. That death was supposed to be an accident. That was how it was meant to appear, a terrible accident. It was a very public event, witnessed by dozens of people in the audience chamber at

Somerset House. And that's how it would have remained – as an accident – if it hadn't been for Jonathan Snell's sharp eyes, or his sharp spectacles perhaps. He spotted that the ropes holding up the chair on which Sir Philip was lowered had been partly cut through, in such a way that they'd sever altogether when the chair reached a certain point in its descent. The fact that the ropes had been cut so nicely suggested that whoever did it was familiar with weights and tensions, and so on."

I paused and looked at the engine-man Jonathan Snell. He said, "My son pointed all this out at the time."

"And then he retracted it," I said.

"Only because I discovered . . . certain facts later," said the son.

"That's as I thought," I said. "You'd been so sure beforehand that someone had tampered with the ropes, even while your father was trying to make light of the whole idea, that when you said you'd changed your mind I concluded that you'd found out something afterwards which you didn't know at the time. There was only one possibility which fitted. It had to be something which implicated . . . a person close to you."

"That's true," said the son.

"Then we had a discussion up in the gallery, you two gentlemen and I, and I said that I would ask some questions about Sir Philip's death, and try to find out more about it."

"I wondered why you offered to do that," said father Snell. "We didn't want it. There was no need."

"*You* didn't want it, true, but I had – private reasons for suggesting it," I said. "There was a man who was demanding that I look into the accident at Somerset House. He had a hold over me."

It seemed appropriate to confess a small item to them since I was expecting so much confession from them in return, even if tacitly.

"But I got nowhere. And when Jonathan here said he'd

changed his mind about Blake's death and that it *was* an accident, it looked as if there was no prospect of finding more."

"Then what has happened to bring us all here if there's nothing to find out?" said Lady Jane.

"I heard that you were about to get married again, my lady."

"I am."

She said this quietly, without apology but without defiance.

"So soon after the death of your first husband?"

"So soon after his death."

"And I'm afraid that was enough to set me thinking. It might have set a saint thinking. You must forgive me, Lady Jane, for attributing base motives to your intentions . . . But it wasn't only that. A friend who also appeared in the *Masque of Peace* told me that he thought Sir Philip had been drugged or poisoned before being placed in the chair."

"What! Impossible! How could he tell?" said Bill Inman with what sounded like genuine puzzlement.

"There was a look on Sir Philip's face. How did my friend describe it now? Like watching someone having a nightmare which you can't wake them from, I think it was. Also he had other – evidence."

(I was unwilling to reveal that Abel had got hold of Sir Philip's flask. In any case, I no longer believed that there'd been any kind of drug or poison in it.)

"So it seemed to me that, in the light of Lady Blake's re-marriage and my friend's story, there was a strong chance that Sir Philip *had* been murdered after all. But there was only one way to put this to the proof."

"To send out accusing letters to all of us," said Maria More.

"Yes. I knew that if anyone came to this – this meeting – then he or she at least had something to hide in the matter of Sir Philip's death. I expected one person, perhaps two. But there are seven of you!"

I almost laughed. Nerves, I suppose. I felt like a fisherman who staggers back home with more than he can carry. I glanced round the little cabin at the array of faces, half illuminated, half shadowed by the lanterns. The only people who hadn't yet spoken were Ned Armitage and, apart from his single "yes", Tom Turner. An hour ago I would have been very surprised at their presence. Now I knew the reasons for it.

"That is not much to build an accusation on," said the older Snell, who seemed to be speaking on behalf of the group. "A story told you by a fellow player about the expression on Sir Philip Blake's face and the fact that Lady Blake desires to get married again."

"No, it is not much perhaps. But when it's combined with other events, with other deaths maybe . . . "

I had their full attention now.

"A moment ago I mentioned a man who had a hold over me. Well, something happened to him, although I can't prove it now since he's dead to the world and the world's dead to him. And then there was that other man called Giles Cass who played the part of Suspicion in Ben Jonson's masque. He died apparently by falling into the river after he'd struck his head on some steps at Somerset House. You remember that? You must do, for you were all present, I think.

"But it's not Cass's drowning which I'm thinking of. That death might have been as accidental as Sir Philip's was supposed to have been. It's what Cass said to me shortly before he died. He was talking about Secretary Cecil and how King James called him his beagle and how Cecil had been on Sir Philip's trail for treason . . . for being part of Sir Walter Raleigh's conspiracy . . . "

For some reason Tom Turner, who'd seated himself in the *deus ex machina* chair, fidgeted impatiently at this point.

"And that did set me thinking but rather late in the day, while I was waiting around up here. I thought about the penalty for treason, the terrible penalty. The hanging . . . and the rest of it."

Maria More shivered again although it was growing stuffy inside this close little hut.

"And I thought of how, if I were a nobleman and being

253

accused of treason, I would do almost anything to escape the terrible penalty. But of course if I were actually accused of treason it would be too late. I'd be in the Tower and facing trial and after that the scaffold and the hangman's bloody hands. Too late. So if I was going to elude the charge of treason, I'd have to take action before that charge was brought. I could run away to a foreign country perhaps – but I do not want to leave my wife, for I am a married man, happily married. And I have great estates in the country and a house in London. I do not want to relinquish any of these things. But I must relinquish them for a time if I am to survive. Survive until my enemies like Cecil are dead themselves perhaps."

"Oh, Cecil is immortal," said Tom Turner. "He will outlast all of us."

This was a surprising observation to come from a tongue-tied artisan.

"When I first visited the workshop which belonged to Master Snell," I continued – taking my time over the story for I was beginning to enjoy myself now, strange as that may seem – "when I went to the Three Cranes yard, I saw a mannequin figure sitting on a pile of tarpaulins. For a moment I thought he was real. But he wasn't real, merely a figure made of linen and stuffed with some material."

"With rags and lead and sand," said father Snell. "The figure's weight has to be judged to a nicety."

"Of course," I said. "Everything in this business had to be done to a nicety. Then exploring further in the Three Cranes yard I came across Master Ned Armitage here. He was asleep at the time but – the silliest thing! – because he'd got red paint smeared across his face I believed for a second that Ned was dead. So I saw how easy it was to play dead accidentally. I ought to know of course, being a player."

Ned Armitage looked faintly, well, sheepish. Perhaps he didn't like being shown up for having fallen asleep in the workplace. As if there weren't greater offences! I paused and looked in the direction of Jonathan Snell senior.

"A body is a body but it doesn't have to be real. That's why there was a strange, distant expression on Sir Philip's face when he fell. When 'it' fell. No wonder he looked like someone who couldn't be woken from a nightmare – no wonder he looked remote, out of this world. The horror was simulated with the figure's gaping mouth and white face. You relied on artificial lighting and the fact that what everyone sees on stage is what they want to see. Or not exactly what they want to see but what they *expect* to see. No one's going to have the chance to examine a man while he's falling down anyway."

There was a silence. Quickly I said to the older Snell, "What was the head made of?"

"Wax, together with a wood frame that would crack with a nasty sound – and other matter inside the head. It was a challenge to our art."

There was pride in the father's tone. I started to understood why he and his workshop had become involved in this dangerous deception.

"That's why almost everyone involved in this came up to the platform beforehand to have a look, it was a work of art," I said. "The image of Sir Philip Blake."

I did not need their half-nods, their half-smiles to confirm this.

"One of you ladies dropped her handkerchief up there."

"It was mine, Nicholas," said Maria More.

"I gave it her, it was a fine piece of work," said Lady Jane.

"And I denied ever having it because I was worried that you were asking questions," said Maria.

"The handkerchief didn't matter after all," I said, conscious that it was now in the hands of a French whore in the Mitre. "It simply showed that there'd been a woman in the gallery. But then everyone had been in the gallery, the whole world and his dog."

"Everyone was curious. Everyone was in on the secret."

"All except your son, Master Snell."

"My father thinks I cannot keep a secret," said Jonathan.

There was no bitterness in his tone, just a matter-of-fact statement. I was inclined to think the father was right. I didn't say, however, that it would have been better if Jonathan had been in the know from the beginning since he wouldn't have then emerged with his murder theory. Did the father rely on the son's dim sight for him not to notice the substitution of the mannequin for the real Sir Philip? No, that wouldn't be enough, he must have found some little task to keep him out of the way on the other side of the gallery.

"Did you use the mannequin from the workshop, the one I saw originally?" I said.

"Heavens no," said father Snell. "That was a crude model. For the masque we constructed a special figure, one with plenty of detail and refinement."

"And it was your good luck that the cloak the mannequin was wearing flew up and over his head as he landed. It prevented anyone getting a close look at the shattered head."

"The head would have looked believable enough, for a moment in poor light. And who is going to look for longer than a moment at such a horrid sight? I tell you, Nicholas, I was almost sorry that no one had the opportunity to examine our handiwork afterwards."

I remembered blood pooling out from beneath the cloak, and someone screaming at the back of the audience chamber and Lady Jane dropping down in a dead faint, then Jonathan Snell hastening forward so that he was first on the scene. I remembered the sound his knees had made as they hit the boards beside the shrouded shape. No surprise that he'd hurried to get there.

"But why use red paint?" I said. "Sheep's blood is more convenient. The players use sheep's blood on stage when we want to simulate a wound. And it washes out more easily, you only have to use milk or salt and water – or spit on it. Red paint is much harder to remove."

"We used what was to hand," said Snell. "In a workshop you have plenty of red paint but sheep's blood is in short supply. We needed a fair quantity of blood to horrify people but also to convince them. And it was convincing, Nicholas. You have to admit that. We fooled – oh, I don't know how many people we fooled."

"You fooled the world," I said. "Everyone outside your little circle believes that Sir Philip Blake is dead."

"Everyone but one person," said Bill Inman.

"Everyone but one," I echoed, fervently hoping that Abel Glaze had made his escape by now but fearing that he hadn't.

Tom Turner stood up from the *deus ex machina* chair. I saw Lady Jane grasp his arm.

"Forgive me, sir," he said, "if I do not remove this, ah, disguise. I have grown used to it and it is safer."

He tugged at the lank hair which more or less concealed his features. A kind of shiver ran down my spine. I was looking at a dead man, though not a ghost. When I spoke I was pleased that my voice betrayed no tremor.

"What disguise will you use as the country cousin, sir?"

"The odd burr in my hair should do it, and the occasional twang in my voice, zurr."

I almost smiled despite myself. Ben Jonson had been quite wrong about Sir Philip Blake. He was a good actor, the very best in one sense since you wouldn't have suspected him of acting at all. His current disguise was almost incidental, although the lank wig allowed him to conceal his otherwise prominent ears and the stubble on his chin was a replacement for the neat, pointed beard he'd worn as a courtier. And Blake was capable of playing several parts. He'd already played himself, and I'd taken him to be a mere nobleman, good-natured, not over-intelligent, with his vague manner and his repetition of 'Very good' at almost every comment. Then he had played at his own death or rather allowed a mannequin to fake it for him. After that he'd taken on the part of a simple artisan. And now he was about to be a fresh husband. But it was the artisan's part I was interested in.

"Why did you do it?" I said. "Hang about in disguise, work in the yard, take a backstage part in the masque?"

"I was curious to see how my death was received. Why do you act, Master Revill? Isn't there a thrill in deceiving people? No one looks at a common workman. And I was not found out."

"Until now," I said.

"Until now," he said.

"And why did you pick such an elaborate means of death? The risks were very high."

"The penalty was very high too," said Sir Philip. It was the traitor's penalty he was referring to, the one which I hadn't been able to get out of my thoughts recently.

"But you might have drowned in the river or fallen from your horse or died in any one of a dozen different ways."

"If I'd fallen from a horse or drowned, then a body would have had to be produced. A real body. I required witnesses too, the more the better, but they had to be naturally present and they had to believe that the person they were watching was me. That way, no one – not even Secretary Cecil – could be in any doubt that I was dead. You said yourself, Master Revill, that my death was very public. It was seen by dozens of people in the most dramatic circumstances. Who would think of trickery in a makeshift theatre, in a place where trickery is taken for granted?"

"Sir Philip posed the problem to me," said Jonathan Snell. "It was a challenge, how we might make the world believe he was dead."

"What are you going to do?" said Lady Blake to me, cutting across Snell. She wasn't interested in challenges and craftsmanship.

"It is rather what *you* are going to do, madam. All of you. You have the advantage, there are many more of you. You might, oh, I don't know, you might throw me from the edge of the roof over there or put me in this chair and cut the ropes."

I said this pretty confident, by the by, that they would do none of these things.

"We are not murderers, sir," said Tom Turner – or Sir Philip Blake.

"What about Giles Cass? What did you do to him? It was he who told me that you were being investigated for treason."

"The charge is absurd, unless every man who has ever made a remark against the Spanish is to be hauled up before Lord Justice Popham," said Blake, ignoring the question about Cass to concentrate on the treason. "Although most of the information brought against me was false, it would have brought dishonour on my family. But Cecil is rightly called the beagle by the King. He will not let go of the prey once he has it in his jaws. He likes bringing prizes to his new master. He more or less told me as much on the day the Spanish first arrived in London – "

Now I recalled seeing Blake in earnest conversation with Cecil on the river bank, my first glimpse of him.

" – I was to be a sacrifice on the altar of our new peace with Spain. Just as Raleigh was persecuted for the same reason. Raleigh has been allowed to live for the time being but I would not have been so fortunate."

His wife put her hand on his arm as if to warn him that, even here in the hut on top of the Globe stage and surrounded by fellow conspirators, it was dangerous to be so outspoken. He paid no attention to her restraining hand.

"It doesn't matter what I say," he said. "I am a dead man either way. Sir Philip Blake is dead as far as the world is concerned, and if you choose to resurrect me, Master Revill, then you'll certainly be condemning me to a real death. Cecil wouldn't let me get away a second time."

"I could not condemn anyone, especially to a traitor's death. But, in return, you must tell me about Giles Cass."

I looked again at the circle of faces. There was a silence before Bill Inman said, "None of us had a hand in Cass's departure, Master Revill. He believed that Sir Philip here was dead, like everyone else. We had no reason to act against him. I swear on my honour that I know no more than that he drowned."

"He was struck on the head first," I said.

"If so, then it wasn't by any of us," said Inman.

"I think he must have tripped and fallen then," I said. "There was blood on the steps leading down to the river."

From the expressions on the faces of the group in the hut this seemed to be news to them. Maybe Cass had died exactly as I'd speculated at first, exactly as the coroner had pronounced. Not all appearances are deceptive. But there was yet another death to account for.

"Someone else died," I said. "I visited the Three Cranes yard for a second time after receiving a certain – summons to go there."

I glanced at Jonathan Snell, the son. He nodded somewhat uncomfortably.

"I wanted to tell you what was happening, Nick. I thought it was only right. Only I wasn't able to do it in public."

(Yes, the father had been correct: Jonathan could not keep a secret.)

"While I was there I saw a dead man, a real dead man, not a mannequin, not someone with red paint smeared across his face. The dead man was called John Ratchett. He was lying on the ground, killed because he had fallen through a trapdoor. Are you going to say he did that to himself?"

I wasn't addressing anyone in particular. I waited to see who would take up the accusation.

"I can tell you about that, Master Revill."

It was Ned Armitage who spoke. These were the first words he'd uttered.

"This gentleman you refer to – what was his name? – "

"Ratchett."

"He came sniffing and snooping round our yard. I challenged him and we – we disagreed – there was a struggle – "

"I came sniffing and snooping round the yard too, Master Armitage, but you did not challenge me. You were courteous and helpful. You were painting a chest in red."

"It's all right, Ned, you should not have to bear this burden alone," said Sir Philip (or Tom Turner), clapping the other man on the shoulder. There was still something unsettling about hearing Blake's refined tones issuing from someone wearing an artisan's gear.

"Ned wasn't alone when Ratchett came calling. I was there as well. Ratchett recognized me. I was not wearing this at the time" – he tugged at his lank hair – "and he recognized me. I knew him too. He used to work for Secretary Cecil."

"Cecil? I thought he worked for the French ambassador," I said.

"Ratchett worked for anyone who would pay him," said Blake. "I believe that he was one of those who was foremost in preparing false information about me to present to Robert Cecil. He was an unscrupulous man. He was a caterpillar. But we did not mean to kill him, not at first. He had seen me, seen that I was still alive. We were trying to stop him getting away. There was a struggle as Ned says. It was not a fair fight, of course, being two men against one. But you have my word, Master Revill, that we did not kill him. We did not even set out to kill him. I may be allowed to murder myself but I would not murder another."

"And yet he died," I said.

"We were struggling as I said," continued Blake. "Ratchett was lying over the trapdoor, battered and hurt. Ned and I had backed away from him, not sure what to do next. I thought he was unconscious. But he was only dazed. He made to get up and without knowing what he was doing he grasped at the lever which opened the trap – took hold of it to help himself up. Even as he exerted his full weight on the lever the trapdoor opened and he tumbled through it. The man fell with a dreadful crack on the floor below. We hurried down but he was already finished. It was ironic that I had simulated just such a death and that now it had occurred in reality."

"*Ironic*?"

"Yes. I won't pretend to a grief I didn't feel."

"And you left him there," I said.

"We went to fetch Jonathan," said Blake. "Later that same night we returned and took away the body."

"All of us helped," said Bill Inman, as if reluctant to be left out of this grisly account.

He meant the men in the business, himself, Blake, both the Snells. That explained the son's near panic when he thought I'd gone to the yard on the previous evening. By the time I'd arrived apparently for our nine o'clock meeting *in the morning*, the case had changed. Maybe the younger Snell had been about to reveal the plot to me – that relatively harmless plot by which an honest man had been saved from a traitor's death – but now another man really was dead. No wonder Snell wanted to assure me that he'd been wrong about everything. It was to prevent me asking any more questions.

"And I saw him in the time between his fall and your return," I said. "Ratchett was gone by the next day. What did you do with the body?"

"The body was sent to our country estate," said Lady Blake. "We were in need of a body."

Of course, the conspirators required a corpse to place in the family vault since the intended occupant of that vault was still alive and above ground. Ratchett would have been interred far from London and well above his station in life. From the set look on Lady Jane's face I realized that she had no qualms of conscience. If a man had to die in order that her husband might be protected, she was prepared to accept it, especially if that man was already her husband's enemy. While Sir Philip had been describing Ratchett's death, Maria More appeared uneasy, looking down at the ground and shifting from foot to foot. But she would never betray her mistress.

They were all involved – Sir Philip and Lady Jane Blake, Maria More and William Inman, the Snells and Ned Armitage – each and every one of them. I'd been looking for guilt in one or two people and found it shared out among seven. The question was not so much: who did it? The question was rather: who did not do it?

But done what exactly? Sir Philip Blake was not dead, either through accident or murder, but standing in front of me. If it's a crime to simulate death, then we actors are guilty every day of the week. As for Giles Cass, he had drowned in the Thames. (Nothing could have been more ordinary. Men, women and children fall into the river every day. Some come out. Some don't.) And when it came to that other death, I was inclined to believe Blake's account of how John Ratchett had perished. The man had pulled the lever that sent him plunging to his own death. An accident of sorts. And if it suited Blake and the others that Ratchett was dead, then it couldn't be denied that it suited me as well. The spy was not around to trick and bribe me, whether he was working for Cecil or the French ambassador or the man in the moon.

So where was the offence? Nowhere (or almost nowhere). *It was all a matter of show.*

"Well, Master Revill, you have the full story," said Blake. "You are free to do what you want with it. We have done no murder but we are all of us complicit in a kind of crime, and I am the most responsible."

"You have done one murder, at least," I said to him. "You have murdered yourself, as you said."

"If any murder may be called justified or honourable, it's that one, I suppose," said Sir Philip Blake.

"You are as good as dead to me," I said. "We should all go home to our beds and forget this conversation."

"In that event," said Blake, "I shall shortly be reborn as Robert Blake, an obscure country cousin who has the good fortune to be marrying Sir Philip's widow."

He turned and smiled at his wife. She clasped his arm tightly.

"My congratulations," I said.

'Twill do me good to walk

I waited until they'd filed out of the hut and across the
roof and down the stairs of the gallery. They took two
lanterns with them, thoughtfully leaving me with one
to find my way out. I delayed until the last footsteps had
died away before saying, "It's all right, Abel, you can come
out now."

My friend came round to where I was standing in the
doorway of the hut. He stretched and bent down, rubbing at
the calves of his legs.

"I was beginning to get a little uncomfortable back there. I
didn't dare to move."

"I hoped you would make your escape."

"And leave you to it?"

"They weren't going to do anything to me," I said. "You
must have seen that just now, or heard it anyway. Sir Philip
Blake is an honourable man and no murderer. He put himself
in my hands."

"So it turns out that you are a judge after all, with the
power of life and death over people."

"Just a poor player. I ought never to have got involved in
this. Not a single thing would be different or changed if I'd
never got involved."

"A mystery is solved."

"Yes, but only to satisfy our curiosity."

"No, justice is done too. Sir Philip Blake will escape a false

264

charge of treason. He'll start a new life and yet keep his wife and his property."

I realized that Abel was intrigued by the idea of someone starting a new life with a new identity. I suppose it was akin to what he'd done himself when he joined the King's Men.

"Do you think he'll get away with it?" he said.

"If he's careful he should manage it. He and Lady Jane can get married – get remarried – in the obscurity of the country and keep out of London for a few months at least. He will grow his beard again but in a rustic style, he'll cut his hair differently. Any similarity can be explained away by the fact that he's Sir Philip's cousin. In a year or two everyone will have forgotten about Sir Philip. And despite what he said, Secretary Cecil won't last for ever."

"I think we should leave this place, Nick."

We were still sheltering in the hut on top of the stage. The single lantern cast its feeble glow over the machinery of the hoist and the vacant *deus ex machina*. Out of doors the moon, pale companion to our strange meeting, had risen almost directly overhead.

Abel and I reversed the process of several hours before, rapidly relocking playhouse doors and replacing playhouse keys. We slipped out of the window into the Brend's Rents alley, and I made a mental note to secure it again first thing in the morning before anyone should notice. Instead of crossing the Bridge and returning to Thames Street, I accompanied Abel to his lodging house in Kentish Street. It seemed the least I could do, since he had risked a great deal to keep me company in this half ridiculous, half intriguing enterprise. We passed a nightwatchman or two, and other less reputable travellers, but there was safety in numbers and no particular danger anyway to two indigent-looking players.

Abel was eager to talk about everything he'd seen and heard. It was still fresh and surprising to him – to me as well, even though the outline of the truth had become clear just before the first 'visitors' arrived on the Globe roof. We both needed to talk.

"This was a very dangerous undertaking for the Snells," he said.

"The father saw it as a challenge to his art and skill, I think. There was nothing exactly wrong with what he was doing, at first. Just pretending that a man was dead. The only mistake he made was in not letting his son in on the secret from the start. Jonathan wanted to tell me everything, suspicions and all. It was only when someone really died – Ratchett – that he clammed up. But if the father had told him the truth in the very beginning then this whole business would have been avoided because there would have been no hint of plots and murder, nothing to set me off."

"That fellow Ratchett would still have died."

"He had the misfortune to go to the Three Cranes yard at the wrong moment. If he hadn't glimpsed Sir Philip when he did – "

"Misfortune! Nick, you don't want any of these people to be guilty."

"I suppose not, they are none of them murderers. Did you believe that story about how Ratchett's death wasn't intended?"

Abel was silent for a moment. We were getting out into the open country which starts quite soon on the fringes of Southwark. We were guided only by the moonlight and by Abel's familiarity with the route.

"If I heard such a story in a play I'd probably disbelieve it," he said. "But listening to Sir Philip Blake describe it, he did not seem to be covering anything up. There was a kind of honesty in what he said. A less straightforward man would have hummed and ha-ed, and tried to shuffle out of things. He admitted responsibility for what happened."

"I thought so too."

"And you weren't exactly mourning Ratchett's death either, Nick."

"The man was a caterpillar," I said, trying to echo Sir Philip's dismissive style. "That was another reason for doing nothing. Ratchett's death was as convenient for me as it was for them."

I let this thought drift away into the moonlight.

"What gave you the truth, Nick? You seemed to know what had happened before anybody'd started speaking."

"Odd ideas that were drifting through my head, I suppose. The idea that some events are staged purely for show. They don't have any real meaning, or not much of a meaning."

"Events such as?"

"The swearing of the oath of peace between England and Spain. That ceremony in the Chapel Royal was as much of a performance as Ben's *Masque of Peace*. People dressing up and saying the lines that were written down for them. In our case we were saying what Ben had told us to say. In the King's case he was saying what Cecil had told him to say."

"It's a jump from that to a staged death."

"Yes, well . . . you can blame Martin Barton too. I'd been looking at my lines for his *Melancholy Man* tomorrow. I remembered how that story turns on a Duke whom everyone assumes to be dead after an assassination attempt . . . "

"Before he comes back in disguise as a hermit to see how they're all getting on without him," said Abel who, like me, had a minor part in Barton's play.

"Yes."

"Far-fetched," said Abel.

"Martin Barton would not like to hear you say so. He thinks Shakespeare is lacking in realism because that play about the Moor turns on a handkerchief. Anyway, it occurred to me that there might be – advantages – for Sir Philip Blake in playing dead, since I'd already heard how Cecil was on his tail. And then other things came together, such as the fact that Bartholomew Ridd's laundrywoman hadn't been able to clean up the 'cloak of Truth' by soaking it in milk or using salt and water on the thing. No wonder she hadn't been able to get the blood out easily, since it wasn't blood but red paint. And I'd seen just such an application of red paint in the Three Cranes yard. Old Ned Armitage had got it over his face by mistake. So one idea led to another . . . "

"Blake is a good actor, he played the artisan well. I'd never have guessed."

"Yes. But he didn't have to speak much, he hid behind that curtain of hair. He probably enjoyed it, just as you or I would enjoy playing the nobleman for a week."

"A year would do."

"The real strain fell on the others who were in on the deception. Lady Blake fainted when her husband apparently died on stage. I thought that was perhaps to distract us from the trick that was being played, but the faint might have been real."

"No feint faint," said Abel.

"Tell it to Shakespeare, he appreciates that kind of joke."

"You're taking that tone because you didn't think of it first. Go on with your explanation."

"Where was I?"

"With Lady Blake."

"Afterwards when I saw her she was sometimes merry and cheerful and sometimes tense and strained. That might fit a new widow, but it would fit even better a woman who was glad that her husband had been preserved alive but was also anxious all the time because he might be found out. The same with Maria More, who denied that the dropped handkerchief was anything to do with her even though the handkerchief was completely unimportant. They were living in expectation of discovery. Even Bill Inman was on edge, for all that he seemed so bluff and cheerful. I saw him and Lady Jane embracing just after her husband's death, but I wonder who was reassuring who."

"So that's it," said Abel. "I can tell you though that I had a nasty surprise when I heard Sir Philip's voice. It was a dead man talking. A ghost."

"So did I," I said, "even though I'd guessed by then who he was. I mean, who Tom Turner was."

"Seeing as it might have been a ghost, I should have slipped into my best Horatio style," said Abel. "Did I tell you I might have the part of Horatio in *Hamlet*?"

"You have mentioned it now and then."

Abel stopped in the middle of the moonlit highway and began to declaim:

If thou hast any sound or use of voice,
Speak to me.
If there be any good thing to be done,
That may to thee do ease and grace to me,
Speak to me.
Or if thou hast uphoarded in thy life
Extorted treasure in the womb of earth,
For which, they say, you spirits oft walk in death,
Speak of it.

The dropping moon gave him a silver tinge. At this moment, such was my state of elation and exhaustion, that I wouldn't have been altogether surprised to see a ghost stalking past us, going about his business by the glimpses of the moon. If Abel could have conjured him with the power of his voice and his earnest tone then he would have done.

But no ghost came. Instead we arrived unscathed at Abel's lodging in Kentish Street. He offered me his bed to share for the night and, in all innocency, I accepted his offer and, in all innocency, we shared it.

Journey's end

I did not return to my Thames Street lodging until the next evening. Abel and I walked up from his place in Kentish Street early in the morning. There was the first touch of autumn in the air, like a dog nipping round your heels in a not altogether playful manner. The mist still lay on the river when we arrived at the playhouse but it was rapidly burnt off by the sun.

There was a Globe rehearsal for *The Melancholy Man* during the morning and the performance of a different piece by another playwright in the afternoon (it was *Love's Triumph* by William Hordle, if you're interested). It was satisfying to be back in our own playhouse, newly renovated – or 'tarted up to buggery' as Sam the doorman would say. It was satisfying to be playing according to our own schedule rather than running around at the beck and call of the court and taking on parts that didn't really belong to us, such as Grooms of the Outer Chamber. Apart from any other consideration, we hadn't been that well remunerated as a company for our attendance on the Spanish mission to London, receiving a total of twenty-one pounds and twelve shillings to cover a period of more than ten days. It sounds a lot but most of the money went on necessary expenses such as barbering, laundering and provisioning ourselves, since the court high-ups never think that the rest of humanity has to be washed, shorn and fed, especially if we're to look and feel our best. And the King's Men didn't even get any new livery out of the whole affair.

So, to get back to our proper business of murder, romance, mayhem, comedy, intrigue and deception was a pleasant relief. While I was practising the not very demanding part of the murderer Lussorio in *The Melancholy Man,* it was curious to reflect that Martin Barton had unwittingly helped me to solve the mystery of the 'murder' of Sir Philip Blake by showing how a man might come back to life under another guise. The playwright himself, with that dainty blue hat on his red head, was in attendance during the morning rehearsal even though he wasn't needed and would have got in the way if Burbage hadn't slapped him down from time to time. Writers need slapping down from time to time in my opinion. Even so, Barton mouthed along to his own lines and mimed the actions, standing to one side of the stage. I was still waiting for his hat to fall off.

I'd forgotten that I had left the passage window unlatched from where Abel and I climbed out the previous evening into Brend's Rents. It suddenly occurred to me in mid-rehearsal that it would still be open. So, in a moment when I wasn't needed, I hurried off to fasten it. I should have left it alone for, as I was leaning out to grasp the catch, William Shakespeare walked past.

"Just shutting this, Will."

I made a bit of a fuss about doing so, turning the catch with precision, and drew attention to the sort of trivial action which is best performed without thought.

WS stopped in his tracks.

"It shouldn't have been open in the first place," he said.

I shrugged casually, but like the window-closing movement this gesture was false, and I felt it as false.

"I'll have a word with Sam about it," said Shakespeare.

"Oh yes," I said.

"As a matter of fact I have just been speaking to him."

"You have?"

I was glad that the light in the passage was dim. It was always dim in this passageway.

"Sam is very worried that the door to his room doesn't shut fast," said WS. "He says that you were most concerned about it too, Nicholas, when you talked to him yesterday."

It crossed my mind to 'forget' the conversation with Sam but then I thought better of it. A partial admission was safer.

"We weren't talking about the door to his room as such," I said.

"That's odd because I got the impression that your whole conversation had been about the door that wouldn't shut. It's unusual for a player to be so concerned about *domestic* matters."

"He did mention it once or twice, yes. *The old bugger* – the door I mean, not Sam. That's how he referred to the door."

I had made the mistake of trying to imitate Sam's style of speech. William Shakespeare did not seem to respond positively to my attempt at lightness. He had more to say.

"But that wasn't what he wanted to talk to me about, the door which doesn't shut and which, in truth, we must see to. What bothered Sam was that someone has been fiddling around with his keys. They were in different places to where they ought to have been. He has a system, you know."

"Labels and so on," I said.

"Yes," said WS.

"Perhaps he put them back in a different place himself yesterday."

"*He* put them back?"

"Well, he's in charge . . . "

"And next, Nicholas, you will be saying that he's an old man, that his sight's going and so on."

"It's true that Sam is getting on . . . "

"Yet we entrust this old man with our money, don't we? He is our principal gatherer and responsible for all our playhouse takings. So we can trust him to know about his own keys, I suppose."

"Yes, we can," I said.

I was in my costume as Lussorio since we were still in mid-rehearsal. Underneath my murderer's gear I was sweating like a pig.

"I've just been having a look round the place to make sure of everything, in case anyone got inside here last night," continued Shakespeare. "I've been examining the Globe from top to bottom. From pole to pole, you might say. I even went up to the cabin on the stage roof. There's a fine view from the roof now that the mist has lifted."

"I must have a look sometime."

"The rushes on the walkway round the cabin are all scuffed and trodden on – although we haven't had cause to use the hut or the lifting-gear so far this season."

"Sightseers maybe," I suggested. "It's a fine view from up there, as you say."

"*Sightseers?*"

"Maybe not sightseers."

"All seems well, though," said WS after a long pause.

"That's good," I said.

"And no damage has been done, Nicholas."

There was – perhaps – just the hint of a question in the remark, a slight lift at the end of his words.

"No damage has been done, William."

"Then we shall have to assume that if anyone fiddled around with Sam's keys it must have been a ghost. If any person – and it was more than one or two from the looks of things – was up on the stage roof, then that must have been a ghost as well."

"Ghosts, yes."

"Playhouses are full of ghosts, on and off the stage."

And with that WS walked away down the passage. I stood there for a minute at least, breathing deep and reflecting that I'd had a lucky escape (although in one sense I had not escaped at all). I recalled how rapid had been Abel's and my relocking of the doors and replacing of the keys on the previous evening. Hardly surprising I'd put them back on the wrong pegs. Sam must be much more sharp-eyed than I'd thought.

Then I remembered that I was taking part in a rehearsal and that if I missed my cue I'd receive a rebuke from Dick Burbage which would be considerably less subtle than the one I'd just had from Shakespeare. I hurried back to the stage, sweaty and distracted. I had to play a scene in which I expressed my 'guilt' for having allowed the Duke to get away from a murder attempt – even murderers may feel uncomfortable over a job badly done or not done at all. On this occasion I did not have to feign shiftiness and guilt.

Shakespeare's reference to the ghosts which haunt playhouses chimed with the moment during the previous night when Abel and I had been walking back to his lodgings. He'd declaimed those lines of Horatio's which are a challenge to the ghost to declare its purpose in returning to stalk the earth.

When I got back to Mrs Buckle's house in Thames Street, it was with an idea in mind.

The widow was waiting for me. I might have expected to be questioned about my whereabouts on the previous night. I might have thought she was going to describe how she'd seen, once again, her husband's spectre. But she had a smile on her face and, quite unbidden, she put her arms about me.

"Oh, Nicholas," she said.

"Oh, Mrs Buckle," I said after a time.

"A most extraordinary thing has occurred," she said. "You could never guess – "

"Have you found something?"

"Why, yes. How did you know?"

I kissed her again for answer. I did not want to spoil her enjoyment in her story, although I had a pretty good idea of what she'd found.

Soon she came out with the story. Preparing to move house, since there was no possibility of deferring this any longer, she had started to sort out the few articles of furniture and other items which she and Lizzie had brought from the St Thomas's parsonage. She'd not been in the mood to do this when they shifted houses shortly after her husband's death. Only now could she decide what should be kept and what might be sold, since she and her daughter had to look to the future and consider all conceivable means of raising money. She'd even contemplated getting rid of the pieces which had been in her husband's family for generations. In particular, the chest which stood in her bedroom.

Opening the chest and examining its contents properly for the first time since the Reverend Buckle's death, she rummaged through some potentially saleable items such as a lace cloth, a silver salter wrapped up in a piece of rag (and which must have been secreted there for safekeeping), and a brooch which she rather thought had belonged to her mother-in-law.

"Then, Nicholas, I felt the strangest sensation. It was as if – as if Hugh was standing behind me and guiding me, telling me to look further, not to be satisfied with what I'd discovered so far but to look further. I got out all the contents of the chest and had them spread across the floor. Still I felt my husband urging me to look further and not to give up. I came to the bottom of the chest and it was bare and empty. I sat back and could not think what to do next. Then, Nicholas, I observed that there was a fair distance between the bottom of the chest inside and where it stood on its base on the floor. I rapped on the wood inside and it sounded hollow. I did not know what to do next but Hugh told me to go to the kitchen and get a roasting-jack. In short I used it to prise up the boards at the bottom of the chest and there I found – what do you think I found? – a hoard of money! Gold coins and more gold coins, and more still. I could not finish counting them but was overcome with amazement."

I thought of those words of Horatio about the reasons why ghosts walk. They come back for vengeance, they come back because they are restless, but they also come back for the

275

most mundane of reasons. They've left money behind. This was a generous ghost though. The Reverend Buckle wanted the money not for himself – what can a clergyman be wanting with cash in heaven (or in the other place, or in the one that stands between)? – wanted it not for himself but so that his wife should have it.

"Why, Nicholas, you do not seem surprised," said Mrs Buckle.

"I am not altogether surprised but I am delighted for you – and for Lizzie," I said.

"What should we do with it, the money?"

"Why, it is yours, Mrs Buckle. Yours and your daughter's. It must have belonged to your husband or to his family maybe. I am sure that his spirit was directing you to find it. Perhaps that is the reason you have, ah, seen him so often. That money is yours now by law and by any other right."

"I suppose so."

"There is no supposing about it. Besides, finders keepers, you know."

"We can afford to move now."

"Yes, you can."

"Where should we go?"

"To the country?"

"Lizzie says she likes the town, even south of the river. But I think that would be a little rough for her."

"Rough for both of you, Mrs Buckle."

"Nicholas, you may move with us, if you like. Grace is coming with us. I could not leave her behind."

"You have a kind heart, Mrs Buckle. But I do not think I can move with you."

"You do not need to feel . . . "

She was going to say something like "coy", I think, but was too coy to express herself.

"It's not that," I said. "I do not think I can house with you – or Lizzie – in the future wherever you're living, in town or country."

"Oh."

"It is nothing to do with you, Mrs Buckle. I shall always have the fondest memories."

She brightened at this and said, "And I. But, do you know, Nicholas, so many coins. I couldn't count them all."

"I don't think you should mention this to anyone else, the gold coins."

"You are the first person I've told."

"Not Lizzie?"

"She is out today," she said.

"Oh yes, out again. Well, please say nothing. Keep the money well hidden. There may be more honesty on this side of the Thames than in Southwark but there are villains and deceivers everywhere. People are not what they seem."

I decided to visit the Mitre brothel for a final time. Before that I dropped in on the Goat & Monkey – for a touch of Dutch courage maybe, considering what I intended to do next – and in that disreputable tavern I had the bad fortune to encounter that disreputable couple Tony and Charity Thoroughgood again. I did not wait to be nudged over, and pointed to and whispered about. Instead I walked straight up to them and told them flat out that I knew they'd been responsible for attacking me on the Thames bank not so long ago, by the Pure Waterman tavern. I'd recognized Charity's voice, I said, and furthermore I had a respectable witness who was willing to give evidence (I did not mention that the respectable witness, John Ratchett, was dead). They could count themselves lucky I'd not brought an action of battery against them. But I would do it if they made trouble for me in future. In fact, I would do it if I ever saw them hanging about the Globe playhouse again.

"What do yew mean?" said Charity. "What are yew talking about?"

It had been a long shot. But Tony looked discomfited and I read the guilt in his face. He was not a violent man by nature.

I guessed that his wife had put him up to the attack in revenge for my frustrating their attempt to rob the Buckles, mother and daughter. I remembered the screeching, "Kick 'im. Kick 'im!"

I walked away from the pair, feeling very superior that I had not resorted to force. I suspected they'd be up to their old tricks again soon but what I'd said might give them pause. Considering everything else which had occurred recently, Tony and Charity's trickery looked fairly trivial. Coney-catchers were as much a part of Southwark life as the cursing ferry-men and the wardens in the bear-pits and the whores in the stews. And talking of whores, talking of stews, I had one final thing to do. From the Goat & Monkey ale-house to the Mitre brothel was only a couple of minutes' walk.

Once there I asked for my favourite girl, the French one called Blanche. It was fortunate that she was unoccupied, although if she hadn't been I would have waited until she was. I made my way to her crib. The room was as dark as usual, with the single wax candle burning by the side of her bed and the sand-glass timer next to it. On the wall were her trophies, the crucifix and psalter, the necklace and pomander. I wondered what she'd done with the handkerchief which belonged originally to Lady Jane Blake.

"Oh, Nicholaas . . . it izz you," she said. "Wot do you want, *mon chéri?*"

"You," I said.

For answer she threw back the sheet which covered her. She was naked. The first thing I noticed, almost the first thing, was that little mole on the upper slope of her right breast. I hesitated.

"Aren't you going to start that?" I said, gesturing towards the sand-glass. "Usually you turn it over before we begin."

"Not ziss time."

I joined her in her bed and for the next half an hour or so we were happily occupied. She said little, and the little she did say was mostly incomprehensible French mumbles. I said little too, just English mumbles. Nevertheless we understood each other well enough, Blanche and I.

When we were done, and she lay in my arms, I said, "You will not need to do this any longer."

"Do ziss? I do not understand what you mean."

"I mean that you won't have to work here in the Mitre now that your mother has discovered money. You know about that? The money that was in your father's chest, the one that is in her bedroom."

Blanche stiffened in my arms but otherwise didn't move. I gave her credit for that. In her position I don't think I would have had that self-command. What I said did not come as a shock. Perhaps she'd been expecting it. When she spoke again it was without a trace of a French accent but in perfect English.

"How long have you known, Nicholas?"

"I think I prefer 'Nicholaas'. Broken English sounds more seductive."

"How long have you known then, *Nicholaas*?" said Elizabeth Buckle, the daughter to my landlady and secret labourer in the Mitre brothel.

"That pomander hanging up on the wall over there, it was the one that that couple tried to steal off you in the spring outside the playhouse. I thought it looked familiar. The last time I was here I noticed it and then almost immediately afterwards I saw Tony and Charity Thoroughgood in the Goat & Monkey, and it made me think . . . although I didn't recognize the connection at once . . . made me think of you, them, the pomander. It's a fine item, with nice engraving. No wonder Charity tried to snaffle it."

"There are plenty of ornaments like that to be stolen. Many duplicates."

"Yes, granted. But when I put the pomander together with one or two other . . . notions . . . "

"Notions, *Nicholaas*?"

"The fact that you were almost never at home in Thames

Street and that whenever I did see you you skittered away like a frightened deer. You hardly ever looked at me."

"Oh, that must have been galling for you, Nicholas, not to be looked at."

Ignoring her, I said, "I remember when we first met not far from here you hid yourself under a great hat. And then there was that time a few weeks ago when your mother was being troubled by one of her nightmares. You were grasping her arm, trying to get her to go back to bed."

"I remember."

"There must have been some echo in the gesture, the way you were holding her, coaxing her, that reminded me of you, I mean of Blanche of the Mitre. I wasn't aware of it at the time. But it was you."

"*Oui, c'est moi.*"

"Why turn French, Elizabeth? Or are you Lizzie?"

"I am Lizzie to my mother. Here I am Blanche, *mon chéri*. You said just now that it was more seductive to be spoken to in broken English. Other men find it so too. They will pay extra for the privilege of being had in French. And since I wanted to get as far away as possible from my real background I made up a new one for myself. No longer the parson's daughter but the strange girl from Bordeaux. That way I don't have to explain myself. I hardly have to say anything. Is that so odd?"

"Odd enough," I said.

"Though you're a parson's son, *Nicholaas*. If there's anyone who ought to understand . . ."

"Tell me why."

"Why another name? I could hardly work here under my own name."

"That's not what I mean. Why do *this* work in the Mitre, the place whose name you pretended not to understand the meaning of, the dirty secret meaning."

"Ze mitre . . . eet ees anozzer zing too?" She laughed but somehow her laughter had lost its innocence and appeal for

me. Then she said, "Why work here when I should be doing
something salubrious, something respectable?"

"Yes."

The conversation was echoing the one I'd had with Sir
Philip Blake. What was the reason for that nobleman taking
on the role of a simple craftsman? The thrill of deception,
he'd answered, more or less.

"Excitement and curiosity and money," said Blanche-
Elizabeth promptly, as though the answer was lying ready.
"Money especially."

"You have money now. Your mother has found money in
your father's chest."

"So you say."

She did not seem unduly surprised at the discovery.

"Well then?"

"It's not only the money and our need for it. My mother
has sheltered me all her life. I wanted to see whether the world
was as dangerous as she said it was."

"And is it?"

"Sometimes it is, I have learnt. Now that I've answered
your questions, *Nicholaas*, you must answer one of mine.
Have you been – familiar with my mother?"

Whatever question I'd been expecting it wasn't that one. I
did not know how to answer her.

"From your silence, I think so," she said. "I zink so."

"Her secret is safe with me," I said, "just as yours is safe
with me. I shall not tell on one woman to the other."

She glanced across at the sand-glass. I took the hint and
climbed out of her bed and started dressing, glancing at her
from time to time. Now that I knew it for a fact, the similarity
between her and her mother was detectable. Not precisely in
their features but in a way of moving an arm or turning the
head.

"Will you visit me again?"

"No," I said.

"Never?"

"If I do come to the Mitre again I shall not ask for Blanche."

"Then Blanche will not charge you this time," she said.

"So you are going to carry on with – all this?" I said.

"That depends."

"But there is no longer any need. Your mother has money. It's true. She found it in the chest in her room. It must have been your father's."

"Where did it come from, I wonder," she said. She still did not seem surprised.

"That's a mystery."

"What's the answer?"

"Not all mysteries have answers," I said.